WITH EVERY KISS
OF SNOW

ANGELA SMITH

Author Angela Smith

www.loveisamystery.com

www.twitter.com/angelaswriter

www.facebook.com/authorangelasmith

❀ Created with Vellum

DEDICATION

Thank you to Katie McGinley. I couldn't have done any of this without you.

To family and the Christmas memories.

CHAPTER 1

Remy Halliburton steered her sedan into the lane leading to Christmas Hills Resort, her pulse pounding in her throat. Two years had passed since her last visit to this fairytale retreat. Two years of ignoring her favorite part of the holidays and disregarding long-standing family traditions.

Her traditions had died with her parents.

She'd anticipated wreaths hanging from pole to pole and illuminating each window. Lights glimmering on the trees leading up to the resort, the breathtaking decorations accentuating the yard and shouting out a welcome.

But nothing welcomed her. She drove into the empty lot and shifted into park, her churning stomach revolting at the solitude. She squeezed the steering wheel and hinged toward it, flustered and confused.

What's wrong?

Everything was dark. Desolate. Bare. The Santa and sleigh should be waving a greeting from the rooftop. The yard was devoid of any customary displays, the lights and sounds of the holiday season non-existent.

Shutting off the engine, she unbuckled her seatbelt and jumped out, not bothering with her luggage, and plodded to the door. The nearby town of Laurel Springs, Colorado, was awash with white but not Christmas Hills Resort. Her favorite place to visit and one that held her most treasured memories was now a broken dream. She had hoped to make new memories and fall in love with Christmas again.

But even snow shunned the resort. It looked shut down, but she couldn't imagine that possibility.

Guilt twisted her throat. She had avoided Seth, and now she was showing up like they were still old friends when she hadn't even spoken to him since the accident. He'd taken over the resort. Her brother and sister had visited the past two years and reported he was doing well. She'd spent every Christmas here since as long as she could remember up until her parents' deaths.

Seth's parents had died, too. Her mouth soured at the memory, eyes burning with the all-too-familiar grief. He'd kept the resort open afterward, so why close now? With no explanation? And why hadn't she checked? She was sure she would have a room. The same room her family stayed in every Christmas.

She jiggled the door. Locked. A sign read *Closed, to reopen March 1*. She knocked, but didn't hold out much hope. Seth wasn't here, and the fairytale in her head would not spark to life.

Her breath hitched in hiccupping coughs. She hadn't needed her warm jacket on the long drive and forgot to grab it from the car. Despite the lack of snow, icy cold prickled her skin. Night had descended, the darkness draining her hope. The spirit of Christmas was supposed to have conquered any negativity. The lights and sounds of cheer and the dancing and jolliness of the season should awaken her soul.

Now her expectations were dashed.

She hadn't visited since the accident because she hadn't had the guts to face the joy and pretend like everything was okay. But now she needed this more than she needed her next breath.

A vehicle drove up. Surrounded by lights but not the glimmering, hopeful, seasonal kind. Seth stepped out of the Jeep. Her stomach dipped, tension mushrooming in her body.

The vehicle resembled a carriage ride to utopia. Lights swathed the roof and along the bottom, more decorated than the resort. He kept it running, the headlights pointed away so they didn't glare at her. The way they illuminated him when he approached made him look like an angel.

But she knew better.

"Remy. What are you doing here?"

Her teeth chattered, and she swiped a piece of hair from her eyes. "Oh. I...I thought I'd see if my room was available." She glanced around, chewing her lip. "Why in the world are you closed during Christmas?"

"You didn't see the sign at the bottom of the mountain?" His forehead crinkled, his voice a sharp accusation.

She closed her eyes and wondered if she had intentionally overlooked the sign or if she was too spaced out to notice. "No. I...guess I didn't."

"Well. We're closed."

"For the holidays?" Her voice rose, a screeching gesture of doubt and confusion. *How could you?* She wanted to ask. *How could you stomp on your parents' memory like that?* This resort embodied the Christmas spirit. It lived for Christmas. His parents had lived for Christmas.

But she couldn't ask such a question. She had done plenty of stomping on memories.

He turned and scurried to his Jeep. She opened her mouth to call out and ask what he was doing, where he was going and why he was leaving her here alone to figure things out by herself, but her voice cracked. Tears burned her throat. He shut down the vehicle and grabbed something. A blanket. A blanket he wrapped around her. She clutched it around her shoulders and nodded her thanks. Her teeth continued to chatter, the cold suppressing any other body movement.

"Let's get you inside. At least for a minute. But I can't promise it'll be any warmer in there."

She huddled into the blanket and followed him to the door. Once she made it inside, she'd see everything was normal. Christmas trees and lights would glimmer in the lobby with the anticipated welcoming spirit. But she stepped over the threshold, and her hope plummeted. Dark. Cold. Dreary. More like a dungeon than anything else.

"The heat is on, but we keep it low." He fingered a keycode to open the thermostat.

She stood near the fireplace, but the bleakness offered no warmth. Seth stuffed his hands in his pockets and leaned against the wall.

At twenty-eight, he was eighteen months older than she, but the deep green of his eyes didn't glitter with the mischief she had known from childhood. His dark brown hair was still thick and unruly, and he was still the most handsome man she'd ever seen.

She wrenched her gaze away.

She couldn't afford to admire him. The casual friendship they'd enjoyed full of snowball fights and strolls around the year-round Christmas village had soured ages ago. Even before their parents' deaths, Seth had brushed her off as if she were an annoying child.

Visiting the resort, launching into the holiday spirit and continuing to ignore her grief by immersing herself in too many activities was now a lost cause.

He might have given her a blanket and let her in, but the torment on his face was enough to reveal his resentment.

~

Seth Lockhart rubbed a hand over the front of his shirt and resisted the urge to study Remy. He should offer her something warm to drink. If he remembered correctly, cocoa had been her favorite. He could putter around the kitchen to stay busy, but it had never been his strong suit. Ignoring her had never been, either.

Her hair was like pine bark kissed by dirt-scuffed snow. Texas snow—almost nonexistent—the light brown highlighted with blonde. She should feel right at home with the outdoor barrenness.

"What brings you from Terrence, Texas?" he asked, making small talk to ease the awkwardness. "You're still there, right?"

"Yes." She glanced around, her gaze bobbing from the window to the fireplace, where a tree usually stood, and back to him. "I was in the mood for snow."

Seth shoved his hands in his pockets. "Not much here. The town has snow and the mountains are covered, but none at the resort."

White powder blanketed the entire city but hadn't touched his property. He'd heard the gossip. The townspeople believed he had caused the lack by shutting down, and thus closing his heart to the spirit of the season. Maybe they were right, since this mountain was usually one of the first to get snowfall.

Defensiveness kinked his skin. He didn't see the need to explain himself to her or anyone else. Yes, he'd closed for the holidays. A travesty. His parents would be rolling in their graves. But he had to, for his own wellbeing.

Had Remy not paid attention to the signs leading up to the resort? Hadn't her siblings told her why they weren't coming? They hadn't missed a season since their parents first

5

brought them here. Then again, she'd never had much respect for anything that didn't suit her needs, so she'd likely ignored all the warnings.

The last two seasons almost did him in, and he'd put his grief on the backburner. He'd never had time to get caught up on his to-do list. With much backlash from the community, he'd closed up the entire resort until March to reevaluate what he wanted to do with his life. After worrying about everybody else at Christmas, spending this time alone was necessary to his mindset.

You can't stay here, Seth wanted to say, but somehow couldn't get those words past his thoughts and into his mouth. His throat thickened with the need to spill out all the hurt and confusion he'd faced when she hadn't come the first two years after their parents died. She hadn't attended his parents' funeral, although he had attended hers.

"Look." He stepped away from the wall that had become his sanctuary. "I'll let you have a room for the night. It's way too late for you to try to get off the mountain now."

Her lips trembled. Her eyes watered. Such blue and potent eyes. Like the massive, powerful ocean luring him. Oh, how he longed for the ocean right now. To escape to a paradise that didn't harbor such bad memories.

He navigated the reception area and found a room key. Should he give her the same room she had every year, or would she prefer something different? He grabbed the first one from the left, which would be the floor above the lobby and the door just off the hall. Something close, where she could get in and get out. He wasn't about to cater to her and give her the room she'd expected.

He handed over the key. "Do you need help getting your stuff? Just for the night," he added.

She glanced at the key and her eyebrows crinkled together, but she didn't say anything about it not being her usual room. He was leery of her having the place all to herself. Not that any big, bad bears would break in, and not that he wasn't stocked to take care of himself and an army of people for the next six months if something terrible happened, but the fact she was all alone two weeks before Christmas. She'd come here expecting to see the festivities, a huge Christmas tree in the lobby and decorations in every nook and cranny.

But he couldn't do it this year.

"Yes, please. I need to grab my purse and two suitcases."

"If it's in your car, I'll get it. You can go in the room and get comfortable. You'll need to switch on the heat. And there's bottled water in the fridge if you're thirsty."

She nodded. "Thanks." She shuffled up the stairs, the blanket—still clenched around her shoulders and waist—trailing behind her.

Seth lumbered to her vehicle and grabbed her purse and luggage. He resented her presence, resented the scent of her car, like a floral luminance of colors. Her brother and sister had known, had even supported him, but as usual, Remy did what she wanted.

Their friendship had waned a long time ago. It had mostly been his fault, since being near her provoked the monsters in his mind. He'd wanted more than friendship back then, and she had rejected him. They were from two different worlds, and she was too self-absorbed to see him as anything but an accessory to her Christmas fantasy.

Nothing much changed. She was here for some illusion she'd probably built in her head and couldn't see past her own goals to notice how others were affected.

When he'd seen her in the security camera at his home a quarter mile away, his entire body had tensed, as if all the snow that hadn't fallen at the resort accumulated in his stomach. He considered just ignoring her until she figured things out and left, but he couldn't let her stay out in this cold. She'd be an icicle by morning. He couldn't let her drive back to town tonight, either. Even though she had made a selfish decision by ignoring his wishes and coming here anyway, he had to take responsibility. She had to have known he was closed, and now he had no choice but to let her stay in the resort, locked up and alone.

Too bad if she was disappointed.

CHAPTER 2

Remy woke the next morning full of life and energy. She sat up in bed and glanced around.

Sunlight beamed into the windows. Light blue walls softened the room, the luxurious bed replete with matching blankets and pillows. The room was smaller than the one she had stayed in with her parents and siblings but was perfect for her.

Her belly flopped. Too bad she would only stay one night. She wasn't ready to leave. The barren resort held no Christmas cheer, but that was an easy fix.

She stretched her arms over her head, letting out a big yawn then a smile. Her pulse thrummed in anticipation. If she could convince Seth to let her decorate, she'd have an outlet for all the anxiety building in her mind over the last few weeks. Anxiety over her life and what she was doing with it, her relationship with Carson, and most especially her job. Which she thought might be the reason for her and Carson's trouble in the first place.

Maybe she made too big of an assumption, considering

the place was closed, but she wouldn't have worried about asking him in the old days.

She needed this holiday. She needed this vacation. She couldn't go back to the way things were and expect any changes. She needed to immerse herself in all the activities of Christmas, to experience it the way she had growing up, and see if her ambitions for living her dream life still existed. Good marriage, great home, but more importantly, a job she didn't dread. She wanted to help people with her creativity, but her life stood at a standstill.

Her good sleep made her eager to tackle the day. At first, she'd hoped to stay in the same room she had for years, and the differences had disappointed her. Once she'd got snuggled in bed though, she'd enjoyed the minor differences. This smaller room didn't have a door attaching to the others. Her parents and two siblings had always stayed in rooms opening to each other so even though they were separated, they were always together. This one overlooked the front yard instead of the back, and thickets of trees surrounded her view.

At any other time, snow would drench those trees.

She checked her phone to find no service but typed a text to her sister anyway. It didn't send. She couldn't even get online with her mobile data and the resort's Wi-Fi password —Christmas, of course—wouldn't work.

Would Carson be missing her by now?

Maybe lack of service was best. If Carson texted, she wouldn't know and couldn't text him back. What better way to make him wonder where she was and what she was doing?

Let him worry and fret.

She shifted the covers and hopped out of bed, quickly showered, then strolled downstairs to the kitchen and sought breakfast. The meager road-trip snacks from yesterday left her starving.

The staircase was immaculate, like a fairytale mansion

that should showcase wreaths and white lights. It ended in the center of the lobby where a massive fireplace—the focal point of the room—usually displayed Christmas decor. Her breath hitched at finding it empty and alone.

Well, of course nothing had changed overnight.

Carson wasn't a fan of Christmas. One of their problems together was his focus on work and goals but never on family or holidays. She devoted her life to family, and after she'd lost her parents, her siblings remained important.

Except the last two Christmases when she'd abandoned them for her boyfriend. And now she was doing her own thing in hopes it would get his attention.

She stopped at the bottom of the steps, blinked her gummy eyes, and glanced outside. The floor-to-ceiling windows in the back that ran the length of the room revealed an outdoor barrenness. How had it not snowed up here on the mountain?

Shivering, she roamed the lobby into the reception area, glad she had brought a light jacket. Although her room was warm and Seth had raised the heat last night, the others were chilly. Before, every main room had a themed Christmas tree. She had never seen the lobby empty.

She stopped in the kitchen, one of her favorite spaces and one where she was allowed to venture into in her younger days. She missed the chef and the rest of the staff and wondered if Maye was still around. A petite woman with a big and burly personality, she had the nicest smile and was always full of surprises. She'd created masterpieces behind this door.

Did Seth not realize how shutting down had affected everyone?

She rummaged through the pantry and found flavored oatmeal and coffee pods. She brewed a cup of coffee and set a bowl of oatmeal in the microwave.

She combed through the freezer to find plenty of frozen

meat. Enough sausage, links, and bacon to feed a small army. She considered throwing some in water to thaw but changed her mind. No sense in pushing her limits. Seth didn't want her here, and he'd want her here even less if she messed with things she had no right messing with.

She was no chef, but she loved to cook and this kitchen was a dream. Sizable and functional, stainless steel harmonized with painted wood and walnut to soften the industrial edge. Plenty of lighting and counter space, with several stoves and cook spaces for Maye's assistants. She had learned to love cooking while staying here during the holidays, where the staff scrambled to serve their guests.

"What are you doing?"

Seth's immense voice boomed through the vacant kitchen, pinging from space to space until landing in her heart. She jumped and turned, almost sloshing her coffee all over. She held up her cup in answer. "Getting coffee and oatmeal. I hope that's okay. I didn't want to disturb you."

He gave a one shoulder shrug, his entire face scowling. "I've got real food at my place."

"Oatmeal is fine," she said, although she wondered what he meant by real food. Was that an offer? Her stomach grumbled, and her face heated at the thought he might hear.

She tried not to admire him, but that couldn't be prevented. He wore a black and gray flannel shirt untucked over jeans and hiking boots, his hair combed but mussed as if he had torn off a beanie. He looked ready to tackle the outdoors.

"Dry oatmeal?" he asked.

"It's flavored."

He nodded. "It wouldn't take much to get some sausage, bacon, eggs, and pancakes. Or we could just step a few hundred feet away to my house."

Curiosity snooped through her. She'd never seen his place.

He and his parents lived in their own home on the property, but as far as she knew he had moved into his own once he'd turned eighteen. She'd visited his parents' house but never his.

"You're doing that on purpose," she teased. "Of course, I want to see it. I mean, have it. Breakfast, that is." *Stupid, stupid*. It had nothing to do with seeing his property and she couldn't let on she'd even considered it.

"Even though we'll be in the Jeep, you might want to grab a heavier jacket. It's cold out there."

"Okay." She drained her coffee, already lukewarm. "I'll run to my room for my coat. Be right back."

Although she'd already dressed for the day, she traded her sneakers for hiking boots and her heavier coat and gloves. Items she'd bought specifically for this trip.

They stepped outside to his Jeep, and she was struck again at the pale property, as if the sun had bleached the colors out of the earth. The trees slumped in sadness. Was the year-round Christmas village still in the back of the building, or had he demolished that, too? She didn't ask. Not yet, anyway.

The Jeep was obviously not her carriage ride to utopia, but was still colossal. Massive tires lifted it up from the ground so much she had to pull herself into the seat by the strap. The lights swarming the roof were turned off this morning, and a huge grill bulged from the front. It growled when he cranked it, and soon they bounced along the road to his home.

The house was situated in the eastern section of the resort, on the opposite side from where his parents had lodged. Tucked behind trees and hills and hidden away from the view of the resort, it wouldn't have been a far walk. The road traversed an exquisite forest, and she relished the view.

"There should be snow on these trees," she mumbled.

Mountains lifted around them. White bordered the peaks on the horizon, but none on the resort property or even within walking distance. *Strange.*

"Well, if you ask the townsfolk, it hasn't snowed because I closed my heart to Christmas."

He spoke with jest, but derision dulled his voice. She agreed with the townspeople but saw no sense in ruining whatever moment she could cling to. "The resort means a lot to them," she said instead.

The resort had meant a lot to everyone.

She hadn't expected him to reply as he steered into the garage, and he didn't. Yet excitement fluttered her belly. This was where she would see his spirit. She jumped from the Jeep and bounced to the door. Her brain danced with the prospect of a festive tree in his living room, twinkly lights hanging everywhere, the scent of berries and cloves, vanilla and ginger, and of Christmas.

"Come on in." Seth stepped aside to let her in.

Remy's heart dropped. The house was cozy and clean, but nothing remotely resembled Christmas and no signs the special day was just around the corner.

"You can hang your coat right here." He shrugged off his and hung it on a rack in the corner near the fireplace.

She removed hers and glanced around. No fire crackled in the brick enclosed fireplace, but the room was warm. Dark wooden beams lined the ceiling, the floor a lighter wood and the paint scheme a muted gray. The charcoal hearth rug finished off the cabin with a touch of masculinity.

She followed him to the kitchen and drew in a stuttered gasp. Another cook's dream, with wood and brick and immaculate counter space. Two sinks, two ovens, a large cooktop, and a stainless-steel refrigerator. Herbs grew in the windowsill above the main sink. "This is..." Her voice fizzled. His kitchen captivated her.

"Almost too much for one person to handle? Yep, you're right."

"A cook's dream," she finished.

"Sure, unless you have an entire staff working for you and can just run to the resort to grab a meal."

Still, a dream.

"So then, why do you have this?" She waved her hands through the air.

He looted the fridge and removed breakfast makings. "I guess my parents thought I'd want my own home. They had it built for me to live in. Of course, they hoped I would one day take over the resort and want to stay. I guess they thought I'd have a family. And I do love the place."

Her throat constricted for a moment while she pictured a happy family in this house, and her not being a part of that.

She swallowed, and shook away that silly thought. "What happened to..." She couldn't finish her sentence. She didn't want to dredge up any bad memories.

"To their home?" he asked.

She nodded.

He cracked open the package of biscuits and dumped them on a pan, his lips compressed. She shouldn't have asked.

"I haven't been in there since. I thought about opening up for space for guests, or offering it to Jonathan or Maye. But I'm just not interested." He lifted his head and wrinkled his nose. "Or maybe I'm just not ready."

Her chest ached. He popped the biscuits in the oven and continued his tasks. She treaded through his living room and glanced at his special touches. Photos of all shapes and sizes lined the walls.

She strolled up to one of an elk standing in the wintery forest. Horns almost bigger than his body, trees sagging with white powder, and a sunset that set the background on fire.

She fingered the cool glass, allured into the picture to experience the chill. "I love the photos," she said.

"Thanks. They're mine."

She giggled. "Of course, they're yours."

"I mean. I took them."

Eyes widening, she stopped in front of the next photo, an elk lounging near the creek, but this time in the summer. The water glittered under the sunlight, the trees blaring dark green. "You took these?"

He nodded and arranged slices of bacon in a sizzling pan. "Yes. You could say I love photography. It's my thing."

"Obviously. Do you sell them?"

"No. Just a hobby."

"Wow. So, you managed to take pictures of all this wildlife?" She studied a photo of a bald eagle perched in the tree, as if safeguarding the world. She recognized the area. She'd taken many hikes through the forest where the mountains dipped into the valley and a creek streamed below. Snow covered the ground and kissed the trees. Even the eagle appeared snow-tipped.

"I am a patient person. And very quiet, too." He mixed the pancake mix and poured them on a griddle.

Obviously. She approached the kitchen, and her stomach rumbled at the scent of coffee and breakfast. "Can I help with anything?"

"Not at all." He nodded to the corner. "But there's more coffee there if you'd like some."

"I would love some. What about you?"

"I'll take a cup."

She glanced outside while he poured them both a cup. "You have a greenhouse?"

"Yes. There's a larger one at the resort. We grow most of our veggies all year long."

"That's new. Have you always had that?"

"We've been working on it for a while, but it's new to you, sure."

What else had changed since her absence? "Who will take care of it while you're closed?"

"I still employ staff who come and look after things. And I am perfectly capable, too."

"Oh." She cringed. "Well, it's lovely." She hadn't meant to offend him. "You want cream and sugar?"

"I'll take it black."

Nose crinkling, she set the cup next to him, then doctored hers. She leaned against the counter while he worked the kitchen like a pro.

He was a beautiful man. Potent green eyes that took her breath away, the varied colors of earth. But they didn't glitter with the mischief she'd once known. Wisps of hair fell into his eyes, and she shoved her hands in her pockets to keep herself from touching the strands.

Her belly tightened. No wonder they had stopped being friends.

Seth found himself enjoying cooking breakfast a bit too much. He hadn't planned to make a large meal. He'd planned to grab toast and eggs for himself and then take his camera out for some photography. Even with the lack of snow, he'd managed some awesome pictures.

But Remy incited the homemaker in him. He couldn't tell her how much he'd missed her. That one of the reasons he'd closed the resort was because he couldn't bear another Christmas without her.

They were from two completely different realities. Remy had lived a normal life. A Texas girl, she rarely saw the snow and only visited once a year. Seth had grown up having to display the Christmas spirit every day of his life.

The resort had robbed him of his independence. Whether he loved it or not, he was host, Christmas character, whatever necessary. Everybody else always came first, and he needed to think of himself this time.

The three-story resort had sixteen luxurious rooms each on the second and third floor, the main floor holding the lobby and reception area, along with the dining, kitchen, spa, and other operations. Guests paid a premium for the top-notch service, including all-inclusive meals and activities.

Seth couldn't recall a time they weren't booked, and most reservations were made well in advance. Some, like Remy's family, held a lifetime reservation for two weeks during Christmas. Which was probably why she'd shown up, expecting a room.

Last night, he had been surly. Their relationship had waned long before she stopped coming for Christmas because of his developing feelings for her. They had been friends, but a friendship was hard to maintain when he only saw her once a year and she treated him like a brother. The thought of her leaving now left a sour hole in his stomach.

He avoided that subject. She had come for the Christmas spirit, and wouldn't find that here. More than likely, she was just as eager as he was for her to leave.

Their forks scraped against plates while they ate across from each other in the dining area near a window.

"Well you know what I do," he said, breaking the silence. "What do you do for a living?"

"Oh." Her face scrunched, and she finished chewing. "I'm in marketing. Right now, I'm working for a corporation, but it's great because of the benefits and time off. I manage branding and website design, along with managing social media and what have you. But what I want to do is graphic design. To help smaller businesses who might not have the opportunity to get noticed."

"That's cool." Some of Seth's employees multi-tasked by running the website and social media. He rarely looked at it, except for approvals on certain occasions. "So why don't you?"

"It's hard to work for yourself." Her shoulders slouched. "Well, okay, so you work for yourself mainly. But I mean, it's hard to get out of a comfortable job and start doing things on your own, you know?"

He knew what she meant. He loved this resort and everything about it, but lately it had become an obligation. He'd lost the optimism when his parents had died on their favorite day of the year. He winced. Their death still hurt, and the way it had happened stung. The plane accident, with his father as the pilot.

He had no idea what he would do if he didn't care for this resort. Take pictures? And how could he make a living?

"I understand." Scooping the last of his pancake and syrup in his mouth, he sat back in his chair and chewed, considering his day. "I was planning to go out to do some photography today. Would you like to come along?" He surprised himself by asking, but it sounded like she needed a chance to remember the joy of discovering what creativity was all about.

She squinted and brushed her hands with a napkin. "Oh, I... I'm sure I would scare away all the animals."

He leaned forward and planted his elbows on the table. "I can teach you to be quiet. Besides, it's not always about the animals. Sometimes it's the landscape. Right now, I can get some pretty good photos of the snow-kissed mountains on the horizon and the bareness of the property here. You'd be surprised at how pretty the picture develops."

Her face beamed in a smile that lightened him, made him

remember one of the reasons he had closed. Made him remember one of the reasons he needed her to leave as soon as possible. But also made him remember why he wanted her to stay longer.

"Okay. I'd love to do it. Part of my graphic design dream is to create and reconstruct images."

"Cool." He scooted back his chair and grabbed her empty plate, his pulse quickening. He could enjoy their day together and send her along her way easy enough. His heart had already been broken enough to avoid more temptation. "Let's see what kind of damage we can do, shall we?"

CHAPTER 3

The mischief she had longed for popped into his eyes then disappeared.

They returned to the main resort, and she grabbed her camera. Then they took the Jeep through a dirt trail that wound downhill, through a forest, and up again. The mountains split in two, leaving a valley between them. An array of colors sprouted on the horizon, muted by cold and fog.

They parked near a drop-off.

"Now we walk." He opened the door and grabbed his camera bag.

She slid out of the Jeep and peered at the view. The way the mountains slumped downhill and erupted on the other side left her anxious, but eager. Her footsteps were slow, cumbersome. She avoided the ledge and focused on the beauty.

She'd never seen it without snow but was amazed at the glory. Still, it held a melancholy that crept into her heart and snatched away any attempt at enjoyment.

Her gaze wandered down the hill toward the creek,

thoughts clustering into something she couldn't pinpoint. She took slow, even breaths to experience the splendor and fight the creeping sadness.

Remy shuffled to Seth's side and waited while he snapped his camera together then strapped it around his neck. They walked side by side until they approached a small incline.

Seth treaded down first then offered his hand in assistance.

Heat spooled down her spine at his touch, even though they both wore gloves, and she shook off the image of them as a couple. They were friends, had been friends for a long time, even though they hadn't gotten along in quite a while, and she was in love with Carson.

Seth held her hand as they trailed through the forest. Trees rose around them, beautiful, green, and luscious, but her chest ached at the scarcity of snow. The farther they walked, the worse the desolation grew. The beauty of the colorful sky braiding with the mountains lacked magic.

Seth stopped, dropped her hand, and kneeled. His lack of touch left her more desolate, longing for something she couldn't name. He aimed his camera at a distant tree and snapped several photos.

She wondered what he was taking a picture of. The landscape was beautiful, yes, but nothing she needed to memorize.

"I know what you're thinking." He dropped his camera where it hung around his neck and then stood.

"What am I thinking?" She put her hand on her hip and cocked her head.

"You're thinking there's nothing out here to photograph. But you couldn't be more wrong."

He had read her mind. He had been good about that in their younger days. Still was, apparently. "No. It's beautiful. I'm not sure I've ever seen it without snow since we only visited at Christmas. It's just..." She wasn't sure how to explain her thoughts in a comprehensible way, and if she tried, the blubbering waterworks might never stop.

"It's what?" He wheeled around, his arms outstretched to showcase nature's potency.

"Lacking something," she muttered.

He turned to her and tapped her heart. "This is lacking something. Because you're feeling all the loss and heartbreak of your parents and the past."

Heat swarmed behind her eyes, her throat tingling. She blinked.

He dropped his hand and walked away.

She followed, her mind reeling with all kinds of questions and comments and accusations. How dare he say she was lacking something! As if he could peer directly into her soul. As if he had the right to judge.

"What about you?" she finally asked. Leaves crunched beneath their feet, amplified in her ears. She didn't want to appear defensive or antagonistic, but keeping her voice on an even keel proved difficult. "You shut down the resort, your parents' life's work, because of such loss. So, you must feel that lack, too."

He dropped his bag and focused his camera, one eye closing as he looked into the lens. "Of course, I do. But not here. This is one of the only places where I don't feel anything lacking." His camera whirred with the *snap snap snap* of photos.

She decided to join him and zoomed in on a clump of pine trees. She spent time framing the background of pine bark and green leaves, then bit back a squeal when a bird landed in her focus.

Seth's words annoyed her. She hoped to experience the spirit of Christmas, fill her heart and rediscover her creativity. The realities of life had overtaken her hopes and dreams, but they nestled somewhere in the marrow of her bones. She had lost the nerve to dig them up.

She no longer had creative control at her job, doing only what she was told and crafting things she no longer cared about. Her company was only concerned about productivity, not originality. Carson loved it and had made it his life. But she longed for something more. She longed to express herself by helping others.

Now she wondered if her problems at work were her fault. They had come out for pictures and she'd resisted the beauty.

How long had she been resisting?

She clicked several shots of Seth, hoping to catch the wisp of his breath, minuscule spirits of the cold. Her own breath released, a huge discharge of pressure and stress.

Life had to be managed. She couldn't afford to take risks. Her brother and sister and their families were successful. They loved their jobs and wouldn't quit something just because it didn't allow them to pursue their creativity.

Her parents had told her to follow her dreams, but Remy wasn't sure what her dreams were anymore.

They hiked for a while, and she was pleased to learn he had water bottles stored in his camera bag. They strolled down to the creek, where she photographed him. She preferred people in her pictures doing normal things. Even mundane things. She loved to capture the essence of a person and loved how lost he got in his work.

He gave her a sideways glance and crinkled his nose. "What are you doing?"

She shrugged and grinned, but took another snapshot of him. "Nothing."

He swaggered toward her. "Come on. I've kept you out here long enough and it's probably already time for lunch."

"Can we go see the Christmas village first?"

The Christmas village was a life-sized replica of a quaint

Christmas town stationed in the backyard of the resort. Vendors sold hot chocolate, ornaments, and gifts, and offered all types of activities for visitors to enjoy. Although her favorite part of the resort wouldn't be active, expectation tingled in her body. She would move forward—she had no choice—but if nothing else, the village would be an expression of her hope.

His shoulders stiffened, mouth banding in a thin line. "Why?"

She followed him to the Jeep. "Because, I want to see it."

"I don't see the point," he said, all surly.

She climbed in and slammed the door, unsure of his abrupt change in mood. With him, it was always as if she could do nothing right. But right now, she didn't care. She had no plans to leave the resort until she visited her favorite village.

"Of course, you don't. But, if you don't mind, I'd like to see it before I leave."

Of course, you don't. Her words berated him, and once again his skin tightened, his eyes narrowing into that scowl that etched in his heart every time she was near. She irritated him like no other.

Might as well take her to the village so she could experience the desolation. Chances were when she left, she'd never want to return.

Pain stabbed his gut.

"I'll take you to see the village," he said. "Then we'll have lunch."

"And then I'll be out of your hair."

You don't have to go, he wanted to say, but couldn't. She wasn't here for him. She was here for something he couldn't provide. And he needed to get back to his life. He'd closed the resort for a reason, and the longer she stayed, the harder it would be to remember to stick to his decision.

"Although..."

He sucked in a breath, his mind reeling in suspicion. What did she want now? "Although what?"

"If it's okay, I'd like to see your pictures before I leave."

He released his breath and nodded. What harm could that do? "Okay."

"Part of my reason for coming here was to find my creativity. I mean, I've been broken for so long." She knocked her knuckles against her chest. "Like you said, lacking right here. And my creativity has been seriously lacking, too."

"This is a wonderful place to rediscover your creativity."

He couldn't ask her to stay. The whole point of closing the resort was to forget this time of year even existed. He didn't need to find that Christmas spirit when he was forced to live it his entire life. He wanted something else. He wanted to figure out who he was beyond who he was expected to be. And he didn't want to think about the memories, the fact he should be celebrating the twenty-fifth anniversary of the resort. Too many reasons pointed in the direction of closing, and asking her to stay would derail his plans.

Seth parked the Jeep and they walked to the village situated behind the resort. As they drew closer, Remy faltered. Her face slackened and paled, her chin pointing down to the ground.

"It hasn't held that same energy since our parents died." He had to say something, at least attempt an explanation. Even if the lights were on and the music played and the carousel twirled, the passion would be absent.

Remy trod the village, her mouth tight, shoulders hunched to her ears. Whether from cold or unhappiness, he didn't know. She stopped at the carousel.

Her strangled sob interrupted the heavy silence.

He approached and pulled her into his arms. She rested the top of her head on his chest, but their coats were so thick he doubted she'd hear how fast his heart was beating. He stroked her hair and supported her while she cried, his own grief long-since buried. He'd visited this place often after his parents' deaths, so much he'd grown detached.

She stifled her tears and withdrew, swiping her cheek. "I'm sorry. I didn't realize..."

"How tough it would be?"

She chewed her lip and nodded.

"We can create snow, you know. When there isn't any. We rarely had to for the village this time of year since it normally snowed, but on those days it didn't, and especially during the summer months, we could create it."

"Yeah," she muttered.

She roamed through the village path, and his gaze followed. The carousel, a fudge shop, a life-sized gingerbread house, all lined the streets like lost souls. Gone were Santa's elves and the people who worked here, offering hope and cheer to the visitors. Even people who didn't stay in the resort came here for shopping, ice skating, and entertainment.

His body ached, numbness reminding him of how much he'd lost.

Remy stopped at a picnic table and slid onto the seat. Her arms rested on the top and she leaned forward, her eyes shimmering with unshed tears. Her gaze landed on the outdoor fire pit. "I remember coming here for hot chocolate."

"We can drink hot chocolate out here before you leave." He slipped into the seat across from her. He was surprised at his offer and was certain she was, too.

Her eyes widened briefly, but she quickly concealed it

with a shaky smile and a nod. "I didn't mean to come here and disturb your plans."

"I didn't mean to ruin your Christmas," he teased.

Her smile didn't reach her eyes.

"You were honest with me. You said you came here to rediscover your creativity."

"Basically," she said.

"So, I'll be honest with you." His mouth clenched, his mind whirling with all the things he could or shouldn't say. He extended his hands forward but didn't reach for hers. "For the past two Christmases, I tried to keep things running. Tried to keep that spirit alive. I tried to give everybody else what they wanted. But I...I got lost." His ears rang, and he swallowed a sob.

And here he thought he had buried his grief. He couldn't afford to let it erupt.

She stretched toward him and clasped his hands.

Even through the gloves, her touch ignited his skin.

"It doesn't help that our parents died on Christmas."

He shook his head, furiously shaking those tears away. "No, it doesn't. It was their favorite time of year."

"You're absolutely right," she said. "Our parents loved this time of year like no other. They would never have wanted bad memories wrapped around the holidays."

Seth closed his eyes, shutting out the image of their plane going down, hitting the snow. His breath hitched.

His dad had flown the plane. Her parents had joined them, like they did many years, as they flew over the mountains to celebrate the season. Something malfunctioned and the plane went down, tumbling into the rocks of the creek and erupting in flames. It hadn't burned completely, and the experts said the two couples were dead from the impact before the fire. As if that would make any of them feel better. One distress call, and then everything went silent.

He'd often wondered if Remy and her siblings blamed his dad and, in essence, maybe that's why Remy never returned to the resort. Her brother assured him that wasn't true, that nobody blamed anybody but the weather and fate. He opened his mouth to ask her, to finally get an answer to a question that plagued him even with her brother's reassurance.

But she blurted, "It doesn't help this is the twenty-fifth anniversary of the resort, either."

Seth drew in a stuttered breath and swiped a hand over his face. He was shocked she knew. Shocked she'd remembered.

She shrugged. "I never imagined you'd want to do something big for the resort's anniversary. And I don't blame you at all. But to shut down?"

Her question ate at him. His ears tingled, tongue burned with unspoken words. What would she know about celebrating a twenty-five-year anniversary?

"I'm sorry," Remy said, again taking him by surprise.

His arms drew into his body. "Sorry for what?"

"Sorry for not being there for you."

"You had your own grief to deal with."

"I know. But I didn't come to your parents' funeral."

"I know." Her absence had cut into his defenses, but no point in admitting that to her now.

"You came to mine."

"Yeah." He bit his lips and leaned back, crossing his arms over his chest. He didn't want to have this conversation. His whole life he had fought his attraction. Easier to stay curt when he thought the worst of her. Her apology wore him thin, chiseled away at the shield of animosity preventing him from falling in love with a fanciful delusion.

Her brows tangled together. "I should have been there."

He wanted to hate her for it, but he couldn't. "You had your own things to do."

"I have no excuse except I was selfish and couldn't deal with what happened. I couldn't come here, be here, see this place that brought my parents such happiness."

He wanted to understand. Her brother and sister had managed to attend the service, but they never made excuses for her. All they said was that she sent her love. But they had also lost their parents, and it'd been a dark day for everyone.

"A place that brought me such happiness." Her voice was low, reserved.

His stomach sank. He rested his chin in one hand, the other holding his elbow. His gaze ping-ponged to the sites he'd seen a million times, trying to avoid watching her. The lifeless storefronts reminded of the ghost town he'd enjoyed visiting with his parents. He imagined the ghosts of his past chastising him for the decisions he'd made, and the hard choices he'd avoided.

The resort had brought many people happiness, including himself. He closed his eyes and pinched the bridge of his nose. He'd expected the shutdown would generate all kinds of emotions he'd grown used to ignoring, but he wanted to be alone when that happened.

"It's snowing!"

Her voice jerked his eyes open.

Remy slid out of the seat and jumped up. White flakes drifted down. She held out her hands and twirled, tilted up her face and stuck out her tongue, laughing. "Why did we stop playing snowball fights?" she asked as snow pranced around her.

His pulse dipped. Skin throbbed. The softness of her features and the play of lights while the sun, muted by the clouds and the snow, cast a gentle glow around her.

He couldn't tell her they'd stopped playing in the snow and anything else that involved her, because he was fighting back his attraction. Although their parents were friends,

Seth's had warned him against getting too close to guests, as if they had seen his growing interest. He blamed it on being a teenager and had sought out plenty of other relationships. Women loved him this time of year, until they realized life with him involved more work than fun.

He couldn't tell her the memory of her kicking his heart to the curb still burned.

His pulse lurched when he caught the telltale sounds of a Christmas song beneath her lips. The snow fell thicker and her voice grew louder. Her smile widened and she held out her hands, lifted her face, and danced under the enchantment of the drifting flakes.

His pain deepened into an all-out defeat.

CHAPTER 4

S now drifted around Remy. Adrenaline spiked her
blood, joy saturating her limbs.

Seth stood with his hands stuffed in his pockets,
the white sticking to his hair.

She laughed and sauntered toward him, brushing the snow
off his cheeks. "Come on, sing with me."

Their gazes touched. Her breath stalled then tingled in
her throat. Her hand paused on his cheek. Despite the cold,
warmth tickled her spine like the first spark of a bonfire.

His breath wisped out of him in a flimsy cloud.

She wondered what his mouth would feel like on hers.
Remy dropped her hand from his cheek and danced away,
distancing herself from him. Although they had fought and
she wasn't sure they could make things work, she was still in
love with Carson.

Their childhood relationship made it easy to reach out to
Seth, to touch him so casually. They shared camaraderie not
unlike siblings, and she trusted him, despite her childhood
infatuation and their past differences. The jolt was unusual
and unexpected.

"It isn't sticking to the ground." She strode to a pine tree and brushed her hand across the bark, shaking off the clumsy bounce in her pulse. "Not even to the trees."

"Maybe it's too warm."

She reeled to face him, tucking her hands under her arms and shivering at the breeze. "It isn't too warm."

"Maybe we'll wake up in the morning to find a snow-covered ground." He nodded toward the resort. "Come on. Let's go get some lunch, shall we?"

Maybe we'll wake up in the morning to find a snow-covered ground. Was this a sign he planned to let her stay? She didn't ask, not yet. No sense in ruining a good moment.

She followed his lead, setting her gear on a table in the lobby and her coat and gloves in the closet. She didn't mind having the place to herself, did she? She could decorate a few things to give it the spirit and take some time to rediscover her creativity.

She didn't have a backup plan if he said no. Since she still had two weeks to go, she'd probably spend some time in Colorado and then head home to spend Christmas with her family. But the whole point of being gone and making Carson miss her would all be for naught if she went back to him.

They entered the kitchen. "What do you have to eat in here?" she asked.

"Soup." He opened the large freezer and fetched a bag. "You want some rolls, too? Crackers, or something?"

"What kind of soup?"

"What kind do you want? Potato, tomato basil, tortilla soup. Broccoli and cheese."

"How about tomato basil?"

He switched the food saver bag for another.

"If that's okay with you," she said, guilt eating her. "We can just do the one you had."

"No. I just pulled the first one I saw. Tomato basil sounds delicious."

"Anything will be delicious if Maye is still cooking."

"She's still cooking."

Memories of Maye warmed her soul. Maye was a temptress in the kitchen and had helped Remy find her love for cooking. Instead of ruling the kitchen with an iron fist, she let Remy accompany many cook sessions.

"How is Maye?" she asked.

He opened the bag and poured it into a pressure cooker. "She's doing well. Just as feisty as ever. She's spending the holidays with her kids and grandkids."

"Didn't they used to come here for Christmas?"

"Yes. But, in spite of her disappointment, she said they could always make new traditions. She understood and supported my decision."

Remy didn't respond. After their earlier conversation, she couldn't judge his reasons. She followed him into the lobby, where he stacked wood into the fireplace.

"My sister said they would create new traditions this year too. But she knew you had shut down, didn't she?"

He nodded but didn't glance at her. "Landon knew."

"And yet they didn't tell me." Remy hadn't stopped wondering why since she'd arrived here to find it closed. Why didn't Tessa tell her he was shut down for the season? She'd sent texts to ask, but all messages failed. "They told me they were going to the coast. Asked if I wanted to join them, but didn't tell me I'd be wasting my time coming here."

"I don't know." Seth stoked the fire and roused a blaze, the wood popping. "I spoke directly to Landon. Maybe he didn't pass on the word."

"Oh, he did." Her older brother had definitely passed the word to her sister, and her sister had let her waste her holidays visiting a shut-down resort alone. But why? Her family had always liked Seth, even teased her about dating him way back when, but surely they wouldn't resort to matchmaking.

A high probability with her sister.

The soup didn't take long. They poured it into bowls and sat on the couch in the lobby to eat near the crackling fire. He told her of events at the resort, funny things that had happened, and they avoided any serious subjects. His eyes lit up when he spoke of the resort, his love for the place evident. Maybe he wanted to find himself, figure out what he wanted to do with his life outside of this place, but his history was a huge part of him.

How could she help him realize the truth?

Once she'd drained her soup, she set her bowl on the end table and stretched. "That was delicious." She dreaded what would happen next. She wasn't ready to go home, and she wondered if she ever would be. "Tessa and Landon have family of their own. Kids with a house full of animals and laughter and joy. Why would they want to pick up and go to the coast for Christmas? Why not just stay home if they couldn't come here?"

Seth shrugged. "Hard for me to say." He spread out his arms. "I've had to experience Christmas here for my entire life. It's almost like being an elf working in Santa's shop."

"Oh, come on. You love it though, right?"

Lips tightening, he slow-blinked, then nodded. "I do. I wouldn't have traded it for the world. And, despite the name, it's not like we celebrate Christmas every day of the year. The resort celebrates every holiday in creative ways. My mom was good at figuring all that out."

She longed to erase the shadow on his face. "I miss them, too. Christmas will never be the same, but you can still make it good. You can still make those plans and have fun events, and if it's something you don't enjoy, someone else will."

His scowl deepened. "I've done nothing but make it good

for people my entire life. It's time I put myself first, don't you think?"

Her breath grew warm in her throat. She retreated and ended the conversation before it got worse. "And that's exactly what you're doing." *But are you really?* Instead of prodding, she asked, "Do you still have your computer room? I brought my laptop, but I'd love to take a look at your pictures before I go. Load them on my laptop, maybe? That is, if you don't mind me having a copy."

"You can have all the copies you want. I'll even sign a release if you want to use them in your graphic design."

"Oh, I couldn't possibly. That wouldn't be fair. Unless I paid you for them."

He stood and went for his camera. "We can discuss that later. Do you remember where the computer room is?"

"I do."

"I'll meet you there."

Once Remy was inside her room, she took a long, deep breath to regain her bearings. Sitting so close to Seth, enjoying their conversation, and then being alone made her more desperate for his company. But she couldn't afford an attraction to Seth.

It was just a silly infatuation. One she'd always had with him.

Neither could she overstay her welcome. Seth needed to work out his issues, and she couldn't help. He wanted to spend Christmas alone, and being alone was the last thing she wanted.

If she went home to Carson, she'd be alone. If she celebrated Christmas with her family, she'd still be alone even with company all around. Sure, she had nieces and nephews to dote on, and she loved them, but she would be the odd-one out. If she stayed in Laurel Springs, she'd be alone, but at least near the place she'd planned to stay for the holidays.

None of her options appealed to her. Her heart had been set on staying here.

She grabbed her laptop and met Seth. Truth was, she didn't need a computer room to do her work, but she loved the atmosphere. The large and open floor plan boasted floor-to-ceiling windows on the back end of the wall. Small desktop computers scattered on solo tables for the patrons who needed them and who wanted to work alone. Other tables stood vacant for those who wanted to sit and read or those who had brought their own computer.

She chose a table and hooked up. He gave her his camera card and before long she got lost in her work.

Remy loved it too much to consider it work. Like Seth had said when he was taking pictures, nothing lacked in her creative endeavors. Energy buzzed her skin, even her bones vibrated with the absolute pleasure of sorting pictures, creating graphics from them, or polishing them to give them a different appeal.

The photos he'd taken were already fabulous, and she was overwhelmed by their beauty. He captured magic with his lens.

She had overlooked the deer in the field, but he caught it, the buck studying them from afar, trees and mountains offering a whimsical backdrop. Despite its beauty, she played with the photo, deepening the red berries and coating it with a subdued overcast. She then used her program to make a postcard and connected to the network to print her creation.

She stood to grab the letter-sized photo, imagining how awesome it would look enlarged. With the right printing and framing, the colors would burst off the page.

Her neck and back ached. She stretched and glanced at the clock, gasping at the time inching over seven.

How long had she hunkered over the computer? Hours. Darkness reigned outside. How had she not noticed?

"Seth?" She strolled out the door, clutching the photo. Guilt chipped away at her happiness. Where had he been this whole time? She shouldn't have taken advantage of this situation. Seth hadn't wanted her to stay, and she no longer wanted to goad him into changing his mind. That wouldn't be fair to him, or their friendship. She would leave and find a hotel. If any were available this time of year.

"Hey." He met her in the doorway and smiled.

"Hey." She smoothed a hand over the top of her head. "I'm so sorry. I lost track of time."

"It's okay. I understand losing yourself in your creative moments. I had some work to do and didn't want to disturb you."

"Oh, I appreciate you letting me work in your computer room."

"It's no problem. It's an inspirational place."

Everything about this resort is inspirational.

"What do you have there?" He nodded at the photo she clutched.

She handed it to him. "Well, it will be better on photo quality paper and all, but it's just something I was having fun with."

His eyebrows rose as he studied it. "Wow. It's beautiful." He glanced at her. His gaze lowered to her mouth, then up again to her eyes.

She swallowed, longing to feel his mouth on hers. The warmth, the taste, the tongue. The fantasy shocked her, the image burning her skin.

He reeled away, breaking their contact and leaving her cold. "This would look incredible above the mantel here." Seth stopped in the lobby. Already, the mantel displayed a photo of a snowy mountain backdrop and trees covered in Christmas lights.

"Did you take this one?" she asked.

"No. My parents bought this somewhere in town. I don't even think it's a local artist. Do you mind if I buy this photo from you? I'd like to enlarge and frame it and put it up here."

"Yes, I mind. It's your photo. And you won't be paying me."

"But you worked so hard on it."

"I won't take your money. Speaking of, I need to pay you for last night's room."

"No," he said, his eyes growing dark. "I won't charge you for last night, and you won't charge me for the picture. Is that fair?"

She nodded, heat swelling behind her eyes. Had he recognized her skill? She gulped back tears. "That's fair."

"And I won't charge you for tonight, either."

Her head lifted. "You what?"

"It's dark out. You might as well stay. That is, if you want to."

Of course, she wanted to. "Are you sure? I mean, I know you had your own thing to do."

"I'm sure. Besides, I still need to get this photo saved. I have a gallery I'd like to take it to where they can print it on canvas for me. I might even let them do the framing this time."

"What do you mean this time? Do you normally frame your own?"

He shrugged. "I usually do, yes. From old wood. Sometimes from old metal or something I see in antique shops I like to use."

"Wow," she said, in awe at his artistry. She glanced around at the photos in the lobby. "Did you take all of these?"

"No. Not all. The ones in my house, and some of the rooms here, yes, but not the ones here."

"Why not?" She longed to know more about him and why his artwork wasn't displayed across every inch of the walls.

"Too busy I guess."

She brushed a stray hair that had fallen across his earlobe. "Or too modest. I know what it's like not wanting to share your work."

Two weeks out of the year was never enough time to get to know this enchanting man, and she longed to know more. They had both been young, and their parents' association had kept any potential relationship from developing past friendship.

She was already feeling better just by spending the past twenty-four hours here, with him.

Now she didn't have much time at all.

How could he explain his reasons for not sharing the vulnerable side of his creativity?

His skin tingled when she touched him. She dropped her hand and nodded as if she understood exactly without him having to explain. But she had no idea, not really, and it wouldn't be fair for him to attempt an explanation.

Modesty was just one part of it. But he'd practically been born into this resort. His parents had expected him to take over one day. He didn't have time for creative nonsense.

"Well, I'd love to see the photo once it's done," she said.

"Absolutely." Maybe next year he'd open the resort. Maybe next year she would visit—maybe she'd even be married—and then she could see the picture.

His parents had supported him, even encouraged him. They knew how much he loved to take and frame photos. As well as his other art. The resort kept him busy, and it took him a long time to find enough faith to share his work with others.

His mom had taken immaculate care in decorating each

room of the resort, so he didn't want to swap the artwork she'd chosen. He had replaced some of the older photos, though.

The memory of him sharing some of his art with Remy and of her turning away almost made him crumble. He didn't bother sharing with her now.

After Seth had left Remy alone to work on her art, he roamed the empty spaces in desolation. He missed the laughter and joy that should be filling the rooms. For a moment, he thought about changing his mind and opening for Christmas.

Her energy, her presence, filled his soul.

And that scared him. He shoved down the idea of opening his heart, and the resort. "Come on. It's time for dinner."

"What's for dinner?" she asked.

He strode into the kitchen and she skipped after him. His pulse romped.

"Maye has all kinds of stuff frozen. Or we can go back to my house where there's food."

"I'm sure we can find something here. Do you mind if I look around for something to cook?"

"You don't have to cook for me."

"You don't have to cook for me, either. Besides, I want to. I love to cook."

"You do?" he asked, surprised at how little he knew about her.

"I do."

Her words wrapped around him, making him dizzy. For a moment, he pictured her in a white wedding dress, in the lobby here at the resort where their paths had always crossed. Lights twinkled around them, her dress sparkling.

He shook the image away. He was not a romantic. Why were these fantasies developing? This Remy wasn't the same

Remy who lived her life outside of this resort. Everyone who came here was in vacation mode. Their lives stalled and they became different people. As if the resort held some magical spell. Sometimes it could change people, but Remy had her own life to live, and not here.

"Do you ever think about picking up and moving?" he asked. Why not prove a point to himself? Remy had her own life. She probably preferred the coast to the mountains, and she'd never consider moving to a place that was colder more times than warm.

She inspected the pantry. "All the time." She opened the freezer and fetched a package of beef.

He wondered what she was making, but didn't bother telling her Maye probably had whatever she planned already frozen. He would let Remy enjoy the process. "What's your fantasy? I mean, where would you live if you could choose any place on earth?"

She dropped the package in the sink and turned on the water. "Here. Right here. In these mountains. At this resort."

His heart thump-thump-thumped. His knees buckled. She had no idea what she was saying.

"What about you?" she asked.

He sucked in a deep breath, reigning in his pensiveness. "I don't know," he said. "But I can tell you that this place, these mountains, are harsh in the winter. It gets cold. Very cold."

She shrugged and rummaged through the freezer again, grabbing a bag of veggies. "I like cold."

"You've never known cold like this."

She tore open a package of onions and okra. "Oh, come on. Now you're just being bitter."

His gut tensed at Remy's words, calling him out on his feelings without trying to understand them.

"You aren't thinking of shutting down the resort for good, are you?" she asked, her face in a worry-frown.

"No. No, nothing like that. I would never shut it down. Perhaps I would sell it, but I doubt I'd do that, either. One day I hope to have kids who will work in it like I did, and who will eventually run it."

And a wife to share it all with. The rest of his dream was now out in the open. At one point, he had hoped to take over and run his parents' resort. Their grandchildren flittering through the halls with them running and laughing after them. But if he were to have children, they would never have the joy of knowing their grandparents.

"Maybe you need help running it, for now," Remy said.

"I have the best help on the planet."

"That's not what I meant. I meant, you know, running the ins and outs of it so you could take some time to yourself instead of shutting it down."

There she went again. Chastising him for shutting down a Christmas resort at Christmas. She meant well, but it got under his skin. And maybe it got under his skin because guilt consumed him every waking moment. He had disappointed a lot of people. The locals, his staff, and the guests who already had reservations. But he needed to endure this season of his life.

He needed to get through this evening and then Remy would be gone.

"Yeah, maybe," he muttered to answer her, but also to answer his own thoughts.

He wanted a partner who loved the resort as much as his parents had. As much as he did. She would have to love the holidays enough to celebrate year-round, and be responsible for the seasons' changing themes. He imagined dancing with her, whirling her around the floor while she laughed and energized the entire resort, much like his parents had.

But every time that image popped into his head, he pictured Remy by his side.

CHAPTER 5

Remy woke the next morning, her stomach tight with dread. Today was the day to leave, and it was best to do so before Seth woke. Leaving would be hard enough without having to say goodbye.

She packed her suitcase and thought of all the ways she could beg him to let her stay. Maybe if she lingered. Joined him for outdoor pictures. Offered to help with chores and keep out of his way.

But she had overstayed her welcome. Finding a hotel would be difficult this time of year but, in her heavy heart, she knew it must be done. She could spend a few days in Colorado, play in the snow, and still make it home in time for Christmas with her family. She would treasure these little moments and make new memories in town. Maybe next year would be ripe for returning.

She wrote him a short letter while eating a granola bar she'd found in her purse.

Dear Seth, thank you for letting me have a room for a few days. Thank you for taking me with you on your photography journey. Thank you... I'm sorry... She stopped and stared at the page, her mind blank, her eagerness waning. She tucked it into her pocket, along with the USB of photos, and carried her suitcases downstairs. She would finish the letter once she had a chance to think.

The cold air struck her face, her throat tingling. She stored her suitcases in her trunk, slammed it closed, and stuffed her hands in her pockets, shoulders inching to her neck. Her pulse dipped when she spotted Seth in the distance, hiking from his home, his attention on her. His footsteps whisked across the trail, a silent staccato rhythm of urgency drumming straight into her chest. She stood at her car door and waited, her hands curling on the note she hadn't finished.

"You were going to leave without saying goodbye?" he asked, a glower cutting into his forehead. He licked his lips, mouth tightening.

"Not at all. Just loading my stuff." She dug in her pocket and pulled out the USB. "Oh, and here's a drive with all your photos." An invisible layer of uncertainty stood between them.

He accepted the USB and slid it into his right pocket, where his hand remained. "Thank you. I appreciate that." His voice was tight, face taut with tension.

"Next time I come, I expect to see the one with the deer you liked hanging above the mantel."

He nodded and smiled a smile that didn't reach his eyes or soften his face. He was upset with her, clearly. He glanced at the ground and kicked the dirt. "You will."

Feeling awkward and ungraceful, she stood near the door of her car, wondering what to do or say next. "I appreciate you letting me stay."

He raised his head and nodded once. "It's no problem. I had fun."

"Me, too." She hesitated but didn't want to leave him

thinking she wasn't appreciative. "I wasn't going to leave without saying goodbye." She pulled out the note, crinkled her nose as she studied it, then crumpled the paper and stuffed it back into her pocket. "I just didn't want to disturb you."

"It's all good." His voice remained stiff, but tempered. His shoulders remained hunched, hands stuffed in his pockets, eyes hooded. "Did you have breakfast?"

"Yes. I grabbed an energy bar."

"Where do you plan to go now?"

A basic conversation, him asking her questions out of politeness. She should lie and say she was going home. "I'm going to see if there are any vacant hotels in town."

One eyebrow rose. "You aren't going home?"

Might as well be honest. She grabbed the door handle, her movements stilted. What else could they say to each other but goodbye? Besides, his countenance made her nervous, like he was ready for her to leave and trying to be polite. Or mad because she was leaving and he still wasn't convinced of her intent. "No. I'm not ready to go home yet."

"So, you'll be alone for Christmas?" His voice lifted the hair on the back of her neck, already chilled by the wisps of cold air.

"I'll probably go home for Christmas, but I would have been alone here, too."

She realized her pointed accusation at the same time his lips pursed. She stumbled over an explanation. "I mean my family wouldn't be here. You would be busy and..."

She sighed, not ready to tell him about Carson. Seth frowned and glanced around, as if he wanted to say something. Wishful thinking on her part. She wished he'd ask her to stay, but she wouldn't dare ask permission.

His mood had soured when she even mentioned him closing down, and she couldn't ask him to change his mind.

She hoped he would see how much the place meant to him, but she understood his reasoning.

Celebrating the holidays with the anniversary of his parents' deaths along with the twenty-fifth anniversary of the resort's opening wouldn't be easy. But he thought he needed this time alone, and she could no longer intrude.

Time seemed to pause. Their breaths, their movements on hold.

She leaned forward and brushed her thumb across his cheek, "I'll be fine, though. Thank you again for letting me stay. And don't be a stranger. If you're ever in Texas, give me a call."

He nodded. "Okay. Will do."

"Have a Merry Christmas."

"Yeah. You, too."

She planted a kiss on his cheek then dropped the hand still resting there, which had remained way too long for her wellbeing. His scent engulfed her, like fresh grass clippings after a long, soaking rain.

She opened the door and waved. "Take care." She slid into the seat and shut the door.

He waved, bumped his palm on the car roof, then turned and walked away. Her pulse battered, her entire body a dance of confused heat, hot and cold. She wasn't parked that far, the first spot from the building since she was the only visitor, and he made it into the resort before she fired up the engine.

Probably eager to be rid of her. She'd wanted to escape the melancholy her Christmas memories wrought, and yet she'd run right toward misery.

She flipped the ignition, but the car didn't start. She pumped the gas and tried again, but it only gave a click. She beat her hands against the steering wheel, frustration welling.

This couldn't be happening right now.

A knock on the window made her jump.

"Is everything okay?" Seth asked.

Jaw knotting, she opened the door. "My car won't start."

His gaze narrowed, lips flattened, and he studied her. Did he think she'd done this on purpose? Like she would be smart enough to do such a thing even if she did want an excuse to stay. His suspicions weren't at all fair, considering she'd never been manipulative. Their friendship waned when he'd copped this horrible attitude and suspected her of being a terrible person. One day, maybe she would ask what she'd done to cause that mistrust.

"Pop the hood and I'll see what I can do. Could be the battery. Weak batteries are always weaker in cold weather like this."

While he checked under her hood, she huddled in the car. The bleak landscape and icy cold crept into her bones. Why had his parents never built a parking garage for their guests?

"I'll run and get my Jeep to see if we can jumpstart it."

"Okay."

"You can go back inside to stay warm."

She fought the urge to huddle into her jacket, refusing to go inside his property. The more detached she could stay away from him, the better. "I'm fine," she said.

She watched him walk away, her heart sinking with each of his steps. Her body ached, throat burned. Homesick for how things used to be between them, when they were friends.

She'd thought she knew what she wanted. The white picket fence with Carson, house full of kids, and an exhilarating creative career. But coming here made her question her motives.

She enjoyed Seth's company. He was the one person she could be herself with, even when he thought the worst of her. At one time in her life, she had fantasized about marrying him and forever living in this resort.

Until she had convinced herself it was all a fairytale, and this place—no matter how beautiful—was no castle.

She didn't want to leave, but more importantly she didn't want to leave Seth. She had missed him.

He was abrupt when he returned.

He shot her an annoyed look as he jumped out of the vehicle and walked to her car to set up the cables. She hugged herself, then dropped her arms lest he berate her for standing in the cold. His pinched expression flustered her, but she could do little about the circumstances.

He flipped the ignition, but nothing happened.

Her heart flopped in her belly, dying a slow death with her car.

"Could be the ignition switch," Seth said. "Or something else fairly simple enough. Why don't you go inside? I'll call Derrick and see if he has time to run out."

"Who is Derrick?" She should probably know something about the man who was going to work on her car.

"Owns the mechanic shop in town. Good guy. I've known him forever."

She followed him inside, her footsteps heavy, and he made the phone call. She dropped to the couch. Nothing at all was going her way this Christmas season. Then again, it hadn't in years. She wanted to like Christmas again, but that desire would remain unfulfilled this year.

"Derrick said he can be here in about an hour."

Overcome with anxiety, Remy rested the back of her head on the couch and closed her eyes. Dizziness assaulted her, heat blanketing her body despite the chill on her skin. Even her toes ached.

Yes, she had wanted to stay, but now it all seemed pointless. He wanted her to leave, and she was ready to decide what to do for the rest of her vacation time.

The Fusion was fine before this trip. She'd stayed up to

date on the maintenance. The warranty had expired, but she had too many other stresses than to plan on a new car purchase.

She jumped up, but nearly collapsed when she grew light-headed. She blew out a breath and regained her bearings. "I'm going to take a walk outside." She needed to be alone. Didn't want Seth to see her cry again.

He stoked the embers in the fireplace, stirring them to life. She didn't know why he bothered, considering she wouldn't be here long. "Yeah, okay," he said.

"The keys are still in the ignition if Derrick comes before I make it back."

Seth's brows bunched together. He nodded and returned his attention to the flames.

Preferring the backyard, where several hiking trails awaited including the one to the village, she strode to the rear glass-encased door, but it wouldn't open. She struggled with the knob then tussled with the lock, letting out a soft groan of frustration.

Seth approached, his warm body a total distraction. She wrenched her gaze away from him.

He unlocked the door and had it open within seconds. The cold air hit her face in welcome consolation.

"Thank you." She rushed out.

Maybe they stopped being friends because they had both gotten older and more attracted to each other. Stress and sadness warped her limbs into a prickly, crampy mess. Her car not starting was a catalyst to unburying years of frustration, disappointment, and grief. Like she was being taunted by every effort she made.

She could barely walk, could barely stand, but she inched her way to the Christmas village to find a safe haven.

None of this was familiar.

She wanted to fall into her mother's arms and hear her

coo about how everything was going to be okay. That her life, her job, her choices, and her relationship would all work out. Since her mom wasn't here to offer comfort, she should picture Carson wrapping his arms around her. But all she imagined was Seth's.

She stopped at the carousel. She'd never seen it so dead, the lack of movement and color aggravating the dread that continued to stuff inside her heart since her parents' deaths. Why had she considered coming here a good idea? As if the memories would help with closure. And why did she feel running would entice Carson to chase?

She wasn't sure she even wanted him to chase her anymore.

She longed to show him this place. Show him all the good memories she'd had growing up. But he didn't love Christmas the way she did, and the longer she stayed with him, the more she resented her favorite holiday. Her parents had died, so being alone made it even more difficult. Easier to just pretend like the holiday was something she had to endure.

But she didn't want to be bitter, and her parents wouldn't have wanted that for her, either. And now Seth was choosing to turn his back on what mattered. Her chest ached.

Moments passed, but the outdoors offered no sanctuary. Her limbs grew cold, toes nearly cracking even under the heavy socks. She should go in and borrow his phone to call hotels. Her cell still wasn't receiving service, and now she couldn't keep a charge. The snow that had teased them yesterday was now a distant memory.

Much like other memories of the past.

"Derrick's here."

She jerked around at Seth's voice.

"If you want to meet him."

She bunched her hands inside her sweater. She hadn't put on gloves or her cap, and the wind was biting. But she wasn't ready to go inside. Being out here had to either offer a cleansing, or a punishment. She just didn't know which.

She wasn't ready to move in case all the emotions pushing their way through her stomach would rise in her throat and burst out in a screaming, aching cry. He was here to fix her car, and maybe her car not starting was a sign.

"I'm good right now. Thank you. But please tell me before he leaves, because I'd like to meet him then and say thank you."

He stepped forward, but not enough to close the distance between them. "Are you okay?"

She blinked away the burn in her eyes. She had wanted to come here, to escape, but also to rediscover herself and her memories. Find closure. Whatever. Just get it away from it all. She could wrap herself in loneliness or find vicarious joy through the other guests. But now, she had no option but to be alone. "Just remembering how things used to be."

He nodded. "You've been out here awhile."

"I thought Derrick got here pretty quickly."

"Forty-two minutes."

"Wow. No wonder my fingers are cold." She brought her hands to her face, as if her fragile breath would heat them.

Seth approached and wrapped his warm, gloved hands around her icy cold ones.

She suddenly had the urge to confess all her thoughts and emotions to him, and her mouth took over before her restraints did. "My brother and sister have everything so put together. Their lives are all figured out. I just can't figure out mine."

He squeezed her hand. "Just because someone seems to have their life figured out doesn't mean it's true."

Her laugh was a stark and stoic sound, blemished by grief and resignation. "Guess that's true. Most people thought I had mine figured out."

"I know the feeling."

She cringed then looked at him. Her breath halted, his gaze holding hers in a potent commotion of attraction. Her mouth grew dry. His warm hands kept holding hers. She swallowed and tamped down on anything that would lure her to him. Nostalgia was heavy, but she had to remember that's what kept her enticed.

She glanced down. "I suppose you do."

He dropped her hands then nodded backward, toward the main building. "Come on. Let's go inside before we freeze to death. I've still got the fire in the fireplace. And coffee sure does sound good right now."

She followed him inside, leaving a safe distance between them, and she made a beeline toward the fireplace while he shuffled toward the kitchen.

"I promised Derrick a cup of coffee. I'll grab you one, too."

"Thanks." She rubbed her hands over the fire as it crackled. Her body prickled with spreading warmth. Her limbs thawed, and she fought the urge to watch him walk away.

Seth brought her coffee, then took one to the mechanic outside.

She sipped hers and considered roaming the resort, checking out the library and pool area to see if anything had changed since her last visit, but doing so didn't feel right. Seth was kind enough to let her stay. She had to remain within her boundaries.

She stood near the fire, studying the flames, when the men's footsteps resounded on the floor. The cold amplified every sound, including her pulse drumming in her ears. She didn't understand where the nerves were coming from when she'd never been nervous with Seth before.

Derrick approached and introduced himself. He was a large man with friendly blue eyes and a thick scruffy beard, sandy brown with gray flecks. A beanie covered his head. She wondered if his shoulders were as broad as they looked or if was the double layers of his worn jackets. He said something about her vehicle that made no sense, but her ears perked up when he said the car was now running and ready to go.

"Thank you. How much do I owe you?"

His gaze flittered to Seth. "Oh, uh, no charge."

"No charge? Really?" She planted her hands on her hips and scowled at Seth. "This isn't your responsibility."

"He offered me a free weekend with my wife." Derrick stroked his beard, eyes wide and hopeful. "Including a babysitter." He cast Seth a sheepish glance, then back to her, square jawed and seemingly determined not to accept money from her. "My wife loves this place, but we can rarely afford rarely a long weekend away from the kids. Her birthday is in January, so it's going to be the best gift ever. I consider it more than a fair trade."

Remy didn't know how to respond to that. She'd didn't want to embarrass Derrick and would have to take up her issues with Seth later. She offered her hand for a shake. "Okay, well, thank you for coming out and fixing my car."

"My pleasure."

Seth accompanied him out the door. When he came back inside, he held up a hand. "Don't say a word. You aren't paying me."

She lifted her chin, refusing to let him win. "I should at least pay for his room."

He stopped near the fireplace and leaned his hand on the brick wall. "No. January is my down time. That room probably would be vacant if I hadn't offered it."

"I doubt you have down time around here."

His jaw tightened. "Well, I do."

"I thought the resort was closed until March."

Seth shrugged. "I can make exceptions."

Heat bubbled up her spine. Her leg gave out as she moved forward, and she planted it on the floor in a sloppy stance of trying to keep balance. She brushed her hand through her hair, but couldn't tamp down on her snide comments. "You'll make exceptions?" *But not for me,* she wanted to add. "Do they want to be alone? Sure, probably, but part of the fun of this resort is being with the other guests. Experiencing it with the other guests. And the staff."

Seth opened his mouth to argue, but Remy recognized a losing battle. His decision was on him, and if it helped him decide to reopen the resort, so be it. Everything was already too awkward. No need to make it worse. She could mail him a check later.

"I don't know," he said, but she was already moving away from him. "It was just a suggestion. I'm sure they're fine with waiting."

She nodded and wave, an awkward attempt to let things go. "Thanks again for letting me stay. And for taking care of things with Derrick. I appreciate it all."

"No problem. I'll walk you out."

The car was still running, the vapors plugging the air. Remy gave him a quick, one-armed hug. No sense in prolonging the inevitable or acting like things were okay between them. She drove away, bottling her tears. She made it to the main road before she cried. Hard, fast tears than had her leaning forward and clutching the steering wheel.

She should have pulled over. Should have let the tears roll without fighting them. Her stomach hurt. Eyes ached. She had to cut the heat down because of the intense sweat behind her neck.

But then she drove into a town covered in white. The stark contrast of the resort's barrenness to the snowy winter wonderland of town bewildered her. She found a spot in the outdoor car park and sat in the car a moment, waiting for the tears to dry.

She cried for herself, but she also cried for Seth. He was so well put together, a good guy who loved the resort, but he didn't realize how much the resort meant to him. She recognized burn-out. He would crawl out of the hole of despair, and she understood why he needed to do what he did, but she hated it, and not only because it ruined her plans.

She wanted to spend more time with him. She enjoyed spending time with him. Always had, even as a child. Even as they grew older and he was always grumpy, like he didn't want her around. She hadn't asked him why. No sense in stirring up old ghosts.

She checked her phone. No texts from Carson. But was she disappointed? She wasn't sure how to recognize her true feelings anymore.

Except for sadness.

She sent one to her sister to let her know she'd made it to Laurel Springs but the resort was closed and she hadn't had any service. *But I have a feeling you already knew that* she typed and hit send. Why hadn't they told her Seth had shut down? Seth had admitted that Landon knew, so how could Tessa not know? And how could they have kept it from her?

She sent another message. *I don't understand why you didn't tell me. Now I have to find a hotel in the middle of nowhere.*

She climbed out of her car, determined to make the best of this situation. Besides, she loved the town and had wanted to do some shopping.

She'd worry about a place to stay later.

Seth roamed the resort, the emptiness thundering with his footsteps. He laundered her sheets and blankets and washed the coffee cups. He grabbed the fireplace poker and worked at extinguishing the fire, leveling the cinders and thinking about his own life, flattened for some time now. His throat tightened as the embers gradually weakened.

Should he have let Remy go? Should he have invited her to stay? What good could have happened if she had stayed? What would that change?

Nothing. It would have changed nothing. He still would have searched his heart for some kind of life left. His hope had died along with his parents, and yet he had kept this resort open and alive. He had tried to live their dream, even if it wasn't his. He could hire other people to take care of it, but he wasn't ready. He wasn't ready to give up control and he wasn't ready to say goodbye. He hoped a break would reenergize and motivate him.

If not, maybe he would consider selling.

He stoked the fire until it formed into a mound of ash, then he grabbed the shovel to cover the ashes over the cooling wood. He continued this process, like a witch stirring her concoction. Stirring, burying, stirring, burying. Burying his memories, his longings, his hopes and dreams, and yet continue to stir out the flames of his life.

He loved the resort. He did. But did he love it as much as his parents had?

The residual ache at closing was now a complex and vivid gash. He'd wanted to be alone. He had no plans for celebrations, lights, festivities, and all the Christmas enchantment. But now he missed it terribly.

He missed the chatter, the joyous laughs and hopes, and helping others experience their dreams. He missed the lights and sounds, the songs and liveliness of the season. How could he ignore that? How could he thrive and live with his decision?

He backpacked through the forest that evening, taking

pictures of the sunset in hopes it would change his feelings and remind him of why he'd decided to shut down. But all it did was exacerbate how completely isolated he felt.

He tossed and turned all night long, then got up early for pictures of the sunrise. He was still conflicted. Still burdened by his decision that affected more than just him. Now he doubted himself.

He roamed his father's office. Technically his now, but Seth hadn't taken over. Not completely. All kinds of plaques, inspirational messages, and photos of the resort guests straggled throughout the open space or on the wall. He picked up one of him and his dad fly-fishing, one of them both golfing. His dad loved many things, but he hadn't loved anything more than his family. And this resort.

Seth loved it, too, but he wanted someone by his side to love it with him. His mom and dad had opened this resort together. He doubted he'd ever find someone who loved it as much as he did. Even to Remy, it offered a fantasy world at Christmas, but she would go on about her life the rest of the time.

He opened the desk drawer where he kept the letter. Seth had read it dozens of times, especially this season, but he hadn't moved it since his family's attorney had given it to him at the will reading. He'd stored it here, the place he'd imagined his father writing it, and only retrieved it when he needed encouragement.

He plopped into the chair where his dad had once sat, and read the tear-stained letter. His eyes burned, the written words he knew by heart blurring on the crinkled page.

Dear Seth. Life is an immeasurable essence. You'll experience bliss, and you'll experience despair. But don't let the sadness ever overtake you or your dreams. Your heart might not be in the same place ours was, and that's okay, but don't overlook the simple things in life. Those simple things often bring us the greatest joy. If something ever happens to us and we have to leave you, remember you will never be alone. Your family is at the resort, even in people you haven't yet met. If you choose not to run it, know you have dozens of friends and family who would love to help. Johnathan, Maye, MacGregor's family, and all the regulars who come every year, even the Halliburtons. They are all family, and they will stick by your side as they have stuck by ours. Don't ever be afraid to ask for help, and don't ever be afraid to experience life as fully as we have experienced ours. Because no matter what happens, the risk is worth it. We love you, son, and we want you to be happy. But happiness is never found in another person or an activity or event. It is in small occurrences that build and spread over a life's term. Know whatever happens, we lived our life to the fullest. By far, you are our greatest joy. With love, Mom and Dad.

He folded the letter and slammed the drawer closed, his throat clenching. He doubted the decisions he'd made. The decisions for the resort, the people he cared about, his family. His muscles tensed with anger at the circumstances he couldn't control, but also the circumstances he had caused.

Why had it taken Remy's visit to the resort for him to realize its importance?

His heart had ached with potential for too long while he fought over following in his parents' footsteps. Never a question until their death, but now he realized what was right in front of him. This resort, his family and friends here, were his purpose.

He pushed away from the desk and jumped up. He was furious with himself, his family, the circumstances he couldn't control. He ground his teeth in that fury, swept his hand through his hair, then walked out into the barren landscape to calm down his nerves.

But seeing the starkness of the trees that should be covered in white only made him angrier.

He stalked down the path leading to his main home.

He'd tried, those first two years, to keep things going, to

keep his parents' dream alive. He'd needed the break, but regretted closing the resort. If he'd known Remy planned to come, would he have shut it down? He didn't think so. But she hadn't visited the past two years, so he hadn't expected her, and he assumed her siblings told her he wasn't open for the season.

He checked his list, all the plans he'd made while he was on break, but realized it was vague. *Take pictures. Go on a trip somewhere. Sleep in.* None of this was real. None of this was what he wanted. He only wanted to stop feeling so alone in a room full of people. To conquer his grief and let go of the guilt caused by his parents' deaths.

He was still alive. Still breathing. He was taking over their dream and failing miserably. And questioning whether he wanted the same thing they had wanted for him.

"Your parents would be so proud," Maye had tried to convince him. But the grief had been too strong.

He could vacation somewhere, but the idea left a hole in his gut.

He blew out a thick breath, stomped his feet on the outdoor rug even though there was nothing but dirt on his shoes, and went inside his house, overcome with a strong realization.

He had been fighting against himself all along.

He didn't want to leave. He didn't want Remy to leave. He wanted to stay and celebrate Christmas with his staff and friends and guests. He longed to experience the sights and sounds, restore the magical moments and make new memories for his patrons.

He wanted to open for Christmas.

CHAPTER 6

R emy spent the night in a drab, dreary hotel. No Christmas spirit here at all. At least Seth's resort had held memories of the season's magic.

She stood by the window and gazed at the beautiful mountain sunrise. The deep cold penetrated the glass and pinched her skin. What to do? Stay here, or go home?

She let out a groan. Neither option appealed to her.

She'd spend one more night then decide. Besides, she wanted to watch tonight's Christmas parade—surely, that would entice her enthusiasm—and shop at the stores here in town.

If she went home and back to Carson, she would be just as lonely. If she stayed with her siblings, she wouldn't have proven anything to herself, or to Carson, and she'd probably be even more depressed.

Carson had chosen work over her, time and time again. She hadn't seen him once this entire season, save for a few hours of dinner where his head was buried in his phone.

It was always about work. Although they both worked with the same agency, he managed the large advertisements with the bigwig companies that brought in a lot of income. It also meant he slaved for long hours and very little time for her.

Most of that was of his choosing, though. He had given his life to the company.

This would have been their third Christmas together. Not once had they done anything Christmasy like strolling down the streets admiring the lights, drinking hot cocoa by the fire, or decorating a tree together. Nothing at all like the traditions she and her family had celebrated. Nothing at all like the traditions she longed for.

He hadn't come for her, hadn't even bothered calling, so deep inside she knew their fate.

She grabbed her jacket and stepped outside, slogging through the white slush. The wind was biting cold. She huddled under her jacket and waddled along sidewalks, waving at people, nodding a hello, smiling at all the joyous energy of the crowds.

Downtown was small, intimate, paths full of people. She bypassed her favorite shops to avoid answering questions on where she was staying and for how long.

Cinnamon and caramel wafted from the pastry shop. Music drifted from each building but the same spirited music engulfed the entire town.

She stopped at the horse carriage ride and wondered how strange it would be if she took one alone. Maybe later tonight.

Then she thought of Carson being here with her, experiencing all that embodied Christmas. She thought of getting up on the seat and laughing with him while they held hands and enjoyed the ride while the horses trotted down the sidewalks. Her face heated. She hadn't pictured Carson, but Seth. Carson was supposed to be the love of her life. She bit the inside of her cheek in uncertainty.

"Do you want to take a ride?"

Seth's voice jolted her. She whipped around to face him and planted her hand over her heart.

He shrugged and smiled sheepishly. "Sorry to scare you."

She dropped her hand. He stood beside her, his hands in his pockets, his face so beautiful. And different. Soft. As if he had let go of resentment and was finally able to enjoy himself.

She pointed at the carriage, a wavy rotation of her wrist. "I was just wondering if it would be awkward to take a ride by myself," she admitted.

His smile caressed her, nestling calm into her body. "You don't have to be by yourself."

She poked his chest, a way to release the fidgety clumsiness she felt around him. "I didn't expect to see you here."

"I came to town to get my photo done."

She dropped her hand, disappointed. Well of course he hadn't come to find her. "Oh. Do you have it with you?"

He shook his head. "It won't be ready until tomorrow, or the next day."

"Oh, okay," she said. Her ribs grew tight. Maybe next year, she would see the photo framed above the mantel.

His head tilted and eyes slid over the carriage. "So, do you want to take a ride, or not?"

"I'd love to." She dug into her purse for some cash.

He grabbed her hand to stop her. "My treat."

He paid for the ride then helped her climb into the seat. Before long, the horses trotted through town. The sun glimmered and snow fell around them. A flake hit his nose, and she laughed.

Everything twinkled. Even under the sunshine, the town glowed.

She shouldn't allow herself to be here with him. Staying at the dreary hotel was bad enough, but spending the day together only to watch him leave would make things even worse. She was supposed to be in love with Carson. She shouldn't be laughing and dreaming about spending time with another man. And she had desperately wanted the Christmas experience she'd grown up with. Seth's resort couldn't give that to her now.

"I've been thinking about opening for Christmas."

Her breath bottled in her chest. Eyes wide, she studied him. "You what?"

"When you left, I realized I didn't want to be alone for Christmas. And I that I didn't need to shut down the resort to grieve, or to find myself. I already know exactly who I am."

She nodded, grateful he had come to this conclusion so soon. She'd seen his excitement when he spoke of the resort. He was born into his calling. Not everyone got the opportunity to follow their dream, and she hated to see anyone flee from theirs.

"I have a lot to do. And I'll have to ask if my staff is willing to return. Or I can just keep it small."

"I'm sure they would love to."

He took her hand in his and brought it close to his mouth, against his chin. "Will you come back?"

Her chest fluttered. She didn't have to think about his request for a second. "Of course I will. I'd love to. And I'll help you with all the decorations I can. It'll be a blast."

"We don't have much time to get things ready."

She squeezed his hands and pulled in closer, their hands against her heart. She bumped her forehead to his. The heat was intense, as if they were lovers, but the quiver in her belly left her too excited to care. She pulled away and clapped her hands together, imaging all the ways they could pull this off. "I know. But it won't take us long. We're going to have so much fun."

~

Remy left him breathless.

Had he made the right decision? Could he stomach being with her for the next few weeks and then watch her walk away?

Snowflakes flurried around them. Remy wore a deep red snowcap, and her hair curled out and down her back. Her eyes sparkled, and Seth had never seen anything more beautiful.

She lifted her chin toward the sky. Her smile lit up the darkest recesses of his heart. She truly appeared happy, but he feared the joy was temporary and would disappear when Christmas was over.

The carriage ride stopped. He helped her out and tipped the coachman.

"Do you have anything else to do in town?" he asked, keeping her hand in his. He found himself wanting to touch her, hold her, and never let go. But he had to practice restraint. Maybe one day he would tell her his true feelings.

"Not really." She shrugged. "I roamed some shops and planned to stay for the parade."

"That'd be fun. Do you mind if I accompany you?"

She whacked his arm. A friendly gesture that left him questioning his plans. Maybe he wouldn't tell her anytime soon.

"I expect you to accompany me," she said.

"Did you reserve a room for tonight?"

She visibly shuddered, then laughed. "The same one I slept in last night. But I'm eager to go get my stuff and tell them adios."

Her eyes glowed, allowing him no room for guilt even if he did feel terrible about casting her out. "That bad, huh?"

Her smile grew, her chin jutting. "Terrible. And I'm pretty sure the heater wasn't working right."

Even if she was teasing, he couldn't help but feel guilty. "I'm sorry about that."

"It's not your fault." She curled her arm through his and lifted her head to give him a smile. "How about we check out of my room and I treat you to dinner?"

"How about *I* treat you to dinner?" he countered.

"Okay, if you want to be that way. I'll treat you, and you treat me. Is Nancy's still open?"

"Sure is."

Nancy's was a good choice. A local restaurant that offered intimacy without being too fanciful or romantic. A good place to talk amongst friends without too much noise. It served comfort food and touted the best coffee and dessert in town.

Arm in arm, they strolled toward the restaurant. But Remy stopped him and squealed, pointing at the fudge shop. "I haven't been there in centuries."

He escorted her forward. "Well, let's go check it out. That is, if you can handle Dani."

"Yes, I'd love to see her."

Seth wondered if she had any idea what she was getting into. Sure, Remy knew Dani from her stay at the resort, but she hadn't been here in several years.

He opened the shop, the door jingling, and rushed inside. He yanked off his cap and stored it in his coat pocket, the heat of the room almost unbearable. Maybe he should have let in some cold air.

"Seth Lockhart, you little rascal." Dani's eyebrows lifted, and she skirted the counter to greet him.

An elderly woman who had owned this shop for as long as he could remember, with dazzling red hair, dark blue eyeshadow, she wore the brightest colors he'd ever seen. Her back slumped with her walk, but her chin stayed lifted. She also loved to call people by their entire name, for whatever reason.

She pinched his cheek and eyed Remy. "Is this why you decided to shut down the resort?"

"I don't know how you keep this fudge from melting." Seth waved his flatted hand near his face. "It's blazing hot in here."

"Oh, bah." She swatted at the air.

Remy patted her chest with both hands. "Dani, it's me. Remy."

Her eyebrows lifted even larger, her face curling in an all-out smile. "Remy Halliburton! I almost didn't recognize you. Well, I didn't recognize you at all." She tugged her in for a hug and, over Remy's shoulder, winked at Seth. "So, are you the reason he shut down for the holidays?"

Remy wouldn't know how to answer that question if she knew the truth. That Seth thought about her way too often and couldn't bear another season without her.

Remy withdrew from Dani's hug and held her shoulders at arm's length. "Actually, no. I didn't realize he'd closed until I came here."

Dani narrowed her gaze at him. "You traveled all this way to celebrate Christmas in your tradition, only to be disappointed?"

Mouth pursing, Remy glanced at Seth and waited for him to tell Dani the news.

He appreciated that. She could have told Dani. Not that he would have cared, but it was just like Remy not to overstep her bounds. Or, at least, the self-imposed boundaries she'd placed in her life. Contrary to what he'd told himself when she'd first shown up on his doorstep—that she was selfish and didn't give anyone any consideration. He was wrong about that on so many levels. "Well, Dani, I have news," he said.

She opened her mouth.

He held up his hands.

Dani crossed her arms around her waist and waited for him to continue. Remy stood nearby, silent. At this point, he wished she'd speak up and help him out.

"I've decided to open the resort for Christmas."

Dani's mouth opened wide and she dropped her hands then pulled him into a hug. "That's fabulous news."

"I need a few days to get ready, so don't put out the word yet. We'll have a Christmas Eve party, like always. Well, it might be a little different, but we'll have a party and dance and everything. We have a lot to do. And, that is, if my staff agrees to come in. They might tell me no."

She drew away and thwacked his arm. "Oh, they won't tell you no. But, if they do, give me a call. I'll round up some help."

"Thanks, Dani." Nostalgia rushed over him, and his breath fluttered in his chest. He glanced at Remy and smiled. "Well, we actually did come in for some fudge sampling."

Dani waved them over to the counter, where fudge of every color and taste was presented under a display case. "I'll bring some to your party too, of course."

"Can I try the peppermint fudge?" Remy tugged off her gloves and stored them in her pocket.

"You may. But only if you agree to try the peppermint coffee with it."

Remy clasped her hands together. "Absolutely."

"I hope it's cooler under those display cases than it is out here," Seth teased.

"Oh, hush." Dani brewed a cup of the peppermint coffee before plating a piece of fudge and sliding it over to Remy. "You're welcome to sample more, if you'd like."

"Oh, gosh. This is probably plenty. But I'll see."

Dani turned to him. "What about you?"

"Let's do the beer fudge," Seth said.

"Of course. But I don't have any beer flavored coffee to offer."

He laughed. "Don't think I could handle that if you did."

She handed him a plate of the fudge and a cup of black coffee.

Just the way he liked it.

"You're welcome to go sit at a table in the corner and admire the Christmas décor."

Seth glimpsed at Remy, and her smile made Dani's offer impossible to refuse. "Sure." He dug in his pocket for his wallet. "Let me go ahead and settle up payment now, if that's okay?"

Her chin jerked up. "That's not okay. It's on the house."

He opened his wallet. Not too long ago, he had denied Remy's offer to pay for her car. Now he knew exactly how she must have felt. Helpless, and desperate. He pulled out bills and handed them over. "No."

She cocked her head and glared at him. "I'm not taking your money. Period." She nodded behind him, where Remy had found a seat with her plate of fudge and cup of coffee. "Don't leave it on the table either."

Defeated, he stuffed his money back in his wallet and held up his hands in surrender. "Okay, okay. But I want to buy some for the party." He kissed her cheek then took his snacks and sat with Remy.

The smell of chocolate, caramel, mint, even beer wafted through the shop, tickling his nose and throat. Wreaths that glittered with white lights and red bows hung on every window, and a vase full of ball ornaments decorated each table.

They ate in silence but the door jangled, announcing the arrival of others. Seth didn't recognize any of them, but Laurel Springs had many visitors this time of year.

Dani greeted her customers and gave out samples.

Seth subtly watched Remy. She glanced around, her eyes twinkling. She bit into a piece of fudge, tipped her head back and swallowed. "Hmm, this is amazing."

A pool of sweat formed behind his neck, but he resisted the urge to fan himself. Dani should really turn this heat down.

He nodded, unable to muster a reply lest he croak on his fascination. He stuffed a piece of fudge in his mouth.

Things would get better. They would go back to the resort and he would be too busy to think about his attraction to Remy. Not that busyness ever helped before, but this time would be different.

When they finished their coffee, Seth carried both plates back to the counter. "Thanks for everything. I hope to see you on Christmas Eve."

Dani skirted the counter and hugged them. "No problem." She faced her other patrons but stationed her hand on Seth's back. "Hey guys, if you're looking for something to do on Christmas Eve, this man has the best party ever at his resort up the mountain."

His jaw went slack and his body flushed. He wasn't ready to tell anyone yet. His staff deserved to know first, and he didn't want them hearing rumors. He had warned Dani but should have known better.

A man stood. "Oh, what resort is that?" he asked.

He glanced at Remy, who stood beside him, her mouth opened and waiting for him to make things right. Or at least, that's how he read her expression. But how could he make anything right? Dani had meant well, and he didn't want to hurt her.

"Christmas Hills," Remy said, then grinned and mouthed *sorry*.

The man's eyes widened and the woman beside him

breathed out a strong sigh. "Oh, that's where we'd intended on staying. But I thought it was closed."

"It was," Dani said as she wiped a vacant table. She was doing a good job of keeping her head down.

"I've decided to reopen for the holidays," Seth interjected before Dani could say anything else.

The man approached and shook his hand. "That's amazing news. I'm Robert, and this is my wife, Stephanie. Will you have any rooms available?"

"I'll make sure to put one aside for you. Why don't you give me a call tomorrow to confirm?" Seth opened his wallet and retrieved a business card. "This has my personal cell number on it, too, but service can be spotty."

"Have you had any snow up there yet?" Dani asked.

"No. Not yet." Annoyance clipped his words. He loved Dani to death, but she could be a handful.

Robert and his wife exchanged a look. "No snow?"

"Yeah, the townspeople told him it happened because he shut down for the holidays," Dani said. "But it's a gorgeous place, no matter what."

Seth bit down on an annoyed sigh. Remy stirred beside him. Maybe she wanted to help, but he hoped at this point she stayed quiet.

Robert flapped the card at his wife, and she took it and put in her purse. "Well, we can't wait to see it," he said.

Others responded in kind.

Seth said his goodbyes and settled his hand on Remy's back, practically shoving her out the door. He couldn't get out of there fast enough. Once the cold air hit him, he let out a long breath. "I should have known better than to go in there."

They shuffled along the sidewalk. Remy folded her arms into his elbow, but she stumbled. He slowed down in case she had a hard time keeping up.

She cuddled closer into him. "Dani means well. And this whole town cares about you."

"I care about them, too." If not for this town, he'd never have survived the past two Christmases without his parents. They had all come together for him, and maybe that's why he had shut down. He'd never had a chance to be alone. Love surrounded him on every level of his life. His parents had taught him long ago family didn't have to be blood, and this entire town was his family.

Despite his love and appreciation, they could sometimes get overwhelming. Just as overwhelming as his attraction to Remy.

Remy strolled along the sidewalks with Seth, enjoying the view. She loved this town and had always meant to come back during the summer but never had.

They did some shopping, deciding they weren't hungry enough for Nancy's and would go later. Seth went his own way and they planned to meet in an hour. Remy chose a few gifts and thought about what she could get Seth. She wanted to find him a little something, but choosing a gift for a man who had everything stumped her. Plus, she had to keep their relationship as friends, nothing more.

They reunited on a bench at the ice-skating park.

"I haven't skated in so long." Remy planted three packages beside her and noted he had none.

"Oh, come on. I remember you being one of the best at the resort."

She rearranged her cap, which had fallen askew on her head. "You remember way wrong. But I know you've got the best rink on the planet. I'll probably avoid it while I'm there if I can."

He nodded toward the packages on the other side of her. "I see you did some shopping."

She fiddled with the tissue and nodded. "I found a few things for my family back home. I see you didn't do any at all?"

"Just some window shopping. What about a significant other? Do you have anyone special back home?"

Remy's breath hitched. Her chest cramped, shoulders tightening. She hadn't thought about Carson all day. But Seth was easy to talk to, a good listener, and maybe she could get a man's opinion. "I thought I did."

His forehead crinkled. "You thought you did?"

She propped her fingers in her lap and tried not to fidget. "Have someone special back home. But why would I come spend Christmas alone if that were true?"

He shrugged and glanced away. His jaw clenched. "I don't know. Why?"

A wistful sigh escaped. "Carson doesn't love Christmas as much as I do." She paused and thought about her next admission. She had wanted Carson to chase her, to care about something more than he cared about his work. But she wasn't sure that was possible.

She'd wanted things to work out with Carson at first but often wondered if he posed as a mask to the pain she'd suffered after her parents' deaths. Maybe she was desperate for any relationship, and he had been good to her at first.

She thought they had wanted the same thing. Coming here was a way for her to find out the truth. "He doesn't really love anything as much as I do."

Seth's brows drew in, and he studied her. "Carson, huh?"

"He's one of the reasons I didn't come here the past two Christmases, although I can't blame him. My heart couldn't take it."

Seth's green eyes drew her into confessing things she

hadn't wanted to admit, even to herself. He blinked, but it wasn't a gesture of judgment or reproach.

"You've been together for two years?"

Carson had offered a nice detour from grief, but their relationship had grown into so much more than a detour. After being here for a few days, she wondered if a healthy connection was wishful thinking. They both wanted different things, and she couldn't see herself continuing to sacrifice her own happiness. "We've been together almost three years actually. But it doesn't feel like we've really dated for the past two. He's full of ambition and strictness. His mom's lips are always pressed into a thin line." She pressed her lips together and zipped her finger across her face for affect before continuing. "They had the most immaculate home at Christmas. But not cozy and comfortable or inviting. I came down here to see if he would fight for me."

Seth coughed into his hands. "You did what?"

And to see if I even want him to fight for me anymore.

She brushed her fingers against the piece of hair escaping from her snowcap. Seth was a friend, she needed to trust him, and why not admit all the reasons she and Seth were bad for each other? Her heart was having a hard time remembering. "I know, it's silly. We work together, which can make things tough, but we're in different departments. Still, I've hated my job for a long time and want something different, and he's pushing me to stay and be more ambitious." She mimicked quotes with her fingers at the word she had grown to hate. Ambitious, as if she should give up her entire life for a job she didn't like to prove she was worthy. "As if me wanting to run my own business isn't ambitious enough."

He shifted on the bench, their knees touching until he moved, ever so subtly, away. Maybe he hadn't meant to and maybe he hadn't noticed, but she did, and her heart ached. When had she ever had a relationship where she could feel comfortable touching knees? Certainly not with Carson. He wasn't loving or romantic or touchy feely.

His expression remained subjective. "So, you broke up because you aren't ambitious enough for his tastes?"

She clenched her hands together drew them to her chin, a means to ward off the chill and his questioning gaze. "Well, we haven't actually broken up. I just got fed up and told him I couldn't do this anymore. I needed to get away for Christmas and he knows where to find me if he decides he wants to come down."

"Woah."

"Yeah" She bent over and scooped snow in her hands. "What do you think?"

"I think...I can't tell you how to feel, but I don't think this is any way to deal with a relationship."

His lack of expression left her dubious. She straightened and worked the snow into a ball, a token of how she had banded her life into a fragile hold that was now on the verge of crumbling. Was she being ridiculous in testing Carson? Of course she was. But maybe she was testing her own strength too. "So you think I should go back and spend Christmas with him?"

"I didn't say that, either."

She broke apart the snowball then let the pieces fall, brushing them off her pant leg. She considered the significance, each moment of her life clinging to her, and she still clinging to the past. She whooshed out a breath. "Then what *are* you saying? I need some good advice here."

"How about we go to Nancy's and put some food in our tummies, and I'll try to make sense of it all."

"Okay. I'm game for food."

Seth held the door open for her, then he escorted her to a seat. Booths lined the walls, and Christmas lights glittered across the ceiling. They stopped to greet a few people. Remy was delighted to recognize many, those who visited his resort for festivities, and for them to remember her in return. She loved feeling like such a huge part of a family. Envy cramped her stomach. Seth experienced this every day and had almost given it up.

Nancy rushed up and gave him a hug. "I heard you were opening the resort for Christmas. That's wonderful." She turned to Remy and took her in her arms. "Hey, Remy. Good to see you, darling."

"How did you hear that?" Seth asked as they slipped into a booth.

Nancy handed them menus. "Dani, of course. The whole town probably knows now."

"Probably," Seth muttered.

Nancy was almost as overwhelming as Dani, but she had a quiet and simplistic nature. She pulled off her pixie hairstyle much better than Remy's disaster when she'd tried it in her teens. Her blonde hair and natural makeup made her look twenty years younger, and the bright red shirt tucked into dark black jeans accessorized with a Christmas scarf showed off a figure that would have left Remy jealous if she wasn't so darn likeable.

She took their drink order and promised to be back in a few. Seth grabbed the menu and let out a long sigh.

"What's wrong?" Remy asked.

"Too many people knowing my business is just unbearable, sometimes."

"Oh, come on. This town loves you. I think it's awesome." Although she could see where it could get stressful.

He dropped his menu and gazed at her. "It is. I mean, I don't know how I would have survived the past two Christmases without them all."

She nodded, her breath in her throat. She regretted not being there for him. Even from a long distance, they could have supported each other. And she had never even tried to reach out to him.

"I'm sorry—"

Seth held up his hand. "Don't even say it."

"Say what?" How could he possibly know all the things she wanted to say?

"You're sorry for not being here, blah blah blah." He opened the menu again. "Did you decide what you want? Their Christmas sandwich is pretty amazing, and they only make it once a year."

She slapped her forehead. "I almost forgot about their Christmas sandwich! Mom and I used to always stop here on our shopping sprees for that sandwich." Turkey, ham, and bacon, toasted with a rich recipe of pumpkin and cranberry and no telling what else, served with decadent sweet potato fries and a chocolate cake. The recipe was a secret they only released for the holidays.

Nancy returned with their drinks and took their order, and while they waited her mind reeled on their previous conversation about Carson. Although she had no plans to leave Seth after promising she would help him prepare, she wanted his opinion. "So, what do you think?"

He leaned back in the booth, his gaze soft as he studied her. "Do you love him?"

She chewed her lip as his question tumbled through her mind. She should have an immediate answer, but she didn't. Her hands curled in her lap, as if displaying them would reveal too much of herself she hadn't even been able to voice yet. Seth was too easy to talk to. Every thought, every emotion wanted to gush out of her with no filter. As if she wanted to shock him, but he couldn't be shocked. "I thought I did. But I don't know. On one hand, I hoped coming here would make us both realize our feelings for each other. But, the longer I'm here, the more I realize maybe I don't love him. I mean, if I did, wouldn't I want to go back? And why would I give up my dreams for him?"

"That's a million-dollar question."

"Argh." She buried her head in her hands, then swiped them over her face and glanced at him. "You haven't really answered any of my questions yet."

"You're the only one who can answer the questions of your heart."

CHAPTER 7

Seth couldn't believe he was giving relationship advice to Remy, but he would never get in the way of her happiness. She was in love with Carson, and she wanted this man to chase her. He didn't bother telling her that if she had to come all the way to Colorado to test his love, then more than likely he didn't love her. Seth never would have left her side. He never would have let her spend Christmas alone.

But he withheld judgment about this guy.

He had no hopes of building a romantic relationship with Remy, even if his buried feelings for her had been renewed with her presence. Until she showed up on his doorstep a few days ago, he never expected to see her again.

No matter how much it cut into his heart, they would remain friends. That meant he'd offer advice, support her, and be there for her if she needed a listening ear. That also meant he had to fight his desire to kiss her. Or give her bad advice.

Night descended. Christmas lights glittered across town, wrapped around trees and buildings and strewn from pole to pole on the sidewalk. They strolled down the street, arm in arm, to catch the parade. As they drew closer, the crowd grew larger. Tears pooled into Remy's eyes.

They stopped at the edge of the street, and Seth gathered her into a side hug "What's wrong?"

She swiped away a tear, her lips trembling in a smile. "I'm crying at the beauty of everything, if that makes sense."

His heart swelled. "It makes total sense." One reason he had fallen in love with Remy so long ago was her sincerity. She had no idea the strength of her mind, her creativity, her inquisitiveness. Her confidence was subtle, but powerful. She wasn't afraid to feel and experience every nuance the world offered.

No wonder she was so miserable now. She was stuck in a mindset that trapped her from pursuing her greatest dreams. If she had come here for answers, he couldn't give them to her. She was better off figuring things out for herself.

"And I'm a bit nostalgic, too," she admitted.

"Of course."

The back of his throat prickled and a dull awareness took over. Maybe he was like her in not realizing his potential. He had almost given up everything. He'd neglected his friends, his family, and nearly made it impossible to meet new ones. Men like Robert, who came with his wife to Laurel Springs to celebrate Christmas and make new memories. Families like Remy's, whose tradition was to come to the resort. His family —the locals who visited for the day or the evening to share the festivities.

Remy bumped her head against his shoulder. "What are you thinking about?"

They stopped under a tree gleaming with lights. A perfect place to stand and watch the parade, which had already started farther up the street. Christmas music boomed around them.

"I was thinking of how I'd almost turned my back on my friends and family."

She faced him and grabbed his hands, her head tilted up and her eyes glimmering with tears. She thumbed the tip of his nose. "You had your reasons, and you aren't responsible for anybody else's happiness. And nobody thinks you turned your back on them. If anything, I abandoned you."

"Well, I was a bit disappointed when you didn't show up for Christmas the past two years." Disappointed enough to shut down, even if it wasn't the only reason, and even if he would never admit it to her.

For a moment, he thought she was going to kiss him. Her eyes darkened. She rose up on her tippy toes, tweaked his nose with her thumb, then settled her feet on the ground and bounced, laughing. Her smile froze on her lips as his gaze held hers and time stood still.

His chest tightened. His body smoldered with the need to get even closer, to sample her lips and discover if she tasted like she smelled—orange and cinnamon and brown sugar. He fought for breath, fought his desires as a rosy flush glistened her skin.

The Christmas music boomed closer, breaking their intensity. The parade marched by. Wheeling around, she squealed and clapped her hands.

He could barely pay attention to the parade. He didn't have to, since the nutcrackers were similar every year. People changed, their themes changed, but the lighted vehicles and decorated trailers remained consistent.

His gaze followed Remy's every move. She tilted her head to the side, giggling and pointing at the floats. His pulse lurched. She cherished Christmas as much as he did, and he had always been attracted to her. But he forced himself to remember that love and attraction were two totally different things. Their strong connection amplified every beat of his heart. But love? No way. He couldn't afford to love her. Especially not when she was in love with someone else. He had to keep his distance.

Friends could hold hands. Friends could bump foreheads. They'd known each other forever. His memory couldn't recall a time without her. She was family, and there was no reason to ruin his mood or his Christmas spirit because she stirred up a longing he would never be able to fulfill.

Nostalgia. That explained the fluttering in his pulse, the constant tension in his chest. Mementos from happier times. A time when he had no fears, no pain, and his one and only goal as a teenager was to get Remy to notice him.

But she hadn't then, and she didn't now.

Once the parade passed, she grabbed his hand again and they ambled through the streets. He was eager to get home and make his to-do list, but he wouldn't rush her.

"You want to make any other stops before we head back to the resort?" he asked, determined to be cavalier about his attraction. "Coffee? Tea? Shopping?"

"No. I'm ready to go on back. That is, if you are. I'm in the mood to start decorating!"

He laughed. "Okay. Are you comfortable driving in the dark and snow?"

"Yes, I'll be fine. And once we turn into your mountain road, it won't be snowing anymore. Remember?"

"True," he said, hollowness filling him. It might not be snowing, but they were going to make the best of it.

Before long, they were both on the way back to Christmas Hills Resort. With the lights of his car, he noticed the snowfall. The trees and road were laced with white. His mouth fell open and he peered in the rearview mirror, slowing to make sure Remy was safe behind him. Fresh snow like this could make the roads treacherous.

Adrenaline spiked him and he yipped in joy. Maybe the

townspeople were right. Maybe him closing his heart to Christmas was the reason it hadn't snowed. Or, maybe the fact Remy was here, opening his heart again, released his negativity.

He had to remember not to get attached.

Remy shrieked in delight as snow drifted down, almost blinding her as she followed Seth's Jeep up to the resort. She clenched the steering wheel and leaned forward, blinking away tears. Although crying was a given during the holiday season, these were happy tears.

Happy, but also full of anxiety. Her heart hammered at the height and breadth of the view. No huge mountain drop-offs awaited her, but it didn't make the drive less scary.

She breathed a sigh of relief once they made it to the resort and parked. She rushed out of the car and clasped her hands to her chest, canting her head back and opening her mouth to catch the falling flurries.

"This is amazing!" The ground was barely covered, but there was enough to dip down and make a snowball, and that's what she did. The soft snow crumbled in her hands. "It's magical."

He grabbed her suitcases from the car. "It'll be even more magical once we get this place lit."

She followed him. "Yes, it will." She couldn't wait for the magic to appear, the illumination of Christmas that had guided so many families to this resort. And the faster they could start decorating, the sooner she would feel more relaxed with Seth's newfound spirit. She was afraid it would be yanked away to leave her in misery again.

He opened the door and left her suitcases in the foyer, then disappeared down the hallway, ducking into a room.

Suddenly, lights erupted outside. She swung around to face the open door, then rushed out.

He emerged with a smile on his face.

"Oh my God," she said. Colored lights illuminated the building's exterior, each doorway and window and rooftop. The trees were wrapped in white and colored lights, one with only red and one with only blue, traveling down the entire roadway into the entrance.

Seth stopped beside her. "These lights stay up year-round. So does the Christmas village, as you know, but each season's theme changes every year. Halloween, Thanksgiving, Valentine's Day, and every occasion in between. My mother always had a fresh vision and her biggest joy was to decorate something new each time."

"That's why every Christmas it looked different," she mused, intrigued by the possibilities.

"Yes. We have a great crew. And of course, each room was different too."

"Yes, I do remember." She twirled in the drifting snow. The sweetness teased her. The punchy treasure of memories, a tangy zing in her nose. Her mind wandered in imagination. "What will the theme be this year?"

"We always let the staff brainstorm with us, too. The foyer was always my mother's idea, since it's the first thing people see when they walk inside. We don't have much time to plan if we're going to open soon."

She clasped her hands to her chest excited by ideas. "How about a theme of hope? And grace? Love lost and found?"

His brows pinched together.

She dropped her hands, disappointment kicking her stomach. She refused to be swayed. A lot needed to be done, but she'd never felt this excited about a project. "What? You don't like it?"

"No. I love it. I'm just trying to get an image for it."

She shuffled toward him and tapped temple. "Don't worry. I've got the image for it right here. But..."

"But what?"

She shifted under the bright lights of Christmas, gazing at the empty yard, and lifted her hands. "What about decorations? And ornaments?"

"My mom has an entire room devoted to all her ornaments."

She pivoted to face him, the snowy ground almost making her trip on her own two feet. Why hadn't she ever known about this room? "Oh my! We must go to see this now!"

He scowled. "This late?"

Anticipation buzzed through her. "It's not late. It's barely eight o'clock." She crossed her arms and pouted. When his gaze darted to her lower lip, Remy wondered if it was too much. "Are you going to be a party pooper?"

His chin jutted. He nodded toward the door. "Come on. I'll show you to this magical room. Let's see if you can keep up."

She followed him inside. He told her to wait while he turned off the outside lights in case someone saw them tonight and tried to come. She studied the lobby and imagined all the things they could do. The stairwell wrapped in lights, of course. Wreaths hanging across the windows. Doves to signify hope. Love, laughter. Lots of red and white. Animals. She remembered all the past white-colored deer displays, so they could show some here, some greenery with red berries, much like the image he had taken yesterday.

He strolled into the room and she smiled, posturing herself for patience. He was being too slow for her liking, and she wanted to bolt to this fantasy room and get started. She thought of all the things she had missed over the years, including the Christmas tree farm that could supply them with unlimited trees of all sizes. She and her family had visited the farm every year, their footsteps tromping through the snow and seeding memories on her heart.

I can't wait.

"Okay," he said. "I hope you're ready for this place."

"I'm ready. Hey, do you still have the Christmas tree farm?"

"I do. And MacGregor and his family still run it."

"Did you shut it down this year, too?" His downtrodden face gave her his answer.

He winced then glanced away. "I did. I thought, if I was going to shut down one thing, I had to shut it all down." He put up a hand. "In case you're wondering, my staff is getting paid their full salary."

She shrugged. "I wasn't wondering." Still, his admission made her admire him even more.

"I've sent texts to Maye and Jonathan to check on who was willing to come back."

"And?" Her voice rose as she waited for an answer. She couldn't imagine anyone telling him no. But if they did, how would they pull this off?

"Everyone is happy to, of course."

"Of course, they are." Seth was a good person, but she was relieved everyone had agreed to come back. She hadn't even considered the possibilities until now, but she was willing and even excited for the hard work ahead of them. "We'll take all the help we can get. And we're going to need a lot of Christmas trees!"

"We don't have much time to get this done. Even with everyone coming tomorrow."

"Then we better get started." Remy skipped toward the basement. They might not have much time, but they had plenty of heart.

And hope.

CHAPTER 8

Seth treaded down the stairs to the basement, switching lights on along the way. Until now, he had refused to visit. His mom had always handled the ornaments, and then his staff. After his parents' death, the pain was too deep to face these memories.

He wasn't prepared for the regret. His knees knocked and muscles clenched. He had neglected his past. Rejected the memories. Refused to revisit the nostalgia for way too long.

He squared his shoulders, determined. He would fight. His parents would want him to continue celebrating. And even though Remy would leave after it was all over—at least until next year—he would give her a Christmas she couldn't forget.

The room stretched far and wide, shelving on both sides stacked with well-organized boxes of ornaments. File cabinets full of his mom's notes and mementos, with a desk and a computer situated in the corner on the back wall. A small hallway led to a bathroom. Despite it being underground, lighting illuminated every nook and cranny. A mini refrigerator and snack bar—mostly empty now—had kept refreshments handy while his mom fashioned her big design. She'd often hosted meetings with her crew, plotting and planning their next theme.

His staff had taken over, kept things neat and structured.

They were always loyal and hardworking. He'd turned his back on them, like the Grinch. They worked Christmas Day because they loved it, and their families came to share it with them. They never considered it work, or that's what Maye told him when she'd argued on all the reasons he shouldn't shut down for Christmas.

Remy frolicked from area to area, opening lids to the boxes and bins of decorations, peeping, then strutting to the next. "This is amazing."

"I was never much of a decorator," he admitted.

"It's like taking a picture." She made a triangle with her hands and put them up to her right eye. "You frame the photo in your lens to get the best angle and perspective and then you click your button. Right?" She dropped her hands and faced him. "But you set it up for a great shot, and that's what you do with the decorations."

He laughed at her analogy. "I'm sure it's a little different than photography."

"It's still an art." She smacked her chest and held her hand there. "If you have an eye for photography, you have an eye for decorating. It'll be fun." She dragged out a box and opened the lid, oohing and aahing and settling on the floor to scour the contents. "I have so many ideas. I can see why your mother loved this." She paused, dropping the wreath she held and glancing up at him. Her mouth drew into a thin line. "I hope I'm not overstepping my bounds."

Her words addled him, and he wanted to reap on assurances that all was okay. As much as he wanted her here doing this with him, he struggled with the balance of wanting too much, and letting things go.

He leaned his hip against the wall and swallowed before speaking, lest he display all the emotion he wanted to hide. "Of course not. I appreciate your help. I have staff who absolutely love the decorating, too. They'll be happy to help."

She pointed her finger and wiggled. "You will at least give it your touch. In the lobby. You have to."

"Why is that?"

"Because I said so. I have this image, but it needs your creative style."

His gut lurched. Why did the thought of decorating terrify him? He'd enjoyed it with his mom when he was younger and had no negative experiences to attach to those memories. The fear of not being good enough had no reason to chime in his ear. His hand fluttered to the back of his neck, and he squeezed out the tension. "Okay, well, you just tell me what to do and I'll do it."

"Do you have a pen and paper? I need to jot down ideas."

"Sure." His mom had always kept a pen and notebook in the top drawer for those moments of insight. He approached the file cabinet, his body tense. When he slid open the drawer, memories assaulted him

He relished the memories. The scent of pine forest and cinnamon, the creamy texture of eggnog laced with bourbon. The candies and salty snacks and festive foods of the season. The glittery decorations, the colored balls, the garland, ribbons and bows, and the lighted stars.

Remy's footsteps thudded into his heart as she approached. He hadn't noticed her getting up.

"What's all that?" she asked, her warm breath landing on his cheek. She was a huge part of his memories, a chunk of time he could never repair. Although mostly good ones, he had pushed her friendship away.

"My mom kept a photo of every decorated room, organized by month and year." His breath clumped in his throat, making his voice choppy.

She flicked through the folders. "Can you imagine some of the things you could do with those photos? Are those the only copies?"

"No. She had digital backups and she printed out extras for visitors. But she wanted them right here, where she planned and dreamed, in case she needed to look back on something."

Her brows screwed together. He handed her the pen and notebook, and she nodded her thanks, her gaze still on the contents in the file cabinet. "I'd love to get my hands on them one day."

"You're welcome to go through any you'd like," he said. "Just keep the hard copies here. The digital copies are labeled and organized well, and she kept a good inventory."

"May I?" she asked, grabbing an album.

"Absolutely." He nodded to the back area. "And, you know, there's a super-large table right there you can use."

She nodded and settled in the same spot. "I prefer the floor right now. Just looking through stuff at the moment." Chewing on her lip, she jotted things down, her back hunching.

He could stand for hours and admire her, but he should be doing something. "What can I help with?"

She spread her hands out around the room. "You said she kept an inventory. Is there a list you can bring me?"

He slid out the drawer and grabbed the folder. Each item had a thumbnail picture attached. As he advanced toward Remy, the lights flickered and then shut down. He stopped midstride, completely lost. Too dark to even think.

Remy's sharp inhale broke his panic.

"Oh my, it's terribly dark," she drawled, her voice shaky.

"The generator will kick on in a minute."

"You have a generator down here?" Her voice rose and warbled as if an untuned acoustical recital.

His main goal was to put her at ease, but he could barely manage to put one foot in front of the other. "We have a generator everywhere. It should have kicked on by now."

A noise whacked the floor, making him jump. "What the..." His skin crawled as he imagined all sorts of critters making a home down here. The basement was clean, and he didn't want to admit his terror at the darkness.

She giggled. "Sorry. Dropped the album. I can't believe I didn't bring my phone. In all my excitement, I must have left it in my purse."

Why hadn't he thought of that? "I've got mine." He dug in his pocket to get his phone and switched on the flashlight. The battery level was only at twenty-five percent, so he switched off everything that would drain it except the light. It didn't illuminate much, but it was enough. They sat together, their breath the only sound.

"This is creepy," she teased. A piece of her hair tingled along his jaw.

He needed to get away from her before he started admitting all his fantasies. "I've got to go check the generator while we still have light."

"Where is it?"

He nodded toward the end of the wall on the other side of the stairs. "There's a storage unit in that hallway."

"I'll go with you."

She inched behind him as he crawled toward the hall on his hands and knees. "Why aren't we standing?"

He shrugged, heat flushing his skin. "Because if the lights go out again, I'd rather be on the floor. Don't ask me why."

"Ah, so you're afraid of the dark?"

"A little bit. But only when it's really dark like this and there's no sky around me."

She followed him to the hallway. "I feel like I'm enclosed in a narrow tunnel. And yet this room is huge."

The light vanished. He dropped his phone and mumbled a curse. Something slid over his ankle and he jerked, then let out a soft squeak.

Remy erupted in her laughter. "You *are* afraid of the dark."

He chuckled, his anxiety melting away. "You're not nice." He stopped, sat, and grabbed her hand as she parked beside him.

"You can keep holding my hand if that brings you security," she teased. He couldn't see her face, but the warmth of her body and the teasing lilt in her voice soothed him.

"This is probably why I never came down here," he admitted. He didn't mind being alone, as long as there were windows and views, and as long as he didn't feel like he was in a coffin. This oblivion elevated his anxiety.

"Has it ever happened before?"

"Not to me. The thought of it was scary enough."

She rubbed his shoulder. Fire burned under his skin at her touch. "My big strong Seth afraid of the dark."

That fire zinged to the base of his throat. "Only dark constricted rooms underground. There are probably flashlights around here somewhere. My mom was always prepared."

Remy laid her head on his shoulder. "Let's get our bearings, and then maybe we can find some."

Getting his bearings was hard on his body. Remy's closeness, the scent of her hair like the crispness of sunshine in the snowy mountains, made it almost impossible to think. His nerves whacked against his ribs.

Now would be the perfect time to share his feelings, admit all the emotional wounds he'd suffered when she and her family had left after the holidays. The deeper wounds she'd carved when she hadn't returned. She'd asked him his opinion on what to do about her relationship, and his only thought was to make her feel better, but maybe he could convince her Carson wasn't right for her.

"You're one of the reasons I wanted to close the resort for the holidays," he blurted. The dark made it easier for such admissions.

Her breathy exhale, the gulp of her words, left him drowning.

"Me? Why?"

He wasn't sure why he'd admitted the truth, but it strengthened him. He squeezed her hand. "I couldn't bear another Christmas without you here."

Words bundled in Remy's throat. She didn't know what to say and her mind reeled with his admission.

She loved the feel of his hand, strong and smooth, but with a roughness that bespoke of hard work. They were usually covered by gloves when they held hands. Her heart battered inside her belly. She was supposed to be in love with Carson, even if she hadn't been this content, this curious, in a long time.

Maybe now she could discover what was going on in Seth's mind.

Despite the chill in the air caused from no heat or power, his palm grew sweaty. Not too bad so she couldn't hold on, but the buzz enticed her. She stationed her other hand on his, sandwiching his hand in hers, a deepening warmth tingling the back of her neck, down her spine, into her toes.

"I couldn't bear another Christmas without being here," she admitted. Eagerness to see him again had eclipsed her worry about how he would react when she showed up. They hadn't been on the best of terms. "But then I was afraid you'd be mean to me," she teased. "Or ignore me."

"I couldn't ignore you if I tried."

His voice gave her goose bumps. The texture of the words, so rugged, raw, and full of an emotion she would love to understand.

"You tried hard enough over the past few years." *Even before our parents.*

"That's because..."

"Because what?" She held her breath, waiting. She'd thought about him several times throughout the year, eager to spend the two weeks at Christmas with him until he'd pushed her away. Then, she'd pulled away.

"Because I was afraid."

"Of me?" She cringed at the squeak in her voice. She wanted to know more. Longed to understand what was going on in that thick skull of his. He'd never been much of a conversationalist with her, and if it took the darkness to draw him out, she'd sit here for hours. Days, even.

"Of my feelings for you."

Her belly fluttered, insides quivering as his words made a home run in her chest.

Feelings for her? The only feelings he seemed to have for her were friendship, then resentment. Even chastisement, before everything in their lives had changed.

The lights flickered. She sucked in a breath and they flickered again, then blared on. The low whirr of electricity emptied her hope. They would go back to normal now. Undoubtedly, he would act like they were just friends and no longer tell her of his feelings.

She squinted at the brightness. He dropped her hand and shielded his eyes. They sat side by side, angled to face one another.

He glanced upward and laughed. "Leave it to my mother," he said, pointing.

"What?" She peered up at mistletoe suspended on the ceiling above them. "What in the world? How did we miss that before?"

"Were you looking at the ceiling?" he asked.

"No." *How silly of me.*

"My mom had mistletoe sprinkled throughout the rooms. Hidden in places you'd not usually notice."

"Does fake mistletoe still count?"

"To her it did." His gaze shot straight into hers.

His eyes smoldered, choking out the void that had filled her since before her visit. Every moment with him filled her with hope.

His lips parted.

Time stood still while they gazed into each other's eyes. Her tongue darted out to wet her lips, then she quickly shut her mouth in case he thought that meant something more.

It did. It did mean something more. She so very much wanted to kiss him. Wanted him to kiss her. She wanted to see if the feelings for him building up inside could be released by a kiss, or only grow stronger. She wanted to know if she could continue forgetting about Carson every moment she was in Seth's presence.

He leaned forward, planted his hand behind her neck, and crept his lips to hers.

His long and drugging kiss was followed by a sweet and sensual flick of his tongue across hers. He explored her mouth, tasting and touching. Her skin tingled.

Time paused, stamping her thoughts with memories and anticipation. Images of Christmas decorations crowded her head. Of hope, memories, the future, and falling in love.

He retreated, leaving her bereft.

"Tomorrow I need to call someone to look at the generator," he said as if the kiss had never happened. "But upstairs has its own separate generator, so we should be fine tonight."

She tilted her head at him, aware of his withdrawal. "So that's it?"

His brows lowered. "Yeah, about that. I'm sorry. I never should have..."

"Kissed me?" Her voice hitched and she felt like an idiot. Her face burned.

He shook his head. "I shouldn't have ever done that. Taken advantage of the situation when you're involved with someone else. It was just the moment, you know?" He took her hands and brought them up to his lips, then dropped them.

Her heart thumped, but she didn't mind being direct. "You said you closed because of me?"

He swiped a hand over his face and kept his gaze on the floor. "Yeah. I mean, because you never came back after our parents. And it was hard. You were like family." He glanced at her, his jaw tense. "Please. I don't want to lose your friendship."

She blinked, her throat aching.

She wasn't kidding when she told him this resort was her dream destination. She'd often longed to pack up everything she owned and move up here. Something had stopped her from doing so. Life, reality, the dread of seeing Seth but unable to act on her infatuation. If he wanted her as much as she wanted him, she'd leave Texas in an instant.

Woah, where had that come from? She liked him. A lot. But anything more than friendship? Impossible in their worlds. Carson was her boyfriend, even if they were at odds right now. She had no right to kiss another man, no matter how long she had known him.

And if she and Carson didn't work out, Seth was family. She couldn't risk hurting him, or herself.

No point in dwelling on whatever feelings he might have admitted before the lights came back on. She still wasn't even sure about her own.

She flicked her thumb across his cheek, determined not to let the kiss made things awkward. "For what it's worth, I'm glad I'm here, and I'm glad I have you as a friend."

"I'm glad you came too."

Heat flushed her body and she nodded, tamping down the tears in her eyes. Best to forget about the kiss or the warmth of his touch before she made even more mistakes.

CHAPTER 9

S eth had lied, and he had lied well, but it had been
worth it. He and Remy went back to normal and
stayed up hours going through decorations and
forming a plan.

His body groaned as he sat up in bed and stretched the
next morning.

He didn't regret kissing her. He would have regretted it if
it made things awkward, but Remy continued on as if nothing
ever happened, unaware of or at least ignoring the feelings
buzzing around him.

He could have said more. But why bother? If he had
learned anything in life, it was that relationships would work
out organically. Their relationship was a deep affection, a
family connection, a companionship that would remain
untied to the boundaries of desire.

After the lights had come back on, magic filled the air. An
enchantment surpassing the spirit of Christmas. Even the
mistletoe seemed real. That magic also helped ease any
awkwardness that might have lingered.

His mom had loved doing this, and for the first time since her death, he experienced that same contentment.

He jumped out of bed, eager to get started. Today would hold many miracles. He had already talked to Maye and Johnathan, and they were ready to come back to work and promised to call the rest of the staff. Johnathan was his right-hand man who helped oversee the running of the resort. He managed the staff and the daily priorities and would take care of the generator. Seth couldn't do any of this without him or Maye.

He expected them here any moment.

The sight of white outside his window filled his heart with joy. The early morning sun cast gold on the ground. He had stayed in the main resort last night since it had been so late when they went to bed. And he hated leaving Remy alone.

He glanced at the time, stunned that it was almost seven. He strolled downstairs and found her in the lobby, hanging up wreaths. The windows offered a backdrop of white, white snow. After all the barrenness, he was astounded that it had come so quickly after his decision to open. It gave him a renewed zest to make it up to everyone who visited, and he was ready to get started.

Remy turned to him, her smile so bright he lost his footing. "Good morning."

"Good morning back." He glanced around and admired all her work. She had already set up lighted deer near the fireplace with white doves floating around them. "You've been busy."

"I thought we could go down to the Christmas tree farm and get us a few trees."

Anything to please you. "Sure. No problem. The staff will be here by noon. We could send some of them."

Her nose crinkled. "And miss out on the best part of Christmas? No way!"

99

He held up his hand. "Okay, okay."

"And I don't want to leave them out, but I really can't wait anymore. Besides, there's plenty to do. This is kind of our thing."

Our thing. His heart jerked. How often had he longed for a woman to tell him that? A woman to spend his life with as his parents had?

But this was different.

"I really appreciate everything you've done," he told her. "I couldn't have done it without you."

She waved her hand at him. "I'm having a blast."

He helped her finish hanging the wreath, enticed by the cinnamon and pine that drifted from her hair. He stepped back, away from the temptation of her. "This is beautiful."

"Does it remind you of anything?" She folded her arms and blinked, tapping her foot and waiting for his reply.

"Reminds me of the picture I took that you structured into something magnificent."

"It was magnificent when you took it." She pointed above the mantel. "I'm hoping that print will be ready soon. I plan to hang it right there. And I'll put some small trees full of red berries to frame the background."

She'd decorated the mantel with a minuscule horse and carriage ride, tiny trees lining a fabricated street and glowing lights all around.

"How long have you been up?"

Remy shook her shoulders. "A couple of hours."

"Have you eaten breakfast?"

"I found waffles in the freezer and had a bite or two." She stopped before him and patted his shoulders with both hands. "You're a late sleeper."

"It's only seven o'clock!"

"Like I said. A late sleeper."

How could he truly express his appreciation for everything this woman was doing? Words weren't enough. He had fallen in love with her as a child, but convinced himself it was just a fantasy. Seeing her enthusiasm made his heart hurt that they weren't a couple.

Easy now, he told himself. Friendship was better. They could spend time together, creating and laughing together without any of the awkward moments. If only he could keep his feelings in check.

He could. He had tamed them for years, but this time he knew how to control them without getting angry. And for his own sake, he would.

They bundled up in their coats and jumped in the Jeep. Instead of turning left on the road to town, they turned right to the Christmas Tree Farm.

Remy knew about the back roads that would take them to the farm, but Seth had wanted to play it safe. The snow on the ground was incredible. Did it have anything to do with Seth's newfound Christmas spirit?

She thought so.

The drive left her breathless. Snow shrouded the earth, the sky open and gleaming and seasoning the landscape with glitter. White covered the trees, but the greenery and bark still glistened their colors.

Seth parked the Jeep and leapt out to open the gate that would lead them into the farm. They continued the drive, a tunnel of trees in all shapes, sizes, and styles surrounding them on both sides.

She'd visited before, but each time brought her to awe. Every year, she and her parents came here to cut down a tree and take it back to their room. A luxury for everyone who wanted their own. She'd forgotten how much she missed the farm. She had no doubt she would find the perfect trees for the rest of her theme, and she was eager to bet back and finish the decorations. The decorations sprawled across the resort were symbolic to the season, and visitors expected their entire holiday to be decked out in Christmas grandeur.

Her belly tightened. For the first time in her life, she had free reign to do whatever she wanted with her ideas.

"MacGregor has taken care of this place as long as I can remember." Seth slowly drove through the cornucopia of trees. They stopped at a cabin where Seth's staff member took shelter during work. Once they parked, Seth didn't shut off the Jeep or get out. "Hold tight if you don't mind. Johnathan was going to call everyone, but I feel like I should be the one to call MacGregor."

She unbuckled her seatbelt and reached for the door. "I'll give you some privacy and start walking through the trees if that's okay."

"Of course."

He gave her a smile, a somber smile that didn't reach his eyes.

Longing to erase his contrition, she leaned forward, kissed him on the cheek, then slid out of the Jeep.

The soft snow fell heavy. Laughing, she sank into the mounds with each step. Trees galore from one end to the other beckoned her. She wanted something large and looming in the corner of the fireplace, small ones behind the deer, and three to place in front of the windows at the back of the room. And she wanted one for her own room.

She grabbed her phone and snapped a few pictures, checking for service and still not having any. She kind of liked it that way right now. Being out here in the middle of nowhere with trees all around her was the best form of meditation a person could ask for.

It also made her realize how unhappy she'd been in her

life lately. She couldn't blame it on her parents' deaths—not completely anyway. It would always affect her, but they had taught her to treasure each moment and that grief couldn't be avoided. No, she was unhappy because she worked at a job she hated and had been pursued by men she had no interest in until she'd met Carson. And even then, she wasn't fulfilled. Carson put more effort in his job than he put in their relationship.

She wondered what Seth would say if she told him she'd considered moving here. Not to the resort, but to Laurel Springs. She could find a job. She'd work at a coffee shop if necessary, and online companies offered many opportunities for freelance graphic design. If Seth would let her, she could take Christmas photos and design holiday cards.

The vehicle door boomed closed, and she turned and waved, then snapped a few photos of him strolling her direction. His mood seemed lightened, his shoulders relaxed and smile slackened. He stooped down, gathered snow in his hands, and took off running toward her. He flung the snow and hit her square in the chest.

She squealed, slid her phone in her pocket, and collected her own snow. It missed its mark, and she fell over laughing.

Once he stopped in front of her, he sank.

She looked past him at the tracks he left and imagined, for a moment, the tracks he'd left on her heart. "I don't know how you ran so swiftly through that snow. I keep sinking every time I take a step."

He shrugged. "What can I say? I'm light on my feet."

She crinkled her nose at him. "Not so much right now. How was your phone call?"

"Good. MacGregor is happy to start working again. He talked me out of my guilt." He clasped her hand and escorted her to the forest. "Now, let's go find us a tree."

"Trees," she corrected. Shutting down the resort had

made him feel guilty, like he'd abandoned his people, but they would never see it that way. Everyone loved Seth and would support his decision. Although she didn't know some of the newer staff members, the team that worked for his family had always considered themselves kin to the long-term visitors.

His eyebrows rose. "Trees?"

"Yes. We might have to make more than one trip."

He laughed. "I should have brought my trailer, then. We can get a bunch on top of the Jeep and some smaller ones inside, but we'll make as many trips as necessary."

Spotting the perfect tree, she stumbled toward it, the snow catching on her boots. She glanced backward to where Seth stood watching her, and waved.

A winter wonderland framed the horizon behind him. Her breath clustered in her throat as snow flaked across his dark beanie and his smile took over his face. And it struck her that she wanted to be so much more than friends.

As Seth watched Remy choose trees, he had to remember that no matter what happened in the future—if Remy never came back or if she married Carson and brought her new family to the resort—he would always cherish these special moments. He could never shut down again. Either with her, or the resort. If he wanted an escape, he had trusted employees to take care of things while he was gone.

His parents had always taken two or three weeks off and left the resort in the hands of their trusted team. Never at Christmas, but the break did them good after working so hard throughout the year. He could do the same.

But this hadn't been about taking a break. This was about finding himself, and he realized who he was all along. A man in love with the life he had lived. A man in love with the resort. He could never turn his back on it or his people.

They hadn't discussed last night's conversation or kiss. She was either ignoring his seriousness or she hadn't grasped the significance of his admission that he hadn't wanted to face another Christmas without her.

Reality was a jerk. She was with another man. Whether here or not, whether they spent the holidays together or not, she would go back to him. Probably marry him and have kids. Seth was supposed to only want friendship. His parents had warned him of such risks, and not with just Remy. As a teenager, a growing adult, many girls had wanted to develop relationships with him during their vacations. Have a fling with the owner's son. His parents made it their priority to keep him interested in the resort so he would one day take over. And he didn't regret that now.

He wanted to prolong the inevitable. Once they were done here, they would return to a room full of people and activities and he would no longer have time to be alone with her. This might be his last chance for a while.

But no more would he share his feelings. The last time he tried had been a disaster, the lights kicking on after a kiss that still burned his skin.

Might as well stop ignoring reality and get on with his business. He unlocked the cabin to grab the tools and saws. He spotted the coffee pod machine and the hot cocoa and asked Remy if she wanted a cup.

She nodded. "I would love a cup."

He switched on the machine and filled it with water, his mind rolling. MacGregor loved his job here during the Christmas season, and his twin boys had always helped. They had everything set up to entertain the people who came here to seek the perfect tree. Coffee, cocoa, water, and all the necessary tools. The visiting family could cut it down if they wanted to, but if not, MacGregor or his sons would do it for them. Then they took immaculate care to wrap up the tree for its journey to its next home.

Remy laid her hand on Seth's shoulder.

Her presence kindled fire in his belly. He tossed her a smile.

Her mouth pursed as she studied him. "A penny for your thoughts."

He tore open the packet of cocoa and dumped it in the cup, then put it under the machine and watched as water gurgled and steamed into the Styrofoam. He handed her the first and then did the same for his. She grabbed a spoon and stirred.

"I was thinking about MacGregor and his boys," he said. He need never tell her the rest of his thoughts, how he wished this could be forever between them. His parents had been in love, her parents had been in love. They might have died early, but they taught the perfect example of romance.

"I hope you're not feeling guilty again."

Jerking out of his reflections, he snapped the lid on the cup and handed her one. "No, no. Just melancholic."

They stood inside the cabin, which MacGregor had set up nicely to use for slow days, take payment for the trees, or let his patrons seek shelter while they waited for their tree. He hadn't visited since his parents died. He'd missed a lot of things since his parents died.

Determined to please her, no matter the heartache, Seth grabbed a large saw and stepped outside.

"I know it's hard to be here." Remy followed him. "I have such fond memories with my parents, and I know you do, too."

He stopped and faced her, holding his cup of cocoa in one hand and a saw in the other. "So, let's make new memories, shall we?"

Remy roamed through the forest to flag her picks, but Seth distracted her by pointing out the sky, birds, and other trees that didn't interest her. Irritation prickled the back of her neck. Urgency filled her. She was eager to get back and get the decorations up before the others arrived so they would be greeted with the spirit.

But then Seth brought out the plastic sled. Excitement replaced annoyance and she promised herself one run. She laughed all the way downhill, her pulse floating on the climb back up.

Seth stood waiting, his smile lifting her doubts. "Ready to go again?"

She dropped the sled and swatted at him. "Come on, you know we have a timetable. You said they would be here by noon and it's almost eleven."

He crossed his arms and simpered. "Didn't you come here to have fun?"

"Yes. And decorating is fun."

He picked up the sled. "So is this. I can tell you're enjoying it."

She was having a blast. More so than she had in a really long time. And she caught herself wanting to please all the visitors, even though the ones arriving today worked for the resort and wouldn't expect things to be finished. She was so used to making sure everything was perfect that she was having a hard time relaxing until it was.

She scowled at him but agreed to another sled run. Although it didn't stop. It was a solo sled so they had to take turns, and she wanted to at least give him one. But one turned into more than she could count. Hours passed and they shared turns sliding downhill.

They stopped to cut down the trees, have a few cups of

cocoa and coffee, and take a few more slides downhill. Adrenaline buzzed through her.

On her way back up after another run downhill, flakes fell harder and she noticed Seth studying the sky.

"We better load up and get back before a storm hits and we get stuck. I'm sure Jonathan and Maye are already there."

She thrust the plastic sled into his chest. "Oh, sure. You entice me with all this fun and now you want to go back?" He ducked his head and gave her an apologizing look, and she giggled. "I'm kidding. I'm ready myself. Let's go."

As they loaded in the Jeep, a dark SUV approached from the gate behind them. "Maybe that's MacGregor." Seth squinted, climbed back out, and shut the door as he waited. "I don't recognize the vehicle."

Remy walked to Seth's side and stood beside him. She was anxious to see MacGregor again and find out if he remembered her. But that definitely wasn't him.

A couple with two young children stepped out, and a woman clapped her hands together once. "Oh, thank God y'all are open. I didn't think you would be."

"About to close up, ma'am. What can I do for you?"

She pointed to the forest behind her. "Well, we've rented a cabin over there and had planned to go into town today to get a tree. But the road is closed."

"The road is closed?" Seth's eyebrows notched up.

"Mountains of snow piled up over the two roads leading to town," the man said.

Seth shot Remy a quizzical look. Her stomach fluttered. Did that mean no one had been able to make it to the resort?

Her only answer was destiny. She hadn't had any phone service, it hadn't snowed until now, and the roads were blocked so nobody could get out or in.

Maybe their parents were up there, conspiring on how to

keep Seth and Remy together. She chuckled to herself. If anything, it wasn't to keep them together but to keep Remy from running away from fun. Lord knew, no matter how much they enjoyed each other's company, they weren't meant for each other. Maybe he had kissed her, but he had never indicated anything other than friendship. Even after the kiss. And she... well, she didn't miss Carson, but that didn't mean she didn't love him. Even if she did picture herself staying here forever.

"You're welcome to choose a tree here," Seth said.

Remy wasn't surprised at his offer. He was a good man who always put others' needs first.

"Are you guys okay? Got enough food?"

The man nodded. "We've got everything else we need. Just wanted a tree."

The young girl, not much more than six, Remy guessed, tugged on her mother's coat. "Mom, mom, mom."

"Yes, Caroline?"

The child pointed. "I like the tree over there. Can we get that one?"

"We can get any one you and your brother choose."

"Let me grab my saw. You want something to drink?" Seth asked, turning to the cabin.

"We're good, thank you," the woman said. She offered her hand to Remy as Seth unlocked the cabin door.

She recognized the woman's twang and felt a familiar comfort.

"My name is Lori and this is my husband, Don."

"Nice to meet you. It sounds like you have a Texas accent," Remy said.

The woman nodded. "Born and bred."

She tapped her chest. "Wonderful. Me, too. I'm in the Austin area."

"Dallas, although I'm ready to get out of the city."

"I hear ya," Remy replied. "Being out here away from city lights, noises, and traffic makes me more so."

They discussed the trip and the cabin they stayed in until Seth returned.

He lifted the saw. "You want to cut it? Or would you prefer I do?"

"I want to do it," Caroline said, bouncing.

"No, baby." Her father smoothed his hand over her head. "That's too dangerous. But you can help Daddy do it."

She jumped up and down and clapped her glove-covered hands. "Okay."

The other child stood next to his dad, watching.

Remy guessed he was about three. She engaged him in conversation while they all walked to the tree.

"I really appreciate this," Don told Seth. "It looks like y'all were loading up and leaving."

"It's no problem. We're down the way there. I did shut down for a while, but we've reopened." Seth told them about the resort and invited them out for activities. "We probably won't officially open until tomorrow or the next day. Now I have to wait on my help to get here."

"I hope the roads clear soon," Don said.

Remy played with the young boy and made snow angels far away from the cutting of the tree. Caroline quickly bored of helping her dad, and frolicked over to play with her brother and Remy.

Remy admired Seth while he worked. He could have refused to help that family, but he had welcomed them with open arms. He helped Don carry the tree to the vehicle and wrapped it up for him. Don tried to pay, and Seth held up his hand. "It's on the house today."

Lori's fingers fluttered through the air. "Oh, we couldn't possibly."

"I won't have it any other way," Seth said. "Have a Merry

Christmas. And don't forget to stop by the resort, if you want."

They loaded the family up with their tree and rounds of hot chocolate, then waved goodbye. The family drove out of the gate and disappeared down the road.

Remy patted his chest and kissed his cheek. "You're a good man."

~

The moment Seth drove out of the gate, his phone binged with text messages. Everyone was stuck and couldn't bypass any of the roads leading up to the mountain. He called Jonathan, who told him all about the snow piled high over the roads.

"We'll try again tomorrow," Johnathan said.

Seth and Remy unloaded all the trees but left them leaning against the resort until he could round up the tree stands.

"This never happens," Seth said. "Usually they have trucks and all clearing the two roads to the mountain and the one to this resort, but something broke down and they can't get to it today. I'm going to drive down and check the road to the resort."

"I want to go with you."

He wasn't sad about the road closure, but eager to get rolling on the resort. They had so much to do. Still, he enjoyed this time alone with Remy.

They stopped at the mound of snow covering the entrance.

"Wow," Seth muttered. "I've never seen anything like this."

"I've never seen anything like a lot of things that have happened since I came here," Remy said.

He angled his head at her. "Like what?"

"Like no snow. And then lots of snow. It's like…"

Her voice trailed, prickling his ears as his imagination took over. He pictured his parents in heaven, dumping snow all around them so they could be alone. He chuckled at the image. He doubted his parents would have taken part in such nonsense.

"Yeah," Seth said, not giving words to his thoughts. If their parents were trying to keep them together, heaven needed a reevaluation. No matter how much he cared for Remy, a pile of snow wouldn't deter her from her goals, and her goals didn't include him. He reached for her hand. "Well, come on, we've got a lot of decorating to do."

Remy eyed her phone then slid it in her pocket. "I don't even have phone service."

"Mine is spotty. But you're always welcome to use it if you need to."

"No, that's okay. It's nice to have no communication with the outside world."

He wondered how long they would be cut off from the outside world. Maybe it was a sign that he should have stayed closed for the season, but he hoped he wouldn't have to disappoint people all over again.

He looped his hand through hers. "Come on. Let's go make the best of this situation."

They spent hours decorating. He turned on Christmas music, and they laughed and sang and hung decorations. The three trees covering the window in the back of the room twinkled with white lights, and Remy declared them sufficiently adorned. Wreaths hung on the walls and lights surrounded the windows.

Seth had to ignore his temptation to kiss her again, but he did grab her hand and twirl her through the lobby in a dance. The smile on her face, one of pure rapture, would remain implanted in his memory forever, like a photograph that never faded.

He enjoyed their time together, but would be disappointed if he couldn't open the resort because of the weather. His heart was set on sharing it with the people he loved, his community and his employees, and he hoped the snow wouldn't stop them.

CHAPTER 10

Remy's back ached, but she wasn't ready to stop. They ate a quick sandwich and took a break to dance through the lobby. She would treasure this magical moment forever.

She'd missed this about Christmas. The joy, the singing, the decorating, and the creativity. Carson was not the kind of man to get excited about Christmas, or much of anything else besides his work.

She squealed at the décor's completion, thrilled at the way the image in her head came alive. Two lighted deer glanced at each other, a third, smaller one, peering up at them. Doves floated above, and a small bunny huddled near the trees behind the deer. Red berries coated the trees, the skirting covered with snow. The mantel held a horse carriage and miniature animals to showcase the hope for all living things. Remy couldn't wait for Seth's photograph to be ready. For now, the wall held a wreath with a red bow, and a small train circled the main tree.

Once they were done for the night, they shut off the lobby lights and stood by the tree. Remy admired the decorations. The staircase was lined with lights, and everything glowed.

"I think I'll stay here tonight, in one of the spare rooms."

Remy bumped his shoulder. "You scared to go outside in the dark?" she teased.

He winked at her. "Scared to leave you here all alone in case you decide to decorate more and we don't have a place to put anyone."

They fixed cups of tea and sat on the couch in the dark, lights twinkling around them.

"I think I've had my fill of hot chocolate for the day." Remy dipped the tea bag in and out of her mug and folded her legs under her on the couch.

"It's beautiful. You did an amazing job."

Heat flushed through her and she took a deep, satisfying breath. "*We* did an amazing job."

"You did most of the imagery."

She blinked at him on the other side of the couch and gave him a teasing snarl, surprised he wouldn't take her compliment. "You helped my imagery come alive."

"Well, you are an amazing, creative person."

She rested her head against the back of the couch and smiled at him. The praise felt good, and something she wasn't used to. Carson never complimented her creative endeavors, and even any accolades at work seemed contrived.

"Why aren't women knocking down your door and demanding marriage, or at least attention?"

He threw back his head and laughed.

The warmth of his voice spread through her chest.

"Why are you laughing?" she asked. "Come on. No women beating down your door?"

His smile created a dip in her pulse, and she longed to know more about him. But he didn't share much about himself. He never had.

She stretched out her legs and wiggled her feet, pressing her back against the couch arm. For a moment, she thought she was probably hogging the couch, but he rested his arm on the back of it and extended his legs in front of him, clearly comfortable. "I bet there are and you just shoot them down."

"I've dated." Seth gave a half shrug. "But nothing to make me want to give up everything for a person."

"You shouldn't have to give up everything for a person." If only she could listen to her own advice. Her limbs tightened, chest growing heavy with tenderness. She jiggled her mug to stir the tea and took a sip.

"No, I shouldn't. But most women I've dated seem to think so. Or then there are the ones who only want to date me at Christmas. Because there's something magical about the season that wraps their heart in joy and they love to be here and experience the resort and everything they think I can give them. But when it's over, the magic is over and they leave."

Her stomach cramped. She was sad for him, but she couldn't ignore the satisfaction that he hadn't found someone to spend the rest of his life with. Not that she wanted him to be miserable, but imagining him happy with someone else left her lonesome. And that was a thought she wasn't fully ready to digest. She fluttered her hand near him, tempted to whisk the hair that had fallen across his forehead. "Oh. I'm sorry."

"Don't be sorry. It was never serious, I assure you. I haven't found anyone I'm serious about."

She glanced at him, and her breath stalled in her throat. Her body flushed.

"Or, maybe I had." He looked right at her, and her world turned topsy-turvy. "But it never worked out."

Everything went still, except her pulse. The tea bag slumped in her mug. Her hand slipped, almost dropping her hold.

The fire popped and she jumped, glancing at the dissolving logs. She wanted to know more about him and this special woman, but she sensed he wasn't ready to share. For a moment, she thought he was talking about her, but that was silly. Or wishful thinking? Maybe. The only relationship they'd had—their friendship and everything in between—had happened at Christmas. Them working anything out beyond that was unimaginable.

Wasn't it?

They both lived in separate worlds a thousand miles apart. In their younger days, there relationship was more like sibling rivalry. Even if her friends would say great relationships start with friendship, they'd had nothing in common.

Although the longer she stayed here, the more she realized they did.

That kiss left her wanting more. But it wasn't just the kiss that wanted to delve deeper into their potential.

She cupped her mug with both hands and held it close to her chin. "If there is a special woman, someone you care about, maybe you should tell her how you feel."

If he cared about her, now was the time to admit it. The fire cracked louder, hissing through the wood as if holding its breath for an answer.

"Maybe." He smacked his legs with his free hand and stood. "It's late. I'm tired. I still need a shower, so I'm heading to bed." He set his cup on the coffee table and waved. "I'll take care of that in the morning."

She pressed her hand into her belly and let out a shaky smile. They both needed sleep, but she didn't want the night to end. She enjoyed their talk. "Okay. I'm going to sit here a moment longer and finish my tea. Goodnight, Seth."

He hesitated. "Do you want me to stay with you?"

Tempting, but she said no. She tucked her legs under her. "I'm a big girl. I've stayed in this resort all by myself before."

He chuckled. "Alright. Good night." He turned and headed for the stairs.

"Oh, and Seth?"

He faced her, the radiance twinkling around him, creating a soft glow.

"Thanks for doing all this. For letting me stay."

He nodded, saluted, and disappeared up the stairs. And as she watched him go, she glanced at the ceiling and wondered what might have happened if they would've been sitting under mistletoe.

Seth woke the next morning and found Remy in the kitchen, cooking breakfast. The scent of maple, bacon, butter and a touch of cinnamon filled the room.

His heart was pleased, but he couldn't hold onto any hope. This was a one-time thing, never to happen again. Remy wouldn't stay. Maye would be back soon, and there was no reason for Remy to cook for him again.

"You're an early riser." He fixed himself a cup of coffee. "I thought for sure I'd be up first this morning."

She shuffled through the kitchen, stopping at the stove. "Nope. Sorry. I've got too much to do."

"You didn't come here to work. You came here to enjoy."

"Well, I've got too much to enjoy to sleep any longer than necessary." She flipped pancakes and eyed him. "How did you sleep?"

"Well. And yourself?"

He'd dreamed of her waking beside him as they imagined their newest adventures for the day. But that was never to be, and he wouldn't ruin their friendship again with illusions of the impossible like he had years ago. "Wonderful," he said instead. He sat at the table and admired her working in the kitchen. His stomach grumbled. "You didn't have to cook breakfast."

"Of course, I didn't. But I wanted to. Besides, once Maye gets here, I won't be able to step foot in this kitchen, so I might as well enjoy it now."

"She's the best of the best. She's probably got all the meals up to next Christmas planned." Seth took a sip of coffee and contemplated what he could do to make it up to his staff. "I gave them all bonuses, but I need to find a nice gift to give her and the others."

Remy dumped another pancake on the stack and slid the bacon from its pan. "Ooh, yes. Let's go shopping. Well, not today, but soon. Besides, we need to go get your photo." She glanced at him and grimaced. "That is, if you don't mind me tagging along."

"Would love for you to. I need all your help to find the perfect gift."

"I've still got a bit of shopping to do for my family back home." She switched off the stove and grabbed two plates and forks. "Breakfast is ready."

They ate across from each other at the kitchen table. The rasp of forks on plates, the occasional sip of coffee, and the chatter about gift ideas filled his heart with joy and created an intimacy he couldn't afford to get used to. But oh how he wished he could wake up to this every morning.

"You have a lot of staff members to buy for," she said. "That complicates things. You could give them champagne, or a framed photo, or chocolate, or some kind of ornament. Something all the same?"

"I probably won't buy for everyone, but I want to give my special long-timers a special gift."

Remy scraped her fork across the plate, gathering eggs, but stopped. "We'll start with Maye. What does she like? Besides cooking, of course."

"I could get her the newest kitchen gadget and she'd be thrilled. But that isn't special enough, and she doesn't use some of the latest and greatest kitchen toys because she's old-fashioned."

An idea formed at something his mom used to do for her personnel. "Every year, my mom would give them a Christmas ornament, but that stopped when she died since I never carried on that tradition. I can gift everyone a small ornament of a dove, with an inscription. My mom used to do that and match whatever theme she was doing."

"I love that idea. We should have a party strictly for the staff members." She bit her lips. "Sorry. I keep saying we."

His heart tumbled. "Don't be sorry. You're in this with me, and I appreciate all your ideas. I still want to give Maye and Johnathan something extra special."

Remy nodded and ate her food, her brows crinkling.

"I need to give Jenny a call and see if she can get me forty-three ornaments for my full-time staff and twenty-eight for the seasonal."

Her gaze snapped to him. "You have twenty-eight seasonal?"

"Yep. Gets crazy around here, you know."

"Who is Jenny?"

"She owns a Christmas store in town. She was a great friend of my mother's. Of course, my mom always gave her a few months to get everything ordered. So, she might kill me for putting this on her at the last minute." He gave a half shrug and tried not to get his hopes up. "It might be impossible."

"If she's like the rest of the folks in town, I bet she'll figure out a way," Remy said.

"And I need an inscription. Got any ideas?"

Her mouth pursed. "I might need some time to think on

that. You could use the word hope. That says enough right there."

They finished their breakfast, and she took the plates. Seth elbowed her out of the way when she tried to wash dishes. "Let me do this. You did the cooking."

She bumped his shoulder. "You have lots to do."

"So do you."

"And this won't take any time. I wouldn't dare let Maye come into a dirty kitchen." She pointed a soapy finger at him. "Call Jenny."

Seth glanced at his phone. Still no calls or messages. "I haven't heard from Johnathan or Maye. I'm worried the roads are still down."

Remy washed the dishes. He grabbed a plate to dry, but she nudged him away again. "Maybe you should go check."

As he exited the kitchen and walked toward the front door, it burst open. Johnathan, Maye, and Cynthia rushed in.

"The roads are clear!" Maye announced, wearing a huge grin and carrying a sack full of groceries.

Maye was a petite woman, her dark hair always pulled into a bun, her lips always lined in red, and her face holding little wrinkles. Despite her diminutive stature, she was boisterous and powerful. When she said jump, one always asked how high.

Seth hugged his receptionist, trying to keep his emotions in check. "Cynthia, hey, thanks so much for coming."

They pulled away, and she smiled. "Happy to be here. Stacey is on her way."

Cynthia and Stacey manned the front and greeted the guests on arrival.

"I'm betting the phones are shut off. I'll go take care of that problem, so we can get this resort filled." Cynthia skipped away to the office in the back, singing a Christmas carol.

Johnathan parked his gear and hugged Seth. "I doubt that'll be a problem."

Seth embraced Maye next. "Do you have anything else you need help bringing in?"

Maye waved her hand at the door. "I've got all sorts of groceries in my car."

From the kitchen, Remy burst into the lobby and squawked. Her footsteps resounded in Seth's heart as she rushed forward to greet Maye.

Maye opened her arms, and she fell into them for a hug. "Remy. It's been so long. It's so great to see you, sweetie."

"You, too, Maye. I've missed you so much."

They spoke to each other, huddling together, and walked to the kitchen. "Don't forget my groceries!" Maye called before disappearing with Remy.

He glanced at Johnathan and wiggled his eyebrows. "Guess I better get those." With Johnathan's help, it only took two trips to carry everything.

"You sure you got enough here?" Seth teased Maye as he set the last bag on the kitchen counter.

"Probably not. But I'll do an inventory." She shooed them away. "Now, everyone out of my kitchen so I can work."

"Do you need any help?" Remy asked.

Maye shook her head and grabbed cabbage out of the grocery bag. "No. The others will be here soon."

"Okay. I've got some stuff to do, too." Remy pranced over and patted Johnathan's cheek. "So great to see you."

Seth spread out his arms, his heart bursting with hope. The perfect theme for this Christmas. "Carte blanche," he told everyone. "Have at it."

∾

Remy loved every moment of her stay. For the first time in a long time, she felt alive and fully capable.

The resort filled quickly with staff, and a decision was made to not open it for visitors until Saturday, three days from now. According to Cynthia, though, the rooms were already booked.

Many staff members came to Remy for advice and permission on the decorations, and she hesitated. She wasn't in charge, but Seth had given her free reign. Still, she encouraged everyone to use their creativity and *have at it*, as Seth had said.

She roamed the Christmas village, redecorating and revamping to make it all in working order. The statues and the buildings exhibited more energy, no longer slumping, and alive with Christmas.

Much like her own energy. She had slumped for too long.

They worked on the large outdoor tree, a permanent fixture at the resort, with plans for a lighting ceremony on Saturday night.

When her romanticism overwhelmed her and she didn't want to cry in front of everyone, she escaped to her room. Not because she was sad, but because she was filled with joy.

Should she feel so happy without Carson? Was it as Seth had said about his previous girlfriends? They got excited for their relationship around the holiday season, but afterwards, when everything turned back to normal, reality staled.

Her and Carson's relationship had grown stale long ago. Christmas wouldn't help them make it work. Carson wasn't here and, at this point, she didn't want him here. But she dreaded going back to reality and pretending like everything was okay.

Nothing was okay when it came to her reality back home. She hadn't been happy for a long time. Her parents' deaths had made it easier to ignore her unhappiness, when all the while it should have given her the wakeup call this vacation was giving her.

But what would she do about it?

Having everyone ask her opinion about the resort gratified her. She thrived when she was creating, and using her creative spirit to inspire others to create. She had neglected the talent for too long. She worked on secret projects—surprises for his resort—and hoped Seth would be as thrilled by them as she was about making them.

Seth empowered her to anything with her dreams. Carson had done nothing but discourage her.

Finding respite in her day, she disappeared into the basement to glance at photos and ornaments for the outdoor tree. She clutched a heavy-duty flashlight in case the lights went out again. Although she hated dark underground places, the room was cozy, bright, and open.

It was likely to stay that way for hours, unless the lights died, and experience taught her exactly how terrifying that would be. Especially alone.

But she was too excited and too eager to worry, and Seth had checked the generator to make sure it would kick on correctly if it happened again. Besides, the resort was now filled with staff, and Seth knew where she was.

She glanced at the mistletoe to see if it still hung. It did, but she didn't reach out to check on its authenticity. Likely, it had dangled for years, put up by his mother when she was still alive.

She scoured the filing cabinet, choosing to inspect the printouts before the disks. Seth told her most everything printed was on the disks, but not everything on them had been printed. They were organized by month and year.

At least one family photo for every year since Seth was a baby, and she smiled at each one. Also, annual photos of her family. Then she came across one with her family and his together, the snowy white forest behind them. The last year their parents were alive.

Her chest tightened, eyes prickled. She remembered the day like it was only yesterday. The breeze across her face, the chirrup of cardinals, and the creek gurgling in the background.

She wondered why that was the only year they all had taken one together. Were they creating a new tradition that never got fulfilled? Everyone was smiling, happy and laughing, dressed in green and red and bunched to all fit in the picture. The photo captured the joy of Christmas.

She placed it on the color copier and continued, being very picky about which ones to choose for the collage she had built in her mind, but also wanting to copy each and every one so she could take home the memories. She'd make it easier on herself and copy the disks later.

She found a file folder named *Seth's photos*, surprised at the quality even when he was so young. They were organized by year, and his mom had apparently seen and encouraged his talent. A lot of landscaping, but snapshots of people, too.

She stopped at the image of her. Her breath bubbled in her throat. The only one he'd taken of her, it spoke of something special. Judging by the year and her memory, she was fifteen years old. They were at the creek. She remembered the day because they had all gone. She had ridden with Seth on the snowmobile and longed to drive. Her parents said no, and Seth teased her. She still considered him a friend, before he turned mean and standoffish. Before he'd stopped wanting anything to do with her anymore.

She knelt along the creek bed, her ungloved hand stirring the water, studying the current with a serious expression on her face. Her hair billowed around her, unrestrained by any cap. Her lips were in a soft pout, and Seth had captured the essence of the picture in a way she never would have known was possible. Bliss. Innocence. Beauty. Enchantment.

She studied his creation, her vision blurring. Even then, she'd had no idea he was interested in photography. Never even noticed he was taking a picture of her. Photos were a huge part of her life. People always around with their camera. *Let's get together for a picture* a mantra for the season.

She had been selfish and self-absorbed. No wonder he could barely stand her.

She copied the photo before she ruined it with her tears, then copied the disks and rummaged through the others. Although fun, reviewing the photos wrung out too many emotions she wasn't ready to name.

After all the disks were copied, she located a large envelope to store everything in and treaded slowly back up the stairs.

The basement area was located in a back portion of the resort, so activity was slim here, but windows in a long hallway revealed an outdoor work area before it entered into the main resort. A loud thwack caught her attention and she jumped. Another *thwack thwack.*

She halted when she spotted Seth chopping wood. Heat flooded her skin. Her senses heightened into unknown territory. He'd removed his jacket, probably because all the chopping warmed him. He grabbed another log, stopped to swipe his arm across his forehead, and whacked the wood in one swoop.

She shuffled away, out into the bustling resort, keeping her chin lowered as she ran up the stairs and into her room.

She wanted to get away. She wasn't ready to see or talk to anyone.

She dropped into her bed and let out a long breath. Her emotions overwhelmed her. Her mind reeled, heart pumped way too furiously.

Her feelings for Seth didn't feel like friendship. But when this was all over—and it eventually had to end—they would go their separate ways. She had to remember she was vulnerable. That's all this was.

Her breath subsided, and she stood, clutching her coat. She could hide her attraction, distract herself with things that needed doing. And eventually, she would remember how much she cared for Seth but how wrong they were for each other.

She glanced at the envelope of memories.

She wanted to make a collage for him. One large frame for several special photos, which meant she'd have to assess them again. Should she include herself? Or would that be too presumptuous? She could place a small photo of her up in the corner somewhere, with the large family photo the focal point and other scattered photos. She was eager to tackle her design, but she also needed rest from the nostalgia.

Grabbing her coat, she went outside and strolled to a table on the outskirts of the village and sat. From a distance, she saw Seth approach, his footprints marking the snow like tracks on her heart. She ducked her head away and watched a finch flitter across a snowcapped pine tree. Safer than observing Seth.

"Hey." He slid on the bench beside her. Her nose tickled with his woodsy scent. "You get everything you needed?"

She bobbed her head, growing tongue-tied. She was afraid if she spoke too soon, her voice would warble and she might prattle off everything she was feeling. Like curious about how his lips would feel on hers again. She cleared her throat and forced away the image. "I made copies of the disks. I hope that's okay."

"Of course. I'm sure there's lots of memories in there for you, too."

She glanced down, blinking away her pain.

He swiped a hand over her cheek. "Is everything okay?"

She looked at him and smiled, her chin quivering. "Yes. Just difficult to go through those photos and see such happy times."

"I haven't managed to do it yet," he said, his voice a steady but low rasp. "But the happy times aren't over."

She shook her head and kicked at the snow. "We have to make more of them."

He bent over and gathered snow in his gloved hands, a twinkle in his eye.

Her pulse stuttered. "Don't you dare!"

He shrugged. "What do you mean?"

"I see what you're doing."

He bunched the snow in a ball. "Just making a small snowman."

"I saw you chopping wood. Don't you have staff for that?" Remy asked.

He planted the snowball on the ground. "I've got plenty of help, but I love to do it myself when I've got the time. Besides, a good boss does everything he'd ask his employees to do."

For a moment, she pictured Carson belting out orders and refusing to do the tough work. He was a hard worker when it came to things he enjoyed, but he wouldn't go above his means to help others like Seth did.

She leaned over and balled a smaller mound of snow, then sat it on the one he'd made, trying to erase the image of her comparisons. It wasn't fair to Carson. They were two different men, each of them with their own strengths. Being selfless just wasn't one of Carson's. "Well, I've got lots to do to get this outdoor tree ready for our opening." As much as she longed for Seth's company, she was feeling way too vulnerable to talk to him right now.

He watched her, his eyes continuing to twinkle.

Her skin tingled at his look, the surge in her chest spreading outward. She tilted her head at him. "What?"

"You said *our*."

"Oh." Her body flushed. Her words had felt natural. "Sorry."

"No. I liked it. Your family was a huge part of this place, too."

She chewed on his words then stood before things grew too serious. She rubbed her hands over his beanie-covered head. "Thanks for letting us be a part of it, Seth. I better get back to work." She waved and shambled away. She couldn't tell him what pulsed through her mind the moment she'd stepped foot on the property.

This felt like home.

CHAPTER 11

Seth chuckled to himself as he strolled through the Christmas village, which flourished under his staff's creativity. A Santa suit draped over a clothesline outside Santa's shop. Each piece dangled individually—the hat, coat, bottoms, and boots. Real logs were tucked into the front of the shop, ready to be used in the outdoor fire pit.

He smiled and continued forward, his thoughts on Remy and all they had accomplished so far.

For the first time in a long time, he felt whole. Remy's smile had awakened him and given him hope. *Hope,* this year's theme. With her help, he ordered engraved ornaments with the word and planned to give them to his staff at the evening's appreciation dinner.

Remy had been super secretive about some of her errands, but he enjoyed watching her. He had a few surprises of his own.

She had transformed since coming here, and he wondered if she realized it. Her eyes glowed. Her shoulders no longer slumped, and the warm flush to her face left him wanting to cradle her in his arms and never let her go. She looked happy.

Maybe it was the season, but he hoped he could take some credit for her contentment.

After his day of activities, he'd escaped to his home to shower and change, then came to his office where they were to meet so she could help him carry the boxes of gift bags to the tree. The slight rap at the door knocked into his ribs, and his breath stalled when she entered.

She wore an elegant green dress with a low back. Her hair was curled and swanked with diamond clips. Her silver heels made her a few inches taller, and he pressed his forehead to hers for a slight second in greeting.

"Wow," he said as he pulled away, his voice hoarse and feeling raw. "You look amazing."

She smiled and straightened his tie. "So do you." She grabbed one box of gifts from the desk and hooked her arm through his. "Are you ready for this?"

He nodded, but warmth filled his eyes and adrenaline rushed through him. Her heels clacked against the foyer as they walked together into the dining hall.

Mellow music floated from the speakers. The noise of several conversations drifted from the area, igniting his nerves. He was eager to see everyone but worried some of them would still resent him for shutting down. This was his third year of owning the resort and hosting this dinner, but his first year with Remy by his side.

Things couldn't have been more perfect.

He almost stumbled when he walked in and noticed the décor. Tables situated together so everyone could fit, with lantern centerpieces displayed every few feet. Etched in silver and gold, each inside held a different display. A cluster of shimmering snowflakes, multicolored beads, and crystal balls hung from the ceiling in one corner. Other tables adorned with snacks and decorations skirted the walls.

His pulse dipped when he spotted the tree. He released Remy's hold and approached.

Photos of past memories were clipped to the limbs. Twenty-five years of memories. He fingered a portrait of him as a young child, barely above his dad's knees as he stood beside him, his mother kneeling forward and offering a poinsettia to the camera. Another of him and Remy, about six years old, walking side by side in the snow. Their fingers were close but not touching, and they were glancing at each other and smiling.

He didn't remember that photo.

A lone one of his mom standing under a blanket of lights wearing a sweater that read *hope*.

He closed his eyes and pulled in an expansive breath. His nostrils burned.

Remy grasped his hand. He turned to her.

Her eyes were watery, her head tilted as she gazed up at him. "Are you okay?"

Grief and gratitude prickled his throat. Grief that this moment was happening without his and her parents. Gratitude for everything she had done. "Is this why you've been so secretive?"

She licked her lips and nodded. "It is. Did you like it?"

He curled her hand to his mouth and kissed her fingers. "I love it. Thank you." He placed the gifts under the tree and noticed one lone package with his name. He bit down on a smile and stood. "Now let's see if I can get through the rest of the evening without weeping."

The staff gathered around the table and remained standing. Several wine bottles were already open, but none yet poured. Seth circulated and poured wine for all those who wanted it then stood at the end and tapped a spoon on the glass. Not that he needed to do so to get everyone's attention. Silence engulfed the room.

He swallowed a lump. "I want to thank everyone for coming tonight." He cleared his throat. "And for helping me get the resort back open. I owe you all an apology."

People murmured, shook heads, and fussed.

He held up a hand. "No. I do owe you an apology for closing for the holidays. But my head and my heart weren't in the right place." He placed his palm over his chest. "They are now. I realized I have so much to be grateful for, and each and every one of you is at the top of that list."

A chorus of sniffling and clapping followed.

"This year's theme is hope. My parents started this dream with nothing more than hope. They carried it through with optimism that it would work out. They praised everything and everyone with the good that happened. And they encouraged each other when things seemed doubtful. Those four words, of course, spell out hope."

Murmurs fell around the table. He ducked his head a moment. He wasn't the best speaker in the world, but he wanted his staff to understand his appreciation, and he didn't know the right words.

He held up his glass, and everything was silent again except for the soft music playing on the speakers. "You've given me all those things and more. I never could have done this without you guys. Cheers to a beautiful holiday season. I love you all."

They extended their glasses and a chorus of "cheers" followed. Everyone sipped, then Johnathan said a prayer before they all sat. Food was passed around and conversations rippled across the table. Remy sat beside him and nodded with a beaming smile.

The dinner was delicious. Maye had cooked her famous prime rib with roasted veggies, garlic green beans, Yorkshire pudding, and a simple gingerbread cake for dessert.

Once everyone had finished eating, Seth grabbed champagne and cracked open a few bottles. Maye and Remy retrieved the flutes and poured while Seth fetched his box of gift bags. He handed them out, hugged everyone and said thank you. They were all almost all in tears. He returned to the head of the table and clasped Remy in a side hug while everyone opened their gifts.

"We got you a little something, too." Johnathan collected the package from under the tree and carried it to Seth.

His belly fluttered. "You shouldn't have."

Johnathan gave a crisp nod. "We wanted to. It's from all your employees. We wanted to say thank you for being such a great boss."

Seth blinked and chewed his lip. He sat down and tore open the package. Thankfully, everyone chattered and mingled and he didn't feel like he was too much in the spotlight. Sniffing, he withdrew a messenger bag, thick and sturdy constructed of full-grain leather and brass accents. He opened it to find a matching camera strap.

Johnathan slapped him on the back. "We thought you could use a new camera bag. Yours is so old and worn and, quite frankly, a bit boring."

Those standing nearby chuckled.

"Man, thank you." He stood and held up the bag. "Thank you, everyone. This is amazing and I can't wait to use it."

He looped it over his shoulder, his gratitude for the employees impossible to hold back. He traversed the crowd to speak to them individually, leaving no one out, and held back tears.

He would reserve those for when he was alone.

Seth's speech rocked Remy's world. Simple and humble, yet graceful.

Carson's family thrived on dressing well and performing dinner speeches for every celebration, but none of them had affected her this way. Everything they did was for appearances, not for making things fun and creative and full of love.

Just like her job.

No wonder Carson hated Christmas. His family had put too many restrictions on it, removing the joy. Being here had reminded her of everything she had missed. While part of her wished he could feel the way she did, another part was glad he had decided to stay home.

She had wanted to dress nice for Seth and his party, and a thrill jolted her when she thought she caught admiration in his eyes. She watched him mingle through the crowd, hugging everyone and spending time listening to what they had to say. Maye handed out hot cocoa. Remy sipped hers and spoke with people too, but her attention kept returning to Seth.

He was a good man, a great man, and she might be falling for him.

Her belly flopped at the revelation.

Many people drifted outside to sit around the fire. Seth set his camera bag down under the tree and returned to Remy. His lips puckered and cheeks puffed as he blew out a breath. "Wow."

She squeezed his hand and let go. "Intense, huh?"

He pinched the bridge of his nose. "Intensely emotional. You want to take a stroll outside?"

They grabbed coats and gloves and joined the others, but strayed off by themselves. Lights glistened under the stars, the main tree not yet lit. They reserved that for tomorrow evening.

"Dinner was wonderful. So was your speech."

His smile dimpled his chin. "Huh, I don't know about the speech part. I'm just glad I didn't cry."

She bumped his shoulder. "Nothing wrong with a few

tears. By the end of dinner, everyone let out waterworks at one point or another."

"Including me." He stopped and turned, tucking a piece of hair behind her ear.

Warmth crawled down her spine, curling into her toes. Laughter from the staff buzzed the air, but she and Seth were hidden between buildings and right now, she felt like they were the only two people in the world.

For two days, they had been. She enjoyed everyone here but cherished this alone time with Seth. She had missed him.

He stroked her cheek with his thumb, the soft leather of his glove shooting tingles down her body. "I couldn't have done this without you."

She didn't have a chance to argue as his head lowered, he cupped the back of her neck, and his mouth came down on hers. His kiss was soft, slow, and tasted like chocolate and cinnamon from the cocoa they'd drank after dinner. Her head spun, and she kissed him back.

He pulled away. "I'm sorry."

Carson's image jumped into her head then, but not when Seth had kissed her. Guilt pinched at her. She should think about Carson, try to call him or something, but she didn't want his foul Christmas spirit to ruin hers. He had barely crossed her mind in days.

She had a decision to make. Lots of them when she returned home.

Her heart beat against her ribcage. She continued to stand there, speechless. How could she explain what she felt? That she was confused. Enamored. Afraid of enjoying a kiss with a longtime friend.

Seth flushed, and when she didn't speak, he continued. "I know you're with someone. I'm sorry. It was just the moment." He swiped a hand over his face. "Man, this is awkward now. I keep messing up."

Goosebumps chilled her arms even through her warm jacket. At one point, maybe they would talk about Carson, but now wasn't the time. Not until she processed her feelings first.

"It doesn't have to be awkward," she said.

He pulled a small package out of his coat pocket. "I meant to give you this at the party when I gave everyone else theirs, but then I doubted myself. And now I'm really doubting myself and feeling stupid."

"Oh." Warmth flooded her belly at his thoughtfulness. She took the package. "You shouldn't have. It's not Christmas yet."

"This isn't a Christmas gift. It's a thank you gift for everything you've done."

She tore open the paper and lifted the lid from the box, her breath in her throat. A necklace with the word hope encrusted with diamonds. "This is beautiful, Seth."

She unzipped her coat to free her neck and removed the chain, struggling with the clasp.

Seth reached for her. "Here, let me help."

She presented her back to him and let him fasten the necklace. She took deep but silent breaths to regain equilibrium and hide her vulnerability.

He dropped his hands, and she faced him once more. "You shouldn't have."

"I wanted to give you something more than the ornament. So that you remember our friendship when you return home and keep your hope alive."

Tears filled her eyes. Her chin trembled. "Thank you. I'll always cherish our friendship."

He closed his eyes a moment, his hands fidgeting. When he opened them and looked at her, they were sheened in tears. "I never meant to hurt you. I never meant to hurt your family."

His unexpected words surprised her. Her eyes widened, she felt the uncontrollable pull, then the frown. As if she had lost control of her facial reactions. And yet, just like the kiss had left her, she was dumbfounded and didn't know what to say.

Why did he think he hurt her and her family?

Any words she might have said jumbled, her doubts taking over any coherency. He nodded once, gave a nervous smile, then wheeled away. Not to leave her, she didn't think, but to put distance between them.

She grabbed his arm. "Whoa, wait Seth. What do you mean?"

He faced her and swiped a hand over his face. "I don't know. I mean, my dad was the pilot."

She lifted her brows. "So? Does that put you at fault?"

He threw out his hands. "I kissed you. When you have a boyfriend. That puts me at fault."

She backed up enough to lean against the pole at Santa's workshop and crossed her arms. "I'm not sure how that relates to your dad being the pilot, but this kiss wasn't terrible."

He arched his brows. "Wasn't terrible?"

"Inappropriate maybe, but not at all terrible." No matter what she felt for Seth, she owed it to Carson to make sure they were really over before she pursued anything with another man, even a kiss with a friend. She held up her palm. "Let's get one thing straight, though. Your dad was the pilot. But it wasn't your fault, and it wasn't his fault. I never blamed you. I never blamed your parents. None of my family did. It's like we said before, no matter how painful it is, our families died together doing something they loved. We might have only visited once a year, but your parents were my parents' best friends. And they loved the holidays. They died way too soon, at their favorite time of year"

His face crumbled into a full-on frown. "I know you're right. Of course, I feel guilty. For a lot of things. I feel guilty for not being a better son. A better boss."

She stepped forward, closer to him, and waved her arms. "Oh, come on. Your parents doted on you and you doted on them. Same for your employees."

His crooked grin sliced a hole in her defenses. "Doesn't mean I don't feel guilty."

"Well I do too about plenty of things." Including the kiss. But Carson hadn't come after her, and deep inside she knew he wouldn't. Deep inside she knew they had broken apart as soon as she'd said goodbye. And deep inside, she knew any relationship between her and Seth would be way too complicated.

He smoothed a hand over his front. "I keep bumbling things, don't I?"

She jabbed his shoulder, the swish of his jacket against her hand another hole in her reserves. They were friends. She could mock punch him. They could bump shoulders and foreheads and not feel strange about it. They could argue and dream, and he was the easiest person in the world to talk to. But that didn't mean anything more would work.

His laugh rippled through her uncertainties. He reached for her. "Now that's out of the way, how about we join the others in ice skating?"

She cocked her head at him and stepped backward. He dropped his hand. "You aren't trying to get out of this conversation, are you?"

He rubbed his chin. "No. I'm glad we had it. This evening has been intensely emotional for all of us. This whole season has been. But I don't want to ruin our friendship."

She toyed with the chain he had given her. Would pursuing a relationship with him be worth the cost of their friendship? Weren't they strong enough to not let that happen?

She hooked her arm through his. Maybe one day she'd be brave enough to find out. And maybe one day she'd find out why he was so focused on keeping their friendship from branching into anything else. Instead, she said, "Neither do I."

CHAPTER 12

The resort quickly filled with guests the next morning. Remy's body tingled as she was met with a whirlwind of activities. She loved experiencing this in a new light, as part of the team who had created the Christmas theme. And yet, a deep sadness filled her when she thought of her family. She had spent the last two Christmases without them. She thought a third away from them would be exactly what she needed.

She was wrong.

She realized how wrong when they burst through the door. Her heart flipped at their unexpected arrival and for a moment she hesitated. Was she imagining this?

Addie's squeal broke her out of her reverie. She rushed forward, twin braids bouncing and freckled-face glowing.

Remy kneeled to the ground, opened her arms and took her in a hug. "Oh, my goodness. What a surprise! I didn't expect you!"

Her eight-year-old niece giggled and pulled away, head bobbing. "We wanted to surprise you."

She moved to Grayson. Her three-year old nephew

garbled out a hello. She hoisted him up and swung him through the air. His brown eyes were darker than his sister's, full of glee, and he grinned as she twirled him.

Breathless, she set him down and ruffled his toast-colored hair. "You're getting too big for that." She went for Ethan, who bounced up and down, waiting his turn. Ethan was nine, Landon's only child, and he tried to act older but couldn't quite accomplish that with his bubbling excitement. "And look at how much you've grown."

Ethan puffed out his chest. "Almost as tall as you now."

She was shocked that his head already reached the bottom of her shoulders. "Almost!"

She hugged her brother next. Landon stood tall and casual and languid, his smile creating dips in his cheeks. His wife, Melissa, pulled her in for a warm embrace. Melissa was a good woman, a good mother, and Remy was thrilled Landon had found someone so sweet. Jason, her sister's husband, laughed and put up his dukes. She jabbed him in the shoulder then hugged him. Jason was retired military and taught Tae Kwon Do, but his strictness bordered on non-existent.

Finally, she hugged Tessa, gratitude filling her that her family was there. At one time, she and her sister were close. They could tell each other anything and share their doubts and fears. Not that they had grown apart, but they had gotten too busy to have more than a few conversations throughout the year.

She withdrew but clasped her sister's hands and stood before her. Tears burned her throat. "Oh my gosh, what a surprise! Did you get tired of the coast already?"

Tessa gave a crinkled-nose smile. "Well, when Seth called to let us know he was opening the resort and our rooms were available if we wanted them, we said absolutely."

Her belly fluttered. "Oh, Seth called you?" Maybe Seth

hadn't told her because he wanted to surprise her. It worked. She'd never expected her family to show up.

Tessa's shoulder-length bob dipped with her nod. "He did."

"But you told me you were staying at the beach."

She gave a half shrug and cocked her head. "Yes, we got tired of the coast. It's hot and humid and doesn't feel at all like Christmas to us there."

Remy hugged her again. "Well, I'm so glad you're here." She dropped away, faced the others, and wrapped her arm behind her sister's waist. "But I can't believe you let me come here knowing Seth had closed."

Tessa's eyebrows rose in mock horror. "He was closed?"

She tweaked her sister's nose. "He was closed, and you know it."

Tessa rested her head on Remy's shoulder. "I know. But I also knew he wasn't going anywhere. And I thought he needed you. I was right, wasn't I? You took away his pain." She lifted her head and swiped her hand over her sister's face. "And I think he took away yours, too."

Remy jutted out her chin. "I have enjoyed myself. And I will more now that you are all here. But we'll have to talk about your machinations later."

Addie bounded forward and pulled on her mom's shirt. "Can we go outside now? I want to see the village!"

"Yes, yes," Remy said. "I've worked hard on it and can't wait to hear what you think of it." She also wanted to find Seth and give him her gratitude. Now that her family was here, her heart was full.

Landon walked alongside her as they made their way outside. The others rushed out the door. On the way, Remy was stopped three times by staff members.

The first was Jennifer, who was still working on the outdoor tree to prepare it for tonight. "We have a problem with the lights. We need more. One string isn't working at all."

"Oh, have you talked to Johnathan?" she asked. "There's more in the basement but he'll have to let you down there."

"I'll message him and find out." Jennifer dashed off to finish her task.

The second was Sophie, an assistant of Maye's who asked her opinion about that night's printed menu.

"What does Maye think?"

Sophie shrugged and pressed the menu toward Remy. "She wanted me to ask you."

Remy accepted the menu and studied the creation. On special occasions, they printed menus for their guests. This one was printed on light peach etched with pearl, the writing imprinted in a charcoal gray that appeared handwritten. Remy was honored Maye had sought her opinion. "It looks fabulous."

The third was from Johnathan himself, who asked permission to change a few things on the tree outside. "I'm about to go down to the basement, anyway," he said.

"Oh, did Jennifer find you? She needed more lights."

"She did."

"What does Seth think?"

"Told me to ask you."

Pride swelled through her. It felt good to be needed and for her opinion to be appreciated. It was also a steady reminder of how little she had mattered in her real job and how much she loved doing this.

Her brother stood next to her, his lips crooked in a knowing smile. She narrowed her eyes at him, winked, then returned her attention to Johnathan.

"Absolutely," she told Johnathan, her body vibrating. "Do whatever you like."

Johnathan disappeared, and Landon hooked his arm through hers. "You work here now, or what?"

"No. Not really. I guess you can say I've volunteered." She ran her fingers through her brother's thick brown hair.

"And I have a feeling you love every moment of this."

"You know what? I do." She could imagine herself doing this for the rest of her life. The lost feeling she had for so long was gone. She felt alive, creative, and ready to share her delight with the world.

They strolled into the village. Addie admired the buildings, ogling Santa's house where his suit hung on the clothesline. "Look at all this snow!" she exclaimed, scooping the white powder in her hands.

"You know, when I first came to the resort, there wasn't any snow on the ground at all," Remy said.

Addie dropped the snow and cocked her head. "What? That's riduck-ulous,"

Remy laughed. "Yep. When Seth decided to open the resort back up, the snow fell."

"And now it's perfect." Addie jutted out her chin "I bet it was the Christmas angels."

Remy glanced at her sister, who watched her, and winked. "Maybe so."

"Hey, guys." Seth's voiced boomed into her chest as he approached, hugging everyone. "So glad you made it."

Remy bit her lip to stifle the beam from spreading across her face, but the heat rose. "Thanks for inviting them. What a surprise."

"We're going to cut down a Christmas tree tomorrow," Ethan blurted.

Seth averted his attention to them and beamed. "That's wonderful. Guess what happens tonight?"

"What?"

"We're lighting the outdoor tree to make it easier for Santa to find us on Christmas."

Grayson's eyes widened.

Addie broke into a giggle and cupped her hand over her mouth.

Ethan bit down on his lips and smiled.

"Be sure to rest up before dinner," Seth said. "We're going to do some caroling, maybe ice skating and other fun stuff. Okay, guys?"

"Okay, Mr. Seth." Ethan held out his hand for a shake, trying to be a big boy.

Remy's heart melted into a puddle at her feet when Seth took his hand.

"Maybe it's time we all go take a nap," Tessa suggested, with much grumbling from the kids. "Hey, remember what Seth said? We've got a long night and we need to rest before dinner."

Remy used her rest time as prep time.

She dressed more sophisticated than her normal jeans and sweater, choosing black skinny jeans tucked into black boots, a red silky top and a black leather jacket. She curled her hair and wore emerald tear-drop earrings along with the necklace she might never remove again.

She didn't feel out of place. Dressing up for the holiday was tradition.

Her ears tickled at the loud and boisterous dinner crowd. Conversations energized the room.

Several tables were pieced together to fit the families and several others set apart for the smaller couples and groups. Remy was certain everyone who stayed at the resort was present, and it was impossible to count the hundreds of people. Her pulse raced in joy and comradeship, and she hoped everyone felt the same inner light she did.

She glanced around for Seth, eager to share this experience with him. Where was he? Too busy to enjoy the moment? She hoped not.

Finally, during coffee and dessert, he mingled and greeted his guests. Once he reached their table, he nodded at everyone and stopped behind her chair, resting his hands on her shoulders. "The tree lighting starts in thirty minutes."

"Awesome," the kids chorused and filled their mouths with the chocolate peppermint cake.

He leaned down and spoke in her ear, his warm breath gliding across her skin, prickling down her back. Her toes tingled and for a moment, her stomach bunched in dread. Dread because she enjoyed his presence a little too much and wasn't supposed to. What had he said about the women who wanted to date him around the holidays? For her, it had nothing to do with the holidays and everything to do with his charm.

"Since this is your tree, I wanted to ask you to be a part of the lighting ceremony."

The tingle spread to her scalp. "I'll be there."

He knelt so he didn't have to continue leaning down. "No. I mean, do you want to do the official lighting?"

"Oh, no. That's better left to you." She kept her side profile to him and forked her cake. She didn't shift in her seat to look at him, not because she didn't want to, but because she didn't want her family to notice the effect he had on her.

"I would like you beside me. Not in the crowd. Stand on the podium with me while we do a toast?"

She glanced at him and nodded, her tongue tangling in her throat. "Okay."

He squeezed her shoulder and stood. "I'll be at or near the podium. Come on over when you're ready. I'll have a place nearby for your family." He nodded, smiled, and waved at the rest of the table and stepped away. "See you guys in a bit."

Tessa planted her elbows on the table and leaned closer, holding her mug near her lips. "What was that all about?"

"Oh, he invited me to help with the lighting ceremony. Says since it's my tree."

Her sister's brows raised then wiggled, a simper spreading across her face. "Your tree?"

"Well, I chose the theme and did most of the decorating." She shrugged and sipped her coffee.

"You two seem very cozy."

"We're friends. We were holed up in the resort for a couple of days, and we decorated this place together. So..."

Steam rose from Tessa's mug, and her eyes gleamed. "I like Seth. He's a good guy. He'd be good for you."

Remy's mouth fell open and she yelped. "Would you stop it?"

Her sister stuck her tongue out at her, then stood. "Come on, guys. We need to get to the ceremony or we won't have a place to stand."

"Seth reserved a place for you," Remy said.

"Of course, he did," Tessa said.

Christmas lights blazed the way on their jaunt to the center of the village, but everything else remained dark. A waitress flittered by with plastic flutes of champagne or sparkling juice.

Seth stopped them and indicated the spot he had saved. Then he guided Remy behind the tree. "I've finally got you alone behind a tree," he said, then snorted. "Sorry, that was a joke. I'm just nervous." He rubbed his hands together and ducked his head. He fidgeted with the light string and shuffled around the limbs.

"Don't be nervous. Everything will go fine."

His cheeks puffed as he blew out a breath. "I hope so. You look beautiful tonight."

"Thank you."

"Of course, you always look beautiful, but..." He shrugged, turned away, and glanced at his watch. "Two more minutes."

His compliment pleased her, but she wondered if it had anything to do with his nerves. His rapid blinking and twitchy jaw concerned her.

She moved closer and rubbed his arm. Her affirmation to him needed a repeat, so she reframed her words. "It's cute that you're so nervous. But it will all be wonderful. So stop. Take a breath." She inhaled, and she motioned by drawing a fist up her belly to diaphragm. He inhaled with her. They exhaled together, and he smiled while she motioned her hand down.

"It's not like I haven't done this a million times," he said. "Lighted a tree for hundreds of people, that is."

He turned toward the blue spruce and fingered the leaves.

The focal point of the Christmas village was rumored to be almost one hundred years old. Because she'd chosen all white in the lobby, she wanted the outdoors to pop with color. Hundreds of colored lights would strand the tree, twinkling and blinking. Or so she hoped. The wildlife theme boasted all kinds of animals in differing colors with branches of flowers and ribbon and bows, even antlers. The tree topper was a large angel glittering in lights, ribbon billowing down to represent her wings.

"It's time." Seth grabbed Remy's hand. "Let's do this thing." He stepped from behind the veil and navigated to the small podium. He grabbed the microphone, fumbled with the cord, and caught it before it fell. He laughed then put up a hand. "Hello, everyone."

The crowd cheered.

Remy's throat thrummed. No wonder he was so nervous. The crowd was enormous. It was way different being up here in front of everyone than sitting with them in a room where their attention was focused elsewhere. Now, as she looked out at the sea of people, they were all focused on the two of them.

She caught her sister's eye and smiled. Let out an awkward wave, then dropped her arm.

Seth let his hold on her go and cupped the mike with both hands. Her coat suddenly became way too hot for her, but she didn't dare move.

"Thanks for coming tonight. I hope you enjoyed your meal, and I hope you'll enjoy tonight's ceremony. After the lighting, there'll be plenty of dancing. Help yourself to ice skating, snowman building, whatever you want to do. There's hot chocolate and all kinds of candies and treats. Probably even some healthy stuff over there." He nodded toward *Santa's Treats*, a part of the village, and everyone laughed. "Everything is included, of course. And for those who aren't staying but came here for dinner and the ceremony, everything is included with your entry price, so go crazy, you guys, okay?"

The applause continued.

"I want to thank each and every one of you. We're a little late on our traditional lighting ceremony, but late is better than never, right?"

Another roar of the crowd with laughter to follow.

Remy's heart filled with warmth, her cheeks hurting with all the smiling. Standing with him overwhelmed her. The crowd's energy wafted under her as if to boost her up and make her float.

She wasn't floating, of course, but her heart soared. Sharing in the season and in the creativity was unlike anything she'd ever experienced. Even in her job where she was told what to create, she only shared it with her boss and a select few.

He raised his flute, and everyone followed. Although lights from the village and the poles brightened the area, the darkness created a sea of sparkles, as if the champagne was on fire.

"For those of you who have made this your holiday tradition, you know how much we have been through to keep the spirit of the resort alive. And for those who are here for the first time, know you are all my family and have helped to keep my spirit alive through the toughest of times. This year is the third anniversary of my parents' deaths. The founders of this resort. As well as their good friends, the Halliburton's deaths. It's also the twenty-fifth anniversary of the resort's opening."

A hushed lull took over the audience. A few jabbered, some sniffled, and soft music drifted from the speakers.

Seth raised his flute and continued. "And now, to a toast to all of you. A very merry Christmas. A happy holiday season, and a prayer this tree actually lights up."

Everyone sang "Oh Christmas Tree." He stepped down from the podium, grabbed the plug, and connected it to the main extension.

Nothing happened. He wiggled the plug. Still nothing. Remy's heart stopped beating, and she closed her eyes, blowing out a breath and a prayer. They had done everything right. Johnathan and Jennifer and several other staff members had worked furiously to finish and ensure it all worked.

When she opened her tear-filled eyes, she realized the outlet they were all connected to was switched off.

"Hey, Seth?"

"Yeah."

Her pulse dipped. She pointed. "Helps if you turn that on."

He chuckled. "Oh, man." His smile tumbled in her chest. The crowd tittered, probably wondering why it was taking so long. He unplugged the two main cords from each other so they wouldn't come on, then switched on the outlet. He grabbed both ends and stood, holding them up to the crowd. "Helps if I turn on the outlet first."

He connected the two. The lights blasted on. The tree glittered and sparkled. Raucous cheers followed.

Tears and laughter bubbled out of Remy.

Seth dropped the plugs and took her around the waist. "What are you crying for?"

She swiped at her cheek. "They're happy tears."

"You did a beautiful job."

She thumbed the tip of his nose. "We did a beautiful job."

The last time she'd seen the lighting of this tree, Seth's dad had executed the speech, and her parents mingled.

The singing continued. Remy's head slanted to meet Seth's gaze, and he glanced down at her and sang. Their bodies swayed in an age-old rhythm of dance.

Joy filled his heart while he danced with Remy. The live band played.

Remy's mouth opened in shock. "You got a live band?"

He nodded. The band had been hidden amongst the crowd, their instruments situated around Santa's house. Remy wouldn't have had time to see it, and Seth had wanted to surprise her. "I did. It's Johnathan's son and his band. He's a musician, and we thought it would be fun."

"You are full of wonders. You said dancing, but I never considered a live band."

"They offered to play every night, including Christmas Eve."

"They're amazing."

He looped his arm through hers and guided her away from the crowd. "I have something else to show you."

"I can't possibly imagine anything else."

He ducked behind the large trees that, if they walked long and far enough, would lead to the creek's trail.

"It's dark over here." Remy shivered. "Where are you taking me?"

"Through the forest."

As they walked away from the resort and through the canopy of forest, the trees shielded the village's glow. Once they got past the first few trees, Seth flicked a switch. White lights bloomed, a glossy sheen surrounding the woods.

"Oh." Remy stopped and looked around at all the trees bathed in a brilliant glow of white. The trail through the trees was completely illuminated until it ended in the darkness beyond. "Oh, my, gosh. I... I... it's beautiful." Her voice cracked, and she swiped tears from her cheek.

Seth had worked on it all day, with Johnathan and a few others who swore to secrecy until he was ready. "I didn't mean to make you cry."

Her lashes fluttered. "They're happy tears. Maybe a few of nostalgia, too."

He sat on the bench in between trees. "For now, it's a secret. You can't see it from the main resort, at least, I don't think so. But you definitely can from the balconies. I can't keep it secret for long, but I wanted to show you first."

She sat beside him, her face gleaming. "Thank you."

He nodded and tamped down his pride. He hadn't enjoyed Christmas like this in a long time, and Remy had a lot to do with that. Every wretched moment of stringing lights around these trees was finetuned to joy when he thought about her reaction and surprise.

"It feels like Christmas already."

Her voice was breathy like a wiry strand of wind entwining his heart.

"It *is* Christmas." Seth said.

Her lips parted, eyebrows rising as she studied the lights. His heart froze, then pounded in his chest

He continued. "I mean, Christmas is an accumulation of things. The joy and laugher, the simple moments shared with family. The love and glittering lights. The songs and parties and food and fun. All accumulating leading to that special day we celebrate with a meal."

She rubbed her stomach. "I've celebrated with a lot of meals lately."

"You're welcome to use the gym anytime you need to. It's open twenty-four seven."

She nudged his arm with her elbow. "Are you saying I need to exercise?"

He shook his head and held up his hands. "No, no, no. Not at all. Besides, all the running around you're doing, you probably need more food. I'm just reminding you it's there."

"What about the observatory?"

The observatory was Seth's favorite. Situated behind the bright lights of the buildings in the northeast corner of the property, it offered an unobstructed view of the stars. Visiting the observatory was also his and her families' Christmas Eve tradition.

"It's still there," he said. "I'm surprised you haven't gone to see it."

"I'm surprised you haven't taken me." She chuckled, then hooked her left arm through his right and placed her head on his shoulder. "I can't possibly imagine anything better than this. Even with all the lights, you can still see the stars."

"You can't possibly imagine any better Christmas present?" he asked. Maybe with this conversation, he could get a hint of what she always wanted for Christmas.

"Not at all," she said.

"Have you ever wanted something for Christmas you never got?"

She lifted her head. "Actually, yes."

"Oh yeah? What?"

She untangled her arm and set both hands in her lap. "It's probably silly, but you know how we always had gifts under the lobby tree from friends or family staying at the resort?"

He nodded.

"One year, when I was seventeen years old, I received this music box. The most beautiful, perfect box I'd ever seen. Handcrafted, I'm pretty sure. I loved it, but I never knew who it was from. No name tag, nothing to indicate the giver. I had to check and double check to make sure it was meant for me, but it had my first and last name. And I had every intention of finding out who it was from. But, well..."

Seth held his breath, waiting for the rest of the story. He knew that music box. He knew it very well. He'd created it and given it to her in secret, and it had broken his heart.

"It got left here. Somehow, some way, it didn't get packed with our belongings. My parents called to check whether it got left here, and your parents said they searched everywhere. But it vanished. I cried like a little baby. My mom said maybe someone who needed it more than I did was able to take it home and enjoy it."

His chest hurt, and he grunted out *huh*. After she'd left, he thought she had discarded it, along with his heart. He had kept it hidden in his room, and now hidden in the back of his closet. Although he'd continued handcrafting things with his father, he'd never put as much effort into anything as he'd put into that gift. Every year thereafter, he had pushed her away, including their friendship.

Some people would have told them him he was too young to know love. His parents had warned him about plenty, but never about being too young.

"You can say I even collect music boxes now. But I've never found anything like it again."

"Wow," he said. He thought she had intentionally left it. "Any idea who gave it to you?"

"Well, there was this guy."

His heart froze.

She tilted her head at him. "Do you remember Andrew? We kind of had a thing that year." She slapped a hand over her chest. "He was so dreamy."

"A thing?" he asked, voice screechy. Jealousy rose. He swallowed the lump in his throat and any other words that might follow. She thought some other guy had given her that box? What would she say if he blurted the truth?

He had spent hours engraving *Love, Seth* on the bottom of the music box. How could she not have seen his handiwork? And how could he have doubted her all these years?

"Nothing serious. Just a flirtation. Never even a kiss. He actually found me later and took me on a date, but it was pretty bland. Come to think of it, I never asked him about the music box. Maybe he decided to take it back." She shuddered. "Probably a good thing."

His throat knotted. He glanced down and swallowed a clump of regret. Would things be different if he knew she hadn't purposely left it behind? If he had told her he was the one who had given it to her? He'd created the special gift to show her how much he cared, and he thought she had trampled over his heart.

Maybe he should have asked her. Maybe he should have never pushed her away.

His body grew cold. Jaw tightened. How could she be so daft? She had never even considered him as anything more than friends. Never considered giving them a try. Because of their relationship, she never even thought he might have been the one. Why bother telling her now?

"What about you?" She squirmed in her seat and faced him.

He coughed in his hand. "Me?"

"Any gift you've always wanted but never received?"

"Well, there was this special Lego kit I never got," he teased.

She nudged her shoulder to his. "Come on. There's got to be more."

"Oh, there was." He flicked a piece of hair out of her eye and time halted. Large flakes of snow spilled from the sky.

Remy stood and grabbed his hand. A sheer sign of her not wanting anything to do with him. His muscles tensed. Irritation bloomed.

"Should we go before it starts snowing too hard? I promised Addie I'd ice skate with her."

He nodded, his heart heavy as they ambled back to the resort.

Remy was that special gift he'd never received. Maybe one day, he'd tell her. But at this point? Probably not. He berated himself, and her, because at this point he was tired of trying.

How could she not give him a second thought? Like *hey maybe I should check and see if Seth was the one who gave me this artwork?*

The cords in his neck tightened.

They stepped out into the village.

Tessa lifted her hand to wave them over. A man stood beside her.

Remy halted.

With a smile, he swaggered forward.

"Who's that?" Seth asked, already dreading the answer. Even though he had never seen her boyfriend, he recognized the man.

Her cheeks puffed as she blew out a breath. "That's Carson."

CHAPTER 13

R emy made her way to Carson, steps faltering. Her heartbeat stuttered, and she hesitated. She was supposed to be happy to see him, supposed to want to run into his arms and profess her love instead of running the opposite direction.

Too many eyes on her had her stepping forward and into his arms. He aimed a kiss on her mouth, but she averted her head and offered her cheek. Her forced smile nearly cracked her face open, the cold shooting ice daggers into her skin.

"Carson. What a surprise." She found her voice at last, but it lacked warmth.

"I wanted to surprise you."

She withdrew from his arms and looked around for Seth. He hadn't followed her. She wanted to introduce him to Carson, but her feelings had fluctuated so suddenly she needed time to process.

Or had the hesitancy been so sudden? She'd left Carson alone, hoping he would chase her but all the while doubting he would. And now here he was, and she wasn't at all happy.

Remy pointed to her left, towards the rink. "I was about to take Addie ice skating. You're welcome to come."

He winced. "Oh, I'm no ice skater."

Of course not. His lack of adventurous spirit was one more thing that had pushed them apart. She propped a hand on her hip. "You don't have to be to have fun."

His brows furrowed. "I thought we could talk."

She shuffled farther away. "Plenty of time for that later."

She wasn't in the mood to talk, and definitely not to him right now. The words that shot out of her mouth might be too harsh to repair any broken relationship. Best to enjoy the rest of the evening and pretend they had a chance.

She was surprised he didn't argue and, in fact, found some skates that fit and followed her out on the rink. They wobbled together. Addie laughed and flew out on the ice, but Remy and Carson both needed something to hold on to. So they held onto each other.

"I don't want to fall into you and hurt you," Carson said, his voice as rickety as his legs.

Other skaters whisked around them, and Remy's confidence soared. Her spine straightened, her legs strengthened, and every memory of years past where she had flown around the ice like Addie bolstered her resolve to skate, have fun, and not fall. She curled her fingers into Carson's and urged him along. "You won't fall on me. Come on."

They skated in small circles, keeping close to the wall and away from the masters.

Addie approached and took Carson's other hand. "Is this your first time skating?" she asked.

Carson's chin tightened, his skin blotching. "Probably."

"Oh, well that's a bummer you've missed out on all this fun all this time."

"Yeah, a real bummer," Carson said, interjecting sarcasm

into his enthusiasm. He glanced at Remy before nodding at the rink. "Why don't you two go skate while I sit in the corner and cry?"

Remy patted his shoulder and teased. "Oh, come on. Don't cry."

Addie squealed and dropped his hand, then raced away, dancing in circles.

"How does she do that?" he muttered.

"Practice and self-confidence." Remy sandwiched his hand between both of hers. "Come on, let's get you to the corner so you can rest. Your legs will be screaming tomorrow."

"They're screaming at me now."

"Trust me, it only gets worse."

They skated to the corner together and relaxed against the wall. Truth was, Remy needed the break, too, before her entire body crumbled.

"This isn't exactly how I planned my first day here," Carson said.

"Oh? How long have you been here?"

"Not long. I haven't even gotten my luggage out of my car."

"You missed the lighting of the tree?" Had he seen her and Seth so cozy together when they disappeared?

He stroked the back of his neck. "I did."

"Won't your mom be disappointed you're missing Christmas with the family?" Although they didn't have the best of celebrations, and Carson would show up only for Christmas dinner, his mom went all out in the most traditional sense. All the carvings and toasts and putting on one's best behavior.

He hauled Remy into his face and snuggled her neck. "Well, either disappoint her, or disappoint you."

Remy palmed his chest and pushed away from him. "I'm gonna go skate with Addie now."

He squeezed her hand before letting her go. "Hey."

She turned back to look at him. "Yeah?"

His forehead wrinkled. "I haven't disappointed you, have I? You're glad I'm here?"

She licked her lips and swallowed her guilt. "I'm glad," she lied. At this point, she was too conflicted to feel anything, especially glee. "But we can't forget the reason I came here without you."

"You came without me because I was too busy."

"We had a small break in our relationship, and I needed some time to process things."

He leaned forward, but didn't release his grip from the railing. "So, I'm disappointing my mother for no reason?"

She fluttered her fingers at him. "That's not what I'm saying, Car. But I won't share my room with you and open my heart back up again as easily as you expect. Our relationship was already growing stale. Otherwise, I never would have come here without you."

His brows crunched together. "Stale? Is that why you were so chummy with that guy before you saw me?"

Her frustration mounted, her body temperature rising. "That guy is Seth, and he owns this resort. He's a great friend and I've known him since I've been in diapers."

His neck corded as he scowled. "And you were here alone with him for several days."

"That has nothing to do with us."

His nostrils flared, and he stuffed his hands in his pockets. "Oh, I think it does."

No matter what she felt for Seth, he had nothing to do with her issues with Carson. Her posture stiffened, and she took a step away. "Well, it doesn't. And if you're going to bring that into our relationship, we were a lot worse off than I thought."

He shrugged and glanced away, out to the skaters who

flowed like a heartbeat around them. His jaw remained clenched.

Remy's pulse pattered.

His attention came back to her, gaze steady, unflinching, and accusatory. "So, if I'm not invited to stay in your room, where am I supposed to sleep? The resort is sold out."

Her stomach knotted. She hadn't realized the rooms had sold out, but she should have known.

"We'll figure out something." She waved at him and skated away, needing to put some distance between them.

She should be excited he had come for her. Hadn't she wanted him to chase her? Express his love for her? Then why did her gaze dart around to find Seth? Why did she worry what Seth might be thinking? And why did she so very much want to find him and tell him things were over with Carson?

Seth watched the two embrace and sucked in a breath. Had he blown his chance with Remy, or had he never had a chance in the first place?

He sat at a table in the corner, away from the crowd but near enough if he was needed or if anyone wanted to interact.

Landon approached and gave him a playful jab on the shoulder, then set his mug on the table. He shook Seth's hand and nodded at the seat across from him. "Do you mind if I join you?"

"Of course not, man. Have a seat."

Landon sat and nodded at the rink. "You're out here alone, in the dark?"

"Just enjoying the crowd."

Landon reached over for his mug and took a sip of his drink. "Watching Remy and Carson."

Seth's nose crinkled. "What do you mean by that?"

"I haven't seen her this happy in a long time," Landon said. "Especially at Christmas. But not because we showed up. And definitely not because Carson showed up."

Seth cocked his head and studied Remy's brother.

"She needed her time away from the resort for the past two years to show her what she doesn't want in her life," Landon continued. "She might not realize that, but I see it. She'd be happy here."

"It's just the joys of Christmas." Seth thumped his fist over his chest. "The spirit of Christmas is in her heart."

"No. She hasn't felt that joy since..."

Seth's ears buzzed with the unsaid words. "Your parents died."

Landon set his cup on the table and leaned forward, giving Seth his full attention. "*Our* parents died. Yours are gone, too."

Seth nodded and blinked, trying not to fall apart in front of his friend. He still missed them, but he didn't want to share his grief. Remy had said she didn't blame him, and he'd had a similar conversation with Landon the first year. So why did Landon want to talk about it again?

"Look, I'm just saying you both seem happy."

Seth *was* happy. Happier than he had been in a long time. He missed his parents and would do anything to have them here, but they weren't and never would be again. He'd spent plenty of remorseful times thinking he would never be happy or have a happy relationship. Why would he, when it could end in trauma? But his parents wouldn't have had it any other way.

Remy was with the man she wanted to be with, and Seth wouldn't dare intrude. "Like I said, it's the joy of Christmas."

"I saw your employees talking to Remy earlier. Asking her for help on some things."

"Good. They trust her. They recognize she's part of the reason I decided to open again."

"And she's part of the reason you decided to close."

Seth blinked and shook his head. Why was his friend pushing for answers?

Landon rubbed his hand over his face. "Look, I'm not trying to pry. And I'm definitely not trying to be a burdensome big brother. But if you care about her as much as I think you do and she cares about you as much as I think she does, you need to tell her."

"I have nothing to tell her." He nodded in her direction, where she and Carson spoke intimately together. "She's with Carson. She hoped he would chase her, and he did. She asked my opinion about their relationship. I would never destroy that. And I would never ruin the friendship we've had."

"You wouldn't take a risk for the woman you love?"

Landon's words slammed into Seth's gut. He shot him a crooked grin and cocked his head, interjecting levity. Anything to downgrade his friend's words. "So, you came out here to lecture me on how I should handle things with your sister?"

He lifted one shoulder. "No. That wasn't my original intention."

"Well, buddy. You're right. I do care about her a lot. I also care about you and Tessa and your families a lot, too."

"Not the same and we know it."

He splayed out his hands, then dropped them to the table. "Okay. What if I do care about her a lot? What if I do want her to stay? We're from two different worlds. My life revolves around Christmas. Not many people can handle that."

His lips pinched together. "Remy can, and you know it."

"And then there's Carson."

Landon snickered, his breath like diamond dust in the

cold air. "Yeah. Carson." His voice projected sarcasm, sharp and sour.

"Well, he's here. He wants to make things work with her, and I'm pretty sure she wants to make things work with him."

"You're kidding me, right?" Landon's brow inched up, almost touching his beanie.

"No." Seth nodded their direction. "You've seen them together, right? Just because you don't like him doesn't mean she doesn't, and doesn't mean you should interfere."

"I've seen them together for the past three years. And Remy never looked happy. But you know what she looks like right now? Pained. Pained that she has to pretend to enjoy being in his presence."

Seth studied them, trying to see what Landon claimed to see. He noticed a hesitancy in her smile, a somberness to her face, but that could be so many things. Carson had hurt her, but he was here now. They were deep in conversation and could work out their differences. Seth would never want to hinder that.

He hadn't even met the guy yet, so he had no reason to cast judgment. Did the dude love her, or not? Would he treat her right and make her happy? That's all that mattered.

"If what you're saying is true, how far do you think she'll take that pretending if he asks her to marry him?"

Landon huffed out another breath and leaned back in his chair, kicking his feet out in front of him. "That's why you should say something."

Seth sneered. If only it were that easy. "Getting involved in someone else's relationship does nothing but cause resentment."

"She left him for a reason." Landon's low-pitched voice grew steady and determined.

"She left him because she wanted him to chase her. And now he is."

"And now she's realizing that's not what she wanted, after all."

"Wishful thinking on your part." Seth refused to become too hopeful. "I don't know why you don't like him. But I have no choice but to give him a chance."

"Sure, you do."

"No, I don't. Look, Lan, I might live in fantasy world with this resort and all, but I've come to reality years ago. I don't go chasing after women who want nothing to do with me. I've got too many other things to do with my life."

Landon leaned forward, his face bunched in a frown.

Seth loved him like a brother, but he didn't appreciate his intrusiveness. Gut tightened and jaw stiffened, he held back his annoyance.

"If you don't tell her you love her—"

"I shouldn't have to tell her anything. Love is a two-way street, and my words won't change a thing."

"So you're saying I should never have to tell my wife how much I love her?"

Seth slapped his palms down on the table. "That's different, man, and you know it."

Landon rubbed his chin. "How is it different?"

"Because it is. You're committed. You've made a life together."

"Because I told her how much I love her and how I can't live without her."

"This is different."

He spread out his arms and shrugged. "How, man? You keep saying that, but I don't understand."

Seth's neck kinked in mounting frustration. Sure, Landon was trying to *reason* with him, but Seth disagreed. Landon had no idea what it was like to live in his world, his life decisions based on the best for the business and the guests. If Remy had any desire to be more than friends, her signs pointed the complete opposite direction, and he wouldn't sacrifice a friendship they'd finally repaired. He opened his mouth to say more, but Addie ran toward their table.

CHAPTER 14

R emy had a blast skating with Addie until her legs screamed to stop.

Carson stood on the side, never budging from the safe place he'd found against the wall.

Remy slid her way to him. "You ready to get off the ice?"

His face softened. "Never been readier for anything in my life." He flinched, then curled his mouth as if he knew he'd said the wrong thing.

At this point, she'd agree with him.

They drifted across the ice and stopped on a bench to remove their skates and don their shoes.

Addie finished before them, so she ran toward Uncle Landon.

Remy's heart thumped when she saw him sitting with Seth. She ducked her chin. "Have you said hello to my brother yet?"

"Not yet. Hadn't seen him."

"Let's go say hi. I'll introduce you to Seth and ask if he has an extra room." She went to stand.

Carson tugged on her hands before she made it all the way up. "Remy."

His brown eyes were dark, muddied by affliction. She cocked her head and remained seated, waiting to hear what he had to say.

"If you don't want me here..."

She brushed her thumb along his cheek, urging herself to feel something potent. Had she ever? Or was he just an excuse not to get on with her life after her parents' death? "It's not that I don't want you here." She didn't want to go back to their life. To a job that stifled her instead of empowering her creativity. To the routine of their day when they barely had a relationship anymore. But this wouldn't be routine, and at one time she'd longed to show him the joy of the resort. Now was her chance. So why wasn't she excited?

Did he love her? Truly, truly love her? Would it make a difference if he did? She wanted the type of relationship where you could share every part of yourself, go on vacation together, play without feeling awkward. And the humdrum days of routine would still make her heart race at his smile. Did Carson know how to love like that, or were they simply not right for one another?

She couldn't explain that to him. Not yet. Not until she had it all sorted out first. And the next few days should answer the questions raging in her mind.

She stood and motioned her hand. "Come on. We'll go say hi."

His footsteps shuffled behind her. Guilt gnawed at her that she didn't walk with him, but she needed to put distance between them.

She approached the table where Landon, Seth, and now Addie sat. Her legs nearly buckled and she fell into the seat.

Landon raised a brow. "You okay?"

She rubbed her upper thighs. "My legs are on fire. Other than that, I'm fine." At least she could blame it on the ice skating, although Seth's presence caused the worst of her turmoil.

Carson shook Landon's hand, but Landon didn't move Addie off his lap so he could stand. He nodded at the chair beside him and Carson sat.

The ring of Addie's sweet laughter fizzled through the air, and everything grew silent. Stilted. Awkward. Even the music was lifeless at this distance.

Something seemed off. Seth's lips pressed together, and he gazed off into the distance. Landon eyeballed Seth, as if he knew something no one else did. Carson was an added weight to the knots in Remy's stomach.

"Did we interrupt something?" she asked.

"Nope." Seth was quick to respond. His eyes flashed, but his aloofness unnerved her. He wouldn't even look her direction. "Perfect timing, actually." He leaned forward and shook Carson's hand. "I'm Seth. Great to meet you. Glad you could make it."

Oops. How had she forgotten the introduction? Her skin burned, pine needles chafing under her jacket.

After the handshake, Carson eased back in his seat. "I haven't had a chance to see much of it, but the resort looks amazing."

"You should see the Christmas village," Addie blurted.

"We'll have to plan that tomorrow." His forehead puckered. "But I've got to figure out what I'm going to do tonight, or where I'm going to stay. Seth, I hear there are no more rooms available."

"Oh, no, we sold out the first day. But—"

"What about your parents' house?" Addie interjected.

Landon winced.

Remy examined her hands, the weight of her gloves growing heavy. Landon fiddled with his mug, his mouth pursing as if he didn't know how to answer. Carson studied them in curiosity, the slight shrill in his breath grating on Remy's nerves.

She refused to look at Seth.

Addie was young, but obviously not too young to remember the great moments they had in that house with Seth and his parents. But she wouldn't know how Seth felt about it now and how much he likely wanted to avoid the place.

After a lengthy silence, she jutted out her lower lip. "Well?"

"Addie." Landon's low voice was a warning that Addie ignored and wouldn't understand.

Her pupils dilated, and gaze darted between the adults. "What? We could all stay together. The house is big enough. So that frees up a room for Carson, and others."

"Wow. She makes a good point." Seth tousled Addie's hair. "You wanna come work for me?"

Addie giggled, her shoulders rising to her ears.

"I mean, the house is in shape. I have staff who keep it clean. The heat is on so pipes don't freeze and such. And like she said, we would have more rooms."

Addie clapped her hands. "Aunt Remy could stay with us too!"

Remy's mouth opened, but no words formed. She loved the resort, but the house would bring them together and offer a nice sanctuary. But only if Seth absolutely agreed. He'd told her he hadn't been in the house since his parents' deaths, and she was concerned about how much this would affect him.

"I like the idea," Seth said when Remy didn't speak.

Remy scratched her nose. "As long as it's no bother to Seth. Your parents would have to agree, Addie. They'd have to move all their stuff."

"We haven't unpacked yet." Addie bounced off her uncle's lap. "Where are my parents, anyway?"

Remy jumped up with her. She hesitated, her legs tight. In spite of the considerable number of lights, it was dim outside, and Remy didn't need Addie straying alone.

Landon stood. "Last I saw, they were sitting by the fire pit. Come on, let's go see if they're still there." He grasped Addie's hand, and everyone followed.

"I didn't mean to be a bother," Carson said. "I can find another place."

Seth darted a gaze at Remy, his cheeks dimpling in a smile, then he looked away. "It's no bother. Besides, Addie is way too excited to disappoint."

Remy hoped that wasn't the only reason he had agreed. She worried it would be too hard on Seth, even if he technically didn't have to go in the house.

Addie pointed. "There they are." She dropped Landon's hand and raced ahead. She ran up to her mother and prattled off her plan, her face animated in excitement.

Tessa stood and watched their approach, her face lined in a worry-frown. Her shoulders bunched. "Seth?"

He held up his hands. "What? No argument. If you want to, it's all yours. But if you prefer the resort, we can put Carson at the house."

"But—"

"No buts. I'm happy to let you all stay there. But like I said, only if you want to."

Tessa tugged on her scarf. "We'd love to. Not that we don't love the resort rooms. But it gets us all together and opens up space for you."

Seth smiled. "Yes, Addie made an argument I couldn't refuse."

Remy's breath hitched at the glow on his face. She ducked

her chin and glanced at Carson, who eyeballed her way too intently.

Did he know? Could he tell that Seth affected her in ways she hadn't yet figured out?

Tessa waved her hands at everyone. "Well, let's get busy moving our stuff so we can settle in and get those other rooms open for you."

They packed and loaded vehicles, and Remy rode with Seth, leaving her car in the main parking lot for now. Addie had begged to ride with them instead of with her parents, and her babble was a nice distraction to the silence that would otherwise accompany the Jeep.

At some point, she wanted to talk to Seth about Carson. Now wasn't the time.

They drove up to the house. Her ears prickled at Seth's breath pulling in and slowly releasing.

He parked. Addie shrieked her happiness and opened the door.

Remy laid a hand on Seth's shoulder. "Are you sure you're okay with this?"

His lips pressed together. He glanced at the house, his face stony. "I'm sure. I never said it'd be easy, but I'm sure."

"You could have said no."

He gave her a sideways glance, his gaze filled with mirth. "Say no to Addie? No way. Besides, I can't avoid the house forever." He opened the door. "Come on before they start to wonder about us."

Remy climbed out of the Jeep and grabbed her stuff.

Seth took everything from her but her purse and camera bag.

Her legs wobbled. She was ready to crash into bed. Not just because of the ice skating creating a burn in her legs, but because of the emotional confliction of the day.

As Seth unlocked the door to the house, Landon set his palm on his shoulder and the family surrounded him. Walking into his parents' home for the first time since their death would be difficult, but they wouldn't give him a chance to breathe, much less grieve. And wasn't that what families were best for?

She let out a silent prayer of gratitude. As tiresome as family could be sometimes, she wouldn't have wanted it any other way.

CHAPTER 15

Seth was happy to accommodate the Halliburton family, even if that meant untold grief when he walked into his parents' home for the first time since their funeral. He left the safekeeping of their home up to Johnathan and his trustworthy staff, and they had kept it clean. Nothing at all had changed, and walking in the door was like stepping through time.

Photos of his family, their memorabilia, his mother's teapot collection, all stood sentry over the home. The worn, but comfy, leather couches beckoned to be relished and sat upon. The scent greeting him was as if his mother's cinnamon bark candle burned the entire time.

The kids tore through the house. His muscles tightened. Addie rushed through the rooms and picked hers while the other kids hollered at the open space of the living and kitchen areas.

Addie stopped to stand at the window and spread out her arms. "A perfect place for the Christmas tree."

His stomach flipped. His mother had put many a tree in that exact location.

He escaped to the bathroom and splashed cold water on his face to wipe away the heartbreak of being here without his mother's warm hugs and his dad's booming laughter. But the Halliburtons filled the home with joy, their presence satiating every crevice and corner. Their warmth and enthusiasm padded the hole in his heart.

Accommodating them was better than Carson rooming with Remy, if that's what the guy planned.

He stepped out of his escape haven, his body still tight with torment but his mind at ease. Remy greeted him with a concerned smile. She squeezed his hand, then let go way too quickly.

"Is everything okay?"

He nodded, his voice too clogged to speak.

"Are you sure you're okay with this?"

"Yes," he croaked. "Just didn't realize how hard it would be coming in here, you know?"

"There's still time to change your mind if you want us to leave."

He clasped both her hands in his and brought them up to his lips. "No. No. This is a perfect solution. And I promise, I don't mind. It's good for me to be here." He kissed both her hands then dropped them and turned to her family. "Looks like they're flipping coins to find out who's getting the master bedroom. You better jump in there if you want dibs."

She shook her head. "That's okay. I'm the only single one, so I can take whatever room."

Seth imagined her in his room. None of his personal belongings were in there anymore, but having her so near and him unable to treat her as anything but friends was like ripping scars from his heart.

Maybe Landon was right and he should tell her his feelings, but he nixed that thought. He'd let her spend her time with Carson. Seth had plenty to do.

Before it got even harder to watch her leave.

Remy slept well in her new room. Seth's old room. His mom had converted it into an office/craft space but kept a small twin bed and a comfy design for guests. Shelves of fabric, books, and accessories lined one portion of the wall next to an elaborate sewing table with all the essentials and the machine itself. Remy loved to sew, and it would be awesome to tackle projects if she had the time.

Carson texted her early the next morning to ask her to join him for breakfast. She didn't respond right away, resentful of him being here and changing her plans. What if she wanted to have breakfast with her family? They hadn't been together for Christmas in the past two years.

You wanted him to chase you. Now he's here. Ashamed for her actions, she texted him to let him know she'd love breakfast and would be there soon.

They needed this alone time together, but maybe tomorrow she'd invite him to eat with her and her family.

She bundled in warm clothing and left a note by the coffee pot. The house was still asleep, doors closed to each room, and she tiptoed out the door.

She decided to walk to the resort and found snowshoes in the mudroom that fit her.

The Lockhart's house was tucked into the mountainside about a quarter mile from the road, hidden by trees and reached by a small dirt road.

She stopped to take in the sunrise, specks of diamond and gold along the freshly fallen snow. The air was cleaner here, lighter, gentler on her lungs. The dryness required more lotion, but she didn't mind. She could wake up like this forever.

How did she feel about Carson being here? At first, she'd wanted it. She'd wanted him to chase her, follow her, and support her dreams. Beg her to never leave him again. Now, she wondered if he'd been her crutch. Something she'd intentionally put in her way to make it easier to handle poor decisions and stay stuck.

She blew out a breath, the cold air giving it a substance, like ghost particles of her past.

She cared about him. He was a good person, and spending time with him might help her remember that and realize what she truly wanted. Spending time with him might make her stop thinking about Seth and all the what-ifs of her life.

When she walked through the back door of the lobby, Carson was waiting, his face tight.

"I was beginning to wonder if you were coming."

Annoyed by his chiding, she took a moment to respond. "Sorry. I got sidetracked by the beauty of the day."

"Did you walk?"

"I did."

His brows dipped together. "I could have come to get you. Or met you halfway or something."

"It's only a quarter mile. And I wanted to walk." In hindsight, it was rude of her to make him wait, but she never said when she'd arrive, and it hadn't taken thirty minutes.

He nodded, his lips pressed together and eyes veiled by the internal mask he often wore.

"You ready for breakfast?"

Determined to make the best of this day, she planted a kiss on his cheek, the curled her arm through his. "I am."

The buffet line was empty, and only four people sat scattered throughout the room. She piled her plate with pancakes, eggs, bacon and fresh fruit, while he only took oatmeal with dry toast and coffee. Carson found a table and sat before she did, and she swallowed her animosity as she slid into the seat. Plenty of available booths—which she preferred—but he chose a table in the center of the room.

"This looks amazing." She eyed his boring bowl. He could have at least piled fruit on top or something, but then again she wasn't a fan of oatmeal. "Is that all you're going to eat?"

Carson's phone buzzed on the table.

He grabbed it and studied the screen, not bothering to answer her. "Sorry. It's the office, and it's an hour later there so they're already at work."

Remy swallowed her pancake and chased it down with orange juice while he typed out a response. "But you aren't."

He glanced at her with squished eyebrows and back at his phone to finish his message.

"At work that is," she added.

As soon as he sat the phone on the table, it buzzed again. He didn't even look chagrined when he picked it up and read the message. She waved her hand in front of him, but he either didn't see, or he ignored her.

His fingers flew across the keyboard, the tap-tap-tapping annoying her. No one else in the room seemed to notice. Everyone enjoyed their breakfast, but a knot of tension skated up her neck. When the phone buzzed again, she threw down her fork.

"Carson. You either have breakfast with me and put your phone away, or—"

"I am, I am." He slid his phone into his pocket and continued eating, scowling with eyes downcast as if his mind was still on the job.

His mind had always been on the job. That was one of the biggest issues of their relationship. Even now, during the holiday season and the slowest time of year in their work, he wouldn't take a break and enjoy her company.

She gritted her teeth, then picked up a piece of watermelon and plopped it into her mouth. The juice exploded on her tongue, and she focused on that rather than on her budding anger. Carson chewed his oatmeal but didn't look at her, and didn't even try to make conversation.

She didn't want to ask what was on his mind, because she didn't want to think about work during her vacation. So they continued to eat in silence.

Her heart skipped a beat when Seth approached. He patted Remy's arm and offered Carson a handshake. They shook hands then Seth dropped his and stationed a palm on Remy's seat. "How was breakfast?"

"Good as always," Remy replied. He stood near enough that the scent of musk he wore drifted toward her.

Carson glared and nodded. No doubt he didn't like Seth standing so close, but Seth was a friend, and she didn't feel awkward. Even if she was lusting over his cologne and enjoying his presence a bit too much.

"Glad to hear." Seth tapped the back of Remy's chair and stepped away. "Look, we're taking a trip out to the tree farm today. Loading a trailer and people who are interested. I know Addie is dying to get her tree."

"Yes. Definitely," Remy said. She couldn't stop thinking about the last time they had gone to the tree farm alone.

He nodded his chin toward the door. "We're meeting in the lobby at ten to get going. Probably be there a couple of hours but back by lunch, if that helps plan your day."

Carson opened his mouth as if he was going to argue all the reasons why they wouldn't be going, but Remy spoke up before he had a chance.

"We'll see you then." She faced Carson. "Carson, you've got to see this tree farm." Then to Seth, "He doesn't need a new tree, only new decorations since I've covered it with a pink princess theme."

Seth's chuckle landed in her belly. "Well, you know where

to find the decorations. I'll see you both later." He waved and walked away.

Carson's scowl etched deep into his forehead. "The princess theme isn't that bad."

She cocked her head and smiled. Not that she would intentionally make him jealous, but maybe she could rile him and finally get him to notice her. "No?"

"No."

"Then why are you scowling?"

"Maybe I wouldn't be scowling if that man didn't interact like you had some kind of intimate relationship."

She snorted. Maybe she wondered what it would be like to have a relationship with Seth, but the comfort she felt around him was natural, developing even stronger over the last few days. "Oh, come on, Carson. You were scowling when I first walked through the door. You were scowling when you looked at your phone."

He gave a one-shoulder shrug. "There's a lot going on at work."

"You can darn sure leave here and go back to work then," she said, then grimaced. Maybe she shouldn't have been so harsh.

He leaned forward and curled his hands in hers. "I don't want to do that."

"You don't want to go to the tree farm either."

His head bobbed once. "I do. I just hoped we could spend some time together alone. And I admit I didn't want to go with Seth."

"The farm is huge. We can talk a walk through the woods and we'll practically be alone. You'll love it."

He didn't seem to love it. All he did was study his phone, texting and cursing the entire time. She pointed out trees and smacked him with snow, but he barely paid attention and didn't appear to be enjoying himself.

"What's wrong?" she finally asked.

"I can't get service here. Only at the front where the building is."

"Thought you wanted to spend time together. What happened to our walk?"

He ducked his head. "Sorry. There's just some really important stuff I need to work on."

Yeah, like our relationship.

Remy nodded toward the building. "There's usually service at the office. Go. I'll meet you there later." She couldn't stand being in his presence a moment longer and he clearly wasn't going to let himself have fun.

He kissed her on the cheek. Nothing intimate, nothing that made her belly flop, just a lukewarm touch on her cold skin. "Thanks, babe. Work stuff is a mess. I'll see you in a bit."

He left, and a geyser of relief shot out of her. She turned to find Seth busy with customers.

She hadn't had a chance to talk to him, explain her confusion and frustrations, but found herself wanting to very badly. She missed their talks, being by his side like she belonged there. She missed him and his laugh and his joy.

She missed the kind of person she was when she was with him.

"Hey, Mac. Looks busy today," Seth greeted MacGregor when he stopped with a trailer load of people. Out of the corner of his eye, he watched Carson and Remy stroll toward a maze and remembered the last time he'd been here, alone with Remy. His heart lurched.

"We've been steadily busy since we opened back up."

Seth nodded and watched as people trekked the trails,

carrying saws. Most visitors wanted their own tree in their room, and the farm gave them the experience of cutting it down themselves. They didn't overprice the trees, but it wasn't an inclusion of the resort price.

MacGregor and his wife had cultivated this farm for over twenty years. Seth's dad had hired him on three years after opening the resort. His two sons now helped, eager to please.

Seth surveyed the crowd. Carson and Remy had stopped near a pine along the edge of the maze of trees. Carson clutched his phone in his hand, kept looking at it, while Remy tugged at his arm as if urging him to pay attention to the view. The branches were frosted with snow. A flicker of light sparkled under the sun and caught the strands of hair flowing from her cap. Seth imagined the perfect photo, but it didn't include Carson, sulking.

He wanted to shake some sense into the man. A beautiful woman stood before him, and he didn't seem to notice or care. Why didn't he take her in his arms and kiss her? Why didn't he run his fingers through her hair tendrils sparkling under the sun? Why didn't he scoop a handful of snow and toss it in her direction?

A pang shot through him. All the things Seth would have loved to do, and this man took it all for granted.

A couple approached, dragging a large fir, three young children frolicking behind. MacGregor's sons wrapped the tree for them then invited them into the cabin for coffee. Since they weren't staying at the resort and had their own vehicle, they didn't wait around long. Their children bounced beside them, eager to get home and decorate.

Mac bobbed his chin toward the departing vehicle. "One of many reasons I love this place. Everyone is so happy when they come here. They're even happier when they leave. Well, except that guy. He doesn't look too happy to be here." MacGregor pointed at Carson.

Seth wheezed out a laugh. "No, he sure doesn't."

Carson looked downright miserable. He'd glowered at his phone almost the entire time.

Seth had kept his distance from Remy, but the hole in his heart grew. He longed to sidle up to her and her family and laugh, but she was with another man and was off limits.

Seth turned his attention away to help customers with their trees. Soon, Carson approached the building.

He waved his phone. "Any good cell service here?" he asked MacGregor.

What a jerk. He was at a tree farm—a romantic one at that—with the most beautiful woman in the world, and all he cared about was his phone.

Seth ignored the rest of the conversation. He'd like to ignore Carson's existence and march right over to Remy and plant a kiss on her lips. He even considered going to her— maybe not to kiss her—but got busy helping.

Once everyone had chosen their trees, he said goodbye and thanks to MacGregor and his sons and left for the resort. He lost sight of Remy as he helped carry trees into rooms. Then he went home and crashed on the couch.

He loved what he did, but it drained him sometimes.

He skimmed his home in censure, his shoulders lowering. He should have chosen a tree. He hadn't decorated at all. He would have invited Remy over to help, or he could have surprised her with a tree, but that wouldn't happen now. He stood and shuffled to his closet, removed a package, and held his breath as he opened the music box.

It was still in pristine condition, playing "Swan Lake," the music he'd chosen. The couple twirled in their dance, lost in time and in each other. A mirror angled behind them, empha- sizing their features. Features he'd created with detailed precision out of hard work and passion.

He closed the lid and whooshed out a breath. Should he wrap it and give it to her?

He had created others, and this wasn't the first, or the last. He had almost stopped when Remy left hers behind, but his parents urged him to continue. They had to have known when Remy's parents called asking about the music box, but they had kept his secret. Why had they never mentioned she'd lost it? He'd never shared his devastation with them.

His body cramped, a heavy awareness of anguish nearly overtaking him. He buried the box deeper in the closet, burying his memories along with it. Then he decided to go back to the farm and get a tree.

Not for Remy, but for himself. He hadn't put up a personal tree since his parents died, and it was about time he did.

He unhooked the trailer. One tree would fit fine in the back of the Jeep. The farm was still busy, but not as much when he drove up and slid out of his truck.

"Back again?" MacGregor asked.

"Decided I needed a tree for my house. So many in the resort, but not one at home."

"Good call. My wife has one in each room. Well, almost each room."

Seth laughed. That's pretty much how the resort was. He grabbed a saw and waved goodbye.

He chose a Douglas Fir, about six feet, nothing too big but something beautiful and simple. Remy would love it. Not that it was for her.

He sawed back and forth, back and forth, trying to saw away her image from his mind. His heart pounded, his mind rambled, and he backed up and grabbed the tree as it fell to the earth.

He didn't bother having it wrapped. Since he was only a few miles from the resort and he'd be going through the private drive to the mountains, he didn't see the need. He said goodbye again and drove away, full of hope and anxiety.

The mountains rose and dipped around him, the trees full and feathery with snow. He stopped to take it all in. When he got into his house and carried the tree inside, he received a text from Remy.

I've missed you. Had hoped to have a chance to visit today at the tree farm. Maybe I'll see you at dinner tonight?

He should be thrilled, but his heart hurt too much to reply.

CHAPTER 16

Remy had breakfast with Carson the next morning. She'd invited him over to eat with her family, but he preferred the buffet and claimed he wanted to spend more alone time with her.

The third time he dug his phone out of his pocket and dipped his head to type a message, she let out a loud sigh. Now was the time to tell him her plans for the day didn't include him. "Carson, I'm going shopping with my sisters and niece today. A girl's day out."

Frown lines cut into his forehead. He set his cell on the table. "What am I supposed to do all day?"

"Hmm, I don't know. Explore the resort. Go ice-fishing with my brother. I know he's asked you." *Or just do what you've been doing on your phone all day.*

He shoveled a bite of oatmeal and swallowed. "I've never been much of a fisherman."

He'd never been much of anything that involved being away from work for long periods of time. "Enjoy the outdoors. Just enjoy nature. You'll have fun."

"Doubtful," he muttered, his gaze returning to his vibrating phone.

She waved out her arms in a shrug. "Okay, well now you have a perfect opportunity to work undisturbed."

Remy didn't feel guilty about leaving him. After breakfast, she met up with her family and soon, they were on their way to town. Once parked, Remy strolled along the sidewalk near her sister-in-law, while Tessa and Addie dawdled behind, Addie pointing and admiring all the decorated storefronts.

Melissa hooked her arm through Remy's. "I love this town. The resort is my favorite place in the entire world. I don't know how anyone ever leaves."

Remy let out a light, carefree laugh. She remembered the terrible feeling of thinking she would have to spend another Christmas away from the resort. "I love it too."

Addie squealed at something and stopped behind them to chat with a miniature elf. They stopped near a storefront to wait. Remy admired a bright red ski suit in the window.

Melissa dropped her hold on Remy and adjusted her beanie. "Are you glad you came back?"

"Absolutely. And I'm glad Seth decided to open. But I also realize staying away the last two years made me appreciate this time even more."

"So, tell me about you and Seth."

Melissa's voice was soft, coy, and caught Remy off-guard. They started walking again, Addie running ahead of them this time. Remy took a while to answer, mainly because she didn't know what to say. *We're just friends* sounded like an easy way out.

Remy's gaze darted around the bustling streets. Shoppers, mostly unhurried except for a haggard mom trying to carry a car seat and two packages, and catch up to her other small child. Until a man came up beside her and took the baby. She glanced at him and smiled, and the other child came back beside them as if they were one happy family.

Christmas blessings.

She brushed a strand of hair away from her eyes and tucked it under her snow cap.

"Well?" Melissa drawled.

Remy shrugged. "What? There isn't anything to tell. We've known each other since, gosh, we were probably Grayson's age."

She wriggled her eyebrows. "You two are very cozy together."

"We've been friends forever. I mean...we kind of grew apart, but we're okay now."

"He's enamored with you."

Remy smiled and bumped her shoulder. "Stop that right now. I'm obviously with Carson."

"Are you, though?" Her nose crinkled, eyes gleaming.

Remy's cheeks burned. She bit her tongue and refused to answer. She wasn't irritated, and she appreciated that her sister-in-law was never one to mince words. She pointed at a store that looked interesting. She'd been meaning to go in it for a while, and now was a perfect excuse to end a discussion she didn't want to have.

"Let's go inside here for a minute," she said, then hollered at her sister, who was sitting on a bench with Addie a few feet away. "I'm gonna check out this store."

"Okay, meet you there in a minute." Tessa fiddled with Addie's shoes.

Remy entered the shop. It appeared small on the outside, but the large interior boasted immaculate handmade items. Shelves displayed wooden, metal, fabric, even bronze and wire type crafts. A tabletop windmill constructed of bronze, a lampshade with frilly fabric, and leather pillows, to name a few.

Melissa's breath hitched beside her. "I didn't mean to overstep my boundaries."

She halted at a curio cabinet full of trinkets. "What?" She swept her thumb across Melissa's forehead. She didn't want to hurt her sister-in-law's feelings, but sometimes she had to be abrupt. "You didn't. Not at all. But Seth and I are friends. We both adore each other. But not in a way that's worth risking a good friendship. Can we shop now, please?"

"I spotted the ladies' room in the corner," Melissa said. "That's where I'm heading."

"Okay. I'll be around here somewhere."

She didn't want Melissa to feel guilty about saying anything, but she didn't want to continue the chatter. She was exhausted trying to think about it all and needed a break. If she had anything to figure out about her life and Seth, she needed to do it on her own without any outside opinion.

She glanced through the shop and when she spotted the music box, her breath stalled in her throat. She tiptoed forward, extending her fingers. The beauty reminded her of a magical mystical being.

She recognized the creation. Not the same one she had lost, but the similarities fascinated her. The wood seemed to hold its own power, having a life, a soul. The detailed carvings, the couple twirling in a dance. Out of all the music boxes she'd seen, all the ones she'd imagined, none had affected her this way. Except for the one she had lost so long ago.

Addie approached, her footsteps matching the soft hammering in Remy's heart.

"It's beautiful," Addie whispered.

"It sure is," Remy said. Should she buy this for Addie for Christmas? Could Remy handle the heartbreak of handing it over and not keeping it for herself? Addie had always enjoyed hers when she visited, but she'd never considered giving her one until now.

She planted her hand on Addie's shoulder and forced herself to turn away from the creation, to escape its magnetic allure. "I'm getting hungry again. You wanna stop for more cocoa?"

Addie laughed. "You and your cocoa."

She found Tessa and Melissa on the sidewalk outside and they all walked together. Remy grabbed Tessa and whispered, "I've got something I need to do. I'll meet you at the skating rink benches later."

"Okay." She tapped at her Fitbit, which also served as her watch. "Whatcha think? About an hour?"

"Perfect."

"Come on, Addie," Tessa said. "I've got some things to show you."

Remy waited until they'd disappeared, then spun around and revisited the gift shop.

She halted at the box. She wanted to give this to her niece, but how could she let it go? Although it wasn't the same, it had been so long ago how could she possibly remember? She grabbed it and approached the counter. "Do you have any more of these?"

The clerk rang up the purchase. "Oh, no. These sell out pretty fast. But you can custom order one. Too late in the year now to get it for Christmas, I imagine."

She dug in her purse for her wallet. "Oh, does the creator live around here?"

"Yeah. You might know him. Seth Lockhart. Owns the Christmas Hills Resort."

She sucked in a quick breath. Her heart thudded to her feet and chills swamped her body. Her mind raced, swimming and dancing in a sea of confusion. Somehow...had she known? Wondered, even hoped? But he had acted so tame about the whole thing when she had told him, she presumed it hadn't been him.

"Would you like me to gift wrap this for you?" the clerk asked, drawing her out of her funk.

She handed over the money, her hands shaky. "Oh, yes. Yes please."

"Give me a few minutes."

"Okay. I'm going to step outside and be right back."

"Sounds great. Do you have any particular preference for gift wrap?"

"No. It's for a young girl. So, anything you think would be a good fit."

"Will do."

Remy practically tripped out of the store. She had to get out of here, had to get her bearings and get her breath. She needed the cold slap of wind to get her back on track. She felt as if she were a train engine, losing course, losing focus, and barreling headfirst deep into the valley. Crash and combust.

She leaned against the building and placed a gloved hand over her face. The fact he had given her a music box when she was seventeen and had never admitted it came from him meant nothing. He had to have known she wouldn't intentionally discard their friendship.

Or had he wanted more, even then?

Stop overthinking things. Seth had never wanted a relationship with her and she had never wanted one with him, no matter how happy he made her.

Why hadn't he told her he was the one who had given her the most perfect gift she had ever received?

She couldn't tell him she knew about the box. He might find out with Addie's gift, but if he didn't admit it to her, she wouldn't admit it to him.

Remy didn't know why she agreed to have dinner alone with Carson. The evening was much the same as the tree farm visit, with his head mostly in his phone. She was upset she'd missed dinner with her family and barely felt like she was celebrating Christmas anymore.

Seth hadn't returned her text, and her stomach twisted at all the reasons he might ignore her. Had she upset him in some way?

She kept thinking of the music box. The one she'd bought for Addie was now under the tree. She knew of Seth's extraordinary talent with his photographs, but hadn't seen any signs of any other woodworking or anything with music boxes. Did he have some workshop somewhere she didn't know about?

After dinner, they met up with her family to walk through the village and enjoy the sights and sounds.

Carson balked, but followed beside her, his nose practically in his phone.

By the time they called it a night, she was fuming.

When he texted the next morning about breakfast, she refused.

Can you stop and see me afterward? He asked. *I have something I need to tell you and would rather not have to do it via phone.*

Okay.

He finally wanted to have a conversation with her? She couldn't imagine.

Remy put too much energy into setting the table, dishes slamming around when they shouldn't be.

"Everything okay?" Tessa flipped bacon at the stove.

She relaxed her shoulders and forced the tension from her muscles. "Yes. Just Carson."

"Did you invite him to breakfast? He's welcome to come."

"I didn't. He'll only sour the mood and continue looking at his phone."

Breakfast with her family calmed her. Although they didn't talk about it—and she didn't want to—she was able to process her thoughts.

Maybe she was being unfair to Carson. His job was important to him, and she had no reason to be upset. He didn't love this place, and how could she expect him to just because she did?

Was her anger masking the emotions she didn't want to admit?

She didn't love him. Not in the forever way. Not in the *I want to be more than friends* sense. She respected him, but she couldn't imagine spending the rest of her life with him.

Now what should she do? Tell him at Christmastime, or wait?

After the kitchen was clean, she escaped into her room to get ready to head to the resort. Her stomach churned, skin clammy. She was a terrible person for leading Carson on, hoping he would come here and now wishing so desperately that he hadn't.

She could really use Seth's opinion right now.

She bundled up and trekked the quarter mile to the resort, stopping to enjoy the whistling birds and freshly fallen snow. Her footsteps cut tracks into the powder. She paused and peered into the small crater a moment, as if it would give her all the answers. But then the snow filled the gap, like patching the cracks in her heart. Reminding her that everything was fleeting.

Could she start over? Could she leave Carson at the happiest time of the year? Could she finally do something for herself for a change?

Her body trembled when she went into the resort. The back lobby held a closet for guests to hang outerwear, so she took her time removing her coat, hat, and gloves. She didn't want to reach out to Seth—he hadn't even returned her text —but if she saw him in the lobby, she could approach.

She slowly treaded her way up the stairs to Carson's room. The same room she had occupied not so long ago. Being here had given her hope again, but now her heart was heavy.

She hesitated at the door. What was her best decision? She pulled in a deep breath and knocked.

When he answered, she spotted luggage all over the bed, clothes tucked neatly inside except for a few items he was still folding.

He lugged her into the room and shut the door. "Look, Remy. I need to get back. There's an emergency at the office."

She dropped onto a chair. Shocked. Surprised. This was not what she expected.

"Mr. Donahue is scheduled to come in tomorrow. We anticipated January. We've worked hard to get our presentation where it needs to be, and it's mostly ready, but I can't miss it. I'm a huge part of it."

Her mind reeled, tongue caking in her mouth. She didn't know how to respond, didn't know if she should respond. Neither did she know what to think. She'd never seen him this nervous, even when he was worried about his newest work creation.

She rubbed the back of her neck. "So, you have to give up your life for a presentation?"

He folded one of his shirts and stuffed it on top of the already flowing suitcase, then fidgeted through his clothing as if checking to make sure he had everything. "It's a huge deal." His eyes darkened, the breath whooshing out of him almost palpable as his shoulders slumped. He dropped to one knee beside her and swiped a hand over his face. "Look, Remy. I..."

She flinched. Why was he dropping to his knee? This was not at all how this was supposed to go. "Yeah, Carson?" she finally managed. Her skin flamed hot, and she could barely breathe. She remained paralyzed to the chair, hoping he wasn't about to propose.

"You said we were different. Wanted different things. At first, I thought you were wrong. I thought you were just in the spirit of the season. But I see you more alive here than I have in a long time. I know how much you love this place, and I see how much you enjoy the creativity you've longed to work with."

"Yes. It's been great for me." Where was he going with this?

"You don't enjoy presentations like I do. You don't come alive like I do. And you're right about us being different."

She held her breath, waiting for him to say *but*. *But I love you,* or something like that. *We can work it out*. "But..." she finally prompted. She would give him his chance to speak, but she had a few words to say herself. And if he proposed, she would have to break his heart.

He cupped her hands and pulled them to his chest. "You deserve to be happy. If you decide to come back to work, we'd all love to have you. But if you decide to leave, I would understand."

"Carson, our differences are a lot more than just you loving your job and me not loving mine."

He dropped her hands and stood. Paced. "I know. I know. And maybe I have known that, but it took me coming here to realize it. I enjoyed it, I really did, and you're right, it is like a piece of heaven. But there's no point in staying anymore. I think we both know that."

Remy stood and came to him. She faced him and placed her hands on his shoulders, making him stop his frantic movements across the floor. "Carson, I will always care about you, too, but you deserve someone who loves you unconditionally, and I deserve someone who loves me the same."

"And we're not right for each other." His voice was resigned.

Her muscles kinked, eyelids gummy. She released her hold and stepped away. "I'm sorry you came all this way to see me and had to stress about being away from work."

He returned to his luggage, seeming more at ease now as he folded the last of his shirts. "It's fine. I'm glad I did." He dropped a tie and shot her a lopsided grin. "Who knows what would have happened if I hadn't. I mean, what if we had gotten married and ended up hating each other?"

He crinkled his nose, making her laugh, and she swallowed the clog in her throat.

He swiped a hand through his hair, then smoothed it over his head. "Besides, honestly, this has been great for me. I had some time to think over my presentation. Getting out of my comfort zone was a huge help."

"I'm glad to hear that," she said, truly meaning it. She chuckled to herself. Seth would have swiped his hand through his hair and left it disheveled, but Carson wanted to always make sure his looks were spot on. And it wasn't a bad thing. He was just him and who he was.

She wasn't sad about the breakup, but she was sad it had taken her a trip here to realize she didn't love him. This season of her life was now over, and a blank canvas awaited her, but the two years she'd spent with him were not a waste. She would always treasure having known Carson. Everything she'd learned in her job, everything she'd learned while being with him, would carry her forward.

She didn't tell him she probably wouldn't be coming back to work or if she did, she probably wouldn't be staying. Her work did not fulfill her. She needed to make a decision soon so she could call them and use the rest of her vacation as her notice time.

She had big plans. She could see herself moving to Laurel Springs. But would Seth be okay with that?

Carson closed his last suitcase. "I've got to get going and get to the airport."

"Do you need any help with anything?"

He lifted one suitcase off the bed and set it on the floor. "No. No. I'm all packed and ready." His chin wobbled and he held open his arms.

She walked into them. No matter how much she wasn't in love with him, she would always care about him and was glad they could part on good terms.

"You know I'll always care about you," he said, as if reading her mind.

Remy pulled away. "Same here. But it's for the best."

"I know it is. You're a good person, Remy."

She rubbed his shoulders before stepping away. "You are, too. Let me call the reception desk so we can get you help with your luggage." She picked up the resort phone and called downstairs, and they promised to have someone there pronto. Then she turned back to Carson. "I wish you the best of luck with your presentation. I know you'll do well."

He swiped his brow. "Thanks. I'm nervous about it, but we're well prepared."

A light knock on the door indicated help had arrived. She opened the door to find Seth. Her pulse knocked against her ribcage and for a moment, she hesitated.

"I happened to be in the lobby when I heard you needed help. Is everything okay?"

"It's great, Seth," Carson said, extending his hand for a shake before he grabbed a suitcase. "I've got to get going, though. I need to get back to the office for some important work."

"Sure. No problem." He wheeled in a luggage cart and stacked the three cases and briefcase on top.

Remy watched Seth work, her heart flipping, toes curling. His face was slack and he barely glanced at her.

Carson winked, but the circles lining his eyes indicated he had worried about his job for quite some time now. Guilt pinched her for never noticing before.

Seth wheeled the cart out the door.

Remy grabbed Carson's hand and squeezed. "For what it's worth, I'm glad you came."

Carson had more luggage than anyone Seth knew. They all rode down the elevator together in silence.

"I've got to get my coat out of the closet," Remy said. "I'll meet you at the car."

Seth helped him load his belongings into the rental. Carson shook his hand. Remy tottered out in her coat, and Carson acted like he didn't want to wait. Seth thought that was strange. Carson gave Remy a salute and was already climbing into the car when Remy stopped beside Seth.

"Bye Carson," she said. Another awkward wave, and Carson shut the door. Seth's chest pounded as they watched him drive away.

"Well, that was awkward." Remy stood in the empty parking area, her gaze on the disappearing car.

Concern tugged at him. "Is everything okay?"

"It's never been better."

He pointed in the direction of where Carson's vehicle had disappeared. "But..."

"Carson and I broke up." A smile spread across her face, lightening her features.

His heart burst open, but he quickly contained himself. "You seem happy."

She squeezed her arms together and shimmied her shoulders. "I am. I thought he was going to fuss about it and list all the reasons we could work things out, but instead he came to the conclusion and said something before I had the guts to."

"Well, I...I'm happy if you're happy." He was happy for a whole lot more reasons but wouldn't dare tell her so.

"Oh, Seth. I've never been happier. I could stay here forever."

"You are welcome to stay here as long as you want."

She twirled around once, nearly stumbled, then stopped and planted her palms on Seth's chest. Her mouth curved, eyes glittering in mischief and face softening. "I've missed you," she said. "I thought you were mad at me or something."

He grimaced. He should have returned her text. "Not mad at all. We've both been busy."

"Yes, and I feel like I've missed out on too many Christmas activities. I think I'll see if Addie wants to go to Snowman Alley today."

"That's great. You'll both enjoy that."

She nodded and dropped her hands, but he missed the contact even though his coat barricaded her touch. They still stood in the middle of the parking lot. No telling what they looked like to observers.

"Carson didn't seem too keen on Christmas," Seth stated.

"Carson isn't keen on a lot of things outside of his job."

"I'm sorry for..."

She play-slapped his shoulders, a crooked grin on her face. "Don't be sorry. I'm only sorry it took coming here to do something we should have done years ago."

"I know the feeling." Her visit, even Carson's, made Seth realize he'd procrastinated too long. Telling Remy how he felt should be at the top of his agenda. "You want to have dinner with me tonight?" he asked. He longed to show her his home and the tree he'd put up. Landon had lectured him and he hadn't accepted his friend's advice. Now, he was ready to tell her how he felt.

"I'd love to."

"At my place?"

She raised her eyebrows, a quirky grin brightening her face. "At your place, where you're going to cook and everything? Even better."

"I do know how to cook, after all."

"I'm finding out you have a lot of talents."

He hooked his arm through hers and escorted her back to the resort. He'd find out tonight if he'd mastered the talent of winning Remy's heart.

CHAPTER 17

Remy spotted Tessa and Addie on the couch and resisted the urge to skip across the lobby. No point in appearing too eager. She planned to tell her family about Carson, but now wasn't the right time. Too many people crowded the room, noise and laughter decking the halls. She'd rather wait until they were alone.

Addie spotted her then shifted aside and patted the seat.

Seth unfurled his arm from Remy's and gave a chin-nod toward the back door. "I've got to run but will see you later."

Remy fluttered her fingers at him, pulse bubbling in her throat. "Looking forward to it." She bounced to the couch and slid on the seat next to Addie. Her heart was full but light, a joyous energy expanding her limbs. Carson was gone. She and Seth hadn't expressed a next move, but tonight's dinner would offer her an opportunity for her to tell him she loved him.

Her stomach rolled. Would he believe her, or blame it on the holiday season like he had his past relationships?

Was she ready? Yes. Absolutely. But first, she would enjoy this moment with her family.

"You look like you've had a good day," Tessa said.

Remy palmed her chest. "It hasn't been bad."

"Oh, so it is true about Carson leaving?"

Remy's mouth drop opened. "What? Where did you hear that from?"

Tessa wriggled her brows. "Maye could barely contain her excitement."

Remy's cheeks burned. She nodded, smiling, barely containing her own excitement. "We broke up. We both realized we weren't right for each other."

"It's about time," Tessa muttered.

"Yeah, the whole family figured it out ages ago," Addie exclaimed matter-of-factly.

Remy finger-brushed her niece's hair. "Is that right?"

Addie bobbed her head once, her legs moving back and forth in a seated dance. "Yup.

Remy dropped her hands. "Well, Addie, I thought I'd see if you wanted to go to Snowman Alley and build a snowman with me." She shrugged, teasing. "But now I don't know."

Addie shrieked and clapped her hands, then lifted her arms in a cheer. "Yes, yes, yes!"

Cringing, Tessa rubbed her daughter's hair. "Calm down, Addie." She tossed Remy a grateful smile. "That would be fantastic. I have some things to take care of. Packages and all that."

Remy got the hint. "Perfect. I do have dinner plans tonight, so maybe we can meet back up at the house, say six?"

"Dinner plans?" Tessa's brow arched.

Remy ducked her head, glancing at the crowded room that seemed to shrink with her confession. "I'm having dinner with Seth tonight." She rose and waved toward Addie. She wasn't about to tell her sister she was in love with Seth until she told him, but if she didn't get out of here, her face would likely give her away.

"Come on. Let's run back to our room and gather a few things. See you later, sis."

"Addie and I drove and I need to get back. Why don't I take you?"

"My car is still here."

"It's fine right where it's at," Tessa commented.

Remy didn't bother asking her what that statement meant. She was too happy, and she had a feeling her sister could read her feelings clearly.

Who else had figured out her love for Seth before she had?

It didn't take long for her to gather a small backpack of water, granola snacks, her laptop, and her camera. Soon, she and Addie trekked the snow toward their destination.

Snowman Alley was situated in an open path past the village, fenced in by a slat of one piece of wood bordering a quarter-sized playing field and an always-open gate. Although the daylight hid the true charm, white lights draped across the fence, and landscape lighting helped highlight the snowmen at night. Several families had already built snowmen there, but Remy was glad to find the two of them had it to themselves.

Her nephews would love to do this, and she planned to bring them all back later, but right now she wanted this time with Addie. Besides, the boys had gone off on some fishing trip and Addie hadn't wanted to go. A perfect moment to create new memories with her only niece.

Addie picked a spot and kneeled on the ground, scooping snow into her hands.

"Your mom and I used to come here when I was your age," Remy said.

Addie set the first mound of the snowman. "Mom has told me stories. I was sad when she said we couldn't come this year."

"I was sad, too. Do you know, when I first came here and found out it was closed, there wasn't any snow?"

Addie threw out her hands and fell backward into the snow, giggling in a dramatic display of shock. "No snow?"

"I kid you not. I have pictures to prove it." She plopped the round portion of the middle belly onto the bottom of the snowman. "You wanna do his face?"

Addie sat upright and gathered snow between her gloves. "My parents told me we couldn't come this year because it was closed."

"I know. But they didn't tell me that."

Addie giggled. "That's kind of mean."

"Kind of!" Remy teased.

The child chewed her lips. She positioned the top portion of the head on the snowman and cocked her head, studying the creation. "I'm glad we're spending Christmas together this year."

"I am, too," Remy said.

Flakes of snow fell around them. Addie glanced at Remy. "I can't believe there wasn't any snow when you first got here. That sounds terrible."

"It was pretty terrible."

"The snow is so magical."

"It sure is." Remy pointed to a pile near the back of the area. "There are the snowman parts."

Addie's face screwed into a frown. "Can you help with the head? It's not in portion...pro...portion. It's too small."

Remy gathered snow. "Okay. You wanna choose your parts while I fix the head?"

"Would love to!" Addie jumped up and rushed off to dig through the bins. She dug out buttons for the body, coal for the eyes, pebbles for the mouth, and a fake carrot for the nose so that it wouldn't attract birds. Piles of sticks for the arms, scarves, hats, and other accessories waited for those who wished to accessorize their snowmen. Addie made several trips and dumped them near Remy.

Since Addie was having so much fun choosing her parts, Remy took her time with the head.

"I think I've found everything we need." Addie settled back on the ground near Remy.

"Awesome. I think I finally got the head fixed."

"Looks good to me."

They placed the face and accessories on the snowman, then Addie stood, backed up, and clapped her hands. "It looks amazing."

Remy stood beside her and planted her hand on the top of Addie's head. "It sure does."

"Did you bring your phone so we can take a picture?"

"I brought something even better." She dug her camera out of the backpack and snapped a few photos, then she handed it to Addie and showed her how to take a few.

"Tonight, when the snowmen glow, we should bring out the family." Addie studied each picture and snapped more.

"Yes, we should," Remy agreed.

Addie fell to one knee and peered through the lens. "This is fun."

Remy's pulse jumped. The best part of Christmas was making memories with loved ones. "It sure is."

Addie snapped a few more photos, then stood and handed back the camera.

Remy waved her away. "You can let it hang on your neck and snap some photos during our hike, if you want to."

"Awesome. Thank you. Can we go on our hike now?"

"I'm ready whenever you are."

Addie's chin lifted, eyes gleaming, and they trekked the forest trail. She occasionally stopped and snapped photos, and Remy's heart swelled.

She should have gotten a camera for Addie for Christmas,

apparently. She'd have to ask Tessa if she knew about Addie's love for photography.

"I miss my grandparents," Addie said out of the blue. "I barely remember them."

Remy's ribs grew tight, and her steps faltered. "I miss them, too. They loved you. They would have loved being here this year."

Addie's eyes filled with tears. She settled her back against a tree and aimed the camera towards the mountains.

Remy's parents should be here, enjoying their favorite time of year. Things were too happy right now, and it scared her. She kept worrying something would come crashing down on her, as it had three years ago.

She barely remembered the day. She was at the resort when she heard the news, but she barely remembered the following days. The only thing keeping her going afterward was the letter from her parents. They had written it for their children in the case of one or both of their deaths. She could recite it by heart now.

Miss us when we're gone, but don't mourn us. Keep the sparkle of your soul alive. Smile when you cry. Laugh through your tears. For we've had a good life and yours doesn't end with us gone.

She blew out a breath, then bent over and gathered snow into a ball, tossing it toward Addie.

Addie jumped, dropped the camera, and stuck out her tongue. "Hey!"

The rest of the letter mentioned much more about living life to the fullest, and that's what she planned to do. Her parents wanted her to be happy. They wanted their children to experience the joy of each breath.

"But you know what?" Remy asked. "They wouldn't have wanted us to be sad. Especially during their favorite time of year."

"That's what Mom says, too. Oh my goodness, look!"

Addie grabbed the camera and pointed it at the tree. A red cardinal fluttered on the branches as snow flittered down and white bunched around the bird.

"That's going to be an awesome picture," Remy said. "Did you know that cardinals signify loved ones who are still with us even though they are gone?"

Addie's eyes widened. "They do?"

"That's what some people say."

Addie placed both palms over her heart. "I believe it. Because I can still feel them."

Remy almost crumbled. Her mom and dad loved Addie. They should have had a chance to see their grandchildren grow. "Me too." Her voice shook. Her parents were strong and wanted their children to be strong. She straightened her shoulders and shook off the nostalgia, determined to create awesome memories for her niece. "Are you ready to go in? We have time to go to the computer room and look at all the photos you took."

Addie bolted forward. "Yes, yes, yes, I do!"

The computer room was empty when they shuffled in, Addie all smiles and chatter. She squealed at the pictures, and Remy helped her create a collage of her favorites. They hooked to the printer in the computer area and found photo paper, then printed the collage.

"I think I'll give this to my parents for Christmas," Addie said. She bunched her lip in a pout. "But I need a frame."

"I bet I can get you one before tomorrow," Remy said.

Her head tilted. "You can?"

She dug out her phone. "I sure can. I bet I can get you one right now."

Addie licked her lips and bobbed her head, her face shining. "Cool."

Remy texted Seth her request, and he was quick to respond.

Meet me in my office.

He stood by the door while they approached, then waved. "Hey."

Addie hid the photo against her chest and put a finger over her lips. "We're working on a super-secret project."

He wiggled his brows. "You are?"

Addie nodded.

The smile he gave Remy tightened her limbs. She wanted to see so much more of his smiles. She could never grow tired of them.

"You must take after your aunt and her secret projects." He shuffled aside and let them in the room, then shut the door behind them. "Well, I think I have just what you need."

Addie displayed her picture. "We took a lot of pictures today. And I want to give some to Mom and Dad for Christmas."

Seth studied the photos. "These are beautiful, Addie. You did these all by yourself?"

She puffed out her chest and cheeks. "All by myself. We did a little bit of treat...uh, tweak...phew, that word. On the computer. But yeah I took them."

"They're amazing. You have a real eye."

Addie shrugged her shoulders and crossed her arms, chin dipping down as she rocked side to side. A tinge of pink touched her cheeks. "Thanks."

Seth opened a door. "Come on. This is my closet here, and you can pick out any frame you'd like."

Remy propped her hand on Addie's head. She could tell Addie was being shy, excited about her work but uneasy with the compliments. She understood all too well how it felt to shrink into oneself when it came to your creation, but she wanted Addie to learn how to accept the well-deserved praise. Her photos were raw, candid, and emotional. She'd touched upon some deep issues within Remy. The angle of the tree, reaching toward an indigo sky, the grayness of the bark with a red cardinal perched upon snow-tipped branches. Maybe because Remy was feeling so nostalgic and eager to tell Seth her feelings. Or maybe because she was still so unsure about her future. Addie and Seth were both so good with photos, but Remy's talent soared in using those creations to expand upon something more.

She was eager to walk past the door and see what secrets Seth hid. His abilities obviously consisted of more than photography. She bit her lips.

He didn't know she knew about the music box. And she wasn't about to tell him. Not yet. But she would love to see his craft room and discover pieces of his soul.

They walked into the room, and Addie whooped. "Wow!"

Wow was right. His closet was like another room, tools and craft tables set up in perfect proportion, with shelving full of his frames and other projects. She wondered if any of the displays were for music box crafts.

"Is this your workshop?" Remy asked.

"Not really. Just some storage. This was my dad's office. Crazy thing is, I haven't taken over the rest of the office, but I've worked on it the past few days during some free time, and I decided to start with this."

"Oh. I'd love to see your real workshop one day," Remy said.

"I like to keep a few things here for when I'm in the resort and want to work on something besides the resort, you know?"

"Like all the photos you've taken?" Addie chewed her lip. "I don't have a camera yet, but I'd love to be able to do that some day."

Seth grabbed several frames and laid four side by side on a table. "And you're already doing so well. Which frame do you like?"

Addie positioned the photo near each of the frames, back and forth between the four. A metallic, two different wood frames, and one white. Remy stood back, watching them work together and keeping her opinion to herself. She wanted her niece to choose.

"I've got more if you want to see more."

"I love them all. But I'm not sure if I prefer the lighter." She laid the photo on top of a pine frame, then picked it up and put it against the darker walnut. "Or this one."

Remy's skin buzzed with warmth as she watched Seth interact with her niece.

Seth tapped the walnut frame. "If you want my opinion, I prefer the dark. Because it brings out the lightness of the snow, the tree, and the bird."

Addie beamed. "That's what I was thinking." She turned to Remy and held up her plan. "What do you think?"

"I totally agree. It looks beautiful."

Seth nodded at a box in the corner of the closet. "Here, I'll put that together for you while you choose the wrappings. I should have whatever you need there."

Addie pulled out several bags and chose a bright red one with a bird and tree. "This kind of matches the photo."

Remy helped her wrap the frame, first in paper then in the gift bag. Her eyes filled with tears.

"Are you crying?" Addie bellowed.

She swiped her cheek. "Happy tears." She glanced at Seth and winked. "Just happy tears."

Addie lifted the bag, full of glittery tissue paper and ribbon. "Let's see if we can get this package under the tree before anyone notices."

"Yes, ma'am."

After realizing Remy left her purse and keys at home, Seth drove them back to the house. Addie bounced in the seat, barely containing her excitement. Remy knew right then and there that if she hadn't already been in love with Seth, today she would have fallen head over heels.

She wondered what would have happened if she hadn't stopped, if she hadn't stayed, if he hadn't seen her at the door and come and instead let her leave on the first day she arrived. But she didn't let herself sink into that worry, because she was here now. Making special memories and expounding upon the ones their parents created.

She had always loved Seth. Maybe it wasn't as deep and pure as it was now. Maybe it was a friendship kind of love. But she kept that secret close to her heart a little while longer.

He loved kids just as much as she did. He loved the holidays, lived for them, made a business out of them. He celebrated life every day and appreciated the small things.

His values matched hers.

He stopped at the driveway. Addie bounded out.

"Careful," Seth warned. "It's slippery."

"Wait up, Addie," Remy said.

Seth opened his door but didn't get out. "I think I'll leave now, so you girls can sneak in and get that package under the tree."

"Thanks for your help, Seth." Addie blew him a kiss.

He caught it, cradled it under his chin, then blew her one. Something they had done when Addie first came here with her parents.

Remy had missed these special moments because she had been too busy trying to hide from her true self.

Seth saluted. "You're welcome. I was glad to help. See you later."

Remy took his hand and squeezed. He brought hers up to his mouth and kissed her knuckles. For that split second when time stood still and they gazed into each other's eyes, words were unnecessary.

Seth couldn't stop the tight beating of his heart. He let the Jeep idle, waiting to make sure the girls got safely inside before he drove away. He texted Remy that he couldn't wait to see her tonight. Seth was eager to ask her to spend the rest of her life with him.

He'd known her forever, and seeing Carson with her made him realize how small of a chance he had and he needed to take it now. She would go back to Texas, meet someone new, and the next time she came out here with another guy, it might be a lot more serious than Carson. Telling her how he felt was worth losing her friendship. They could get past it if she didn't want to give him a chance, but he would rather gamble his friendship than lose out on something deeper they might have together.

He would do it tonight. At dinner. And he couldn't wait to show her the Christmas tree he'd put up and decorated all by himself.

He arranged a carriage ride to pick Remy up that evening.

The bells notified him of her arrival. They would have their ride together later, but for now he wanted her to enjoy the experience by herself. The vastness of the resort, the profundity of how majestic it was, and also the immensity of being alone once the crowd was gone.

He stepped outside to greet her. His breath caught in his throat, and he almost stumbled. The driver caught her hand and helped her down, and she walked forward.

But Seth couldn't take a step. He was too busy admiring her. Too busy trying to breathe.

Curls cascaded around her shoulders. Her silvery earrings dangled like ice crystals and sparkled with the colors of snow. The deep blue of her shirt bought out the depth in her eyes, and her denim jeans tapered at the ankles to display black furry booties.

For a moment, he imagined her coming to him in a marriage ceremony. Her father wouldn't be available to walk her, but Landon would. For now, the driver assisted. Seth swallowed and fought the urge to remain standing.

This was no wedding ceremony. At least not yet.

He stepped forward. Bowed to Remy and took her hand. Gave the drive a handshake and thought about how later he'd like to ask him to come to work for him fulltime.

Remy was all smiles when he took her hand and led her inside.

He'd wait a little while longer to take her in his arms and kiss her like there was no tomorrow. And he'd learned all too well if he didn't tell her his feelings soon, there might not be a future with them.

Remy's eyes widened once they went inside. "Oh my gosh, Seth." She danced to the tree. She twirled once, holding up her hands. "This is amazing. The carriage ride was amazing. The kids were disappointed they had to stay behind."

"He's going back for them and giving them all a ride through the lighted trees and up to the resort." The driver was instructed to return to the house afterwards and give the rest of the family an unexpected treat. Seth had already cleared it with Landon, and the driver would take them through the forest before going to the resort where they would have dinner.

Seth was doing something new this year. He'd rented a carriage ride up until Christmas Eve, and reservations were required because of its popularity. At one time, his parents had considered getting horses and doing their own, but they never did. Maybe Seth would add that to his bucket list.

He told her of his plans to hire a driver year-round.

She clapped her hand over her mouth. "That's an

awesome idea." She faced the lighted tree that blinked out a welcoming chorus of color. His mantel was lined in garland, more colored lights, and wreaths.

He'd chosen a simple, old-fashioned theme, his body tightening and tingling at each placement of the ornaments and the memories they developed.

She angled her body toward him and tilted her face up to his. "Did you do all this yourself?"

He nodded. "I did."

"Oh, I would have helped you."

"I know. But you were busy, and Carson was here." Her face fell, and he continued in a joking manner. "What, you don't think I did a good enough job?"

She planted her hand on his arm. "You did a fantastic job."

"The tri-tip is out on the grill. I need to go check it."

Her brows arched. "The grill?"

"Yep." He nodded to the door behind the kitchen. "In my grill space outside. I've got a heat lamp and fire, but we don't have to sit out there."

"I'd love to be outside."

"Good, because there's more to show you."

She followed him. His porch was covered with wooden beams, besieged with colored lights strung across the roof's ceiling and illuminating the space. Large, comfy chairs gathered together near a small fire pit, and a heated patio lamp—which blazed—stood sentry in the corner. His outdoor kitchen was any man's dream. Brick, a slot for wood, lots of counters, cabinetry, and a huge gas grill along with a smoker and wood grill.

"Wow, Seth."

He opened the wood grill and poked the thermometer into the meat. Temperature was perfect, so he removed the steaks and wrapped them with foil. He wanted to impress her. And judging by the looks of the food, she would be. "The potatoes will take a bit longer, and the meat needs to sit a few moments."

"Fine by me."

"I hope you like it. I know you're a Texas girl who likes her barbecue."

She settled into a seat near the blazing fire pit. "I sure do." She leaned forward and rubbed her hands near the fire.

Seth sat in the chair beside her, the herbal and peppery scent of the smoke teasing his nostrils. Soft strains of music from the live band at the resort filtered through the air.

"It's amazing how quiet it is over here," Remy said. "I can hear the music. The kids laughing. The celebrations. I swear I even hear the skates clinking against the ice."

He flattened his lips together and nodded. "The quietness can be pretty barren when everyone is gone."

Remy laughed. "I remember how barren it was when I first came. Kind of eerie."

"It can be," he agreed. In a crazy way, he'd wanted her to experience that during the carriage ride. If he asked her to stay and she said yes, he wanted her to understand the intricacies of her decision. She'd helped him manage the activities and offered her own ideas, and although the resort was usually booked, there were days that could get lonely.

Snow sprinkled down. Remy stood and exited the shelter of the roof, lifting her head up and opening her mouth to enjoy a morsel. She twirled around and laughed. "I can't ever get enough of this snow." She shifted closer to the fire and rubbed her hands together. "But it's cold once you get away from this fire."

"We can always go in if it's too cold for you."

"No way. I love it out here. Nothing better than sitting around a fire at night."

He stood and held out his hands. "True that. But there's also nothing better than dancing under the stars near a fire in the middle of the night. In this case, we'll dance under the glimmering lights of the ceiling." His heart knocked against his ribcage.

They danced, the music a hushed melody as it muted the air.

"Do you still play?"

Remy's words skated across his cheek in warmth. His parents used to sing at least one song together at the Christmas Eve celebration, and Seth played guitar. "I haven't."

"You haven't?"

Seth shook his head. "Not in a while."

"Not even on Christmas Eve?"

"No."

"Maybe you should this year."

His throat grew thick, prickling. By a while, he'd meant since his parents died, and he wasn't sure he was ready. Too many emotions attached to that memory. No matter how honest he wanted to be with her, right now it was easier to make excuses. "Oh, I'm not sure my fingers would cooperate. Besides, it's time for new traditions."

"I'll sing and play the piano if you'll play the guitar."

His heart jerked. He pulled away and studied her.

"You sing and play the piano?"

She blinked, her eyes flashing, sparkling, synchronizing with the outdoor lights. "Yes. I mean, I might be as shaky as you are. I haven't done it in a while. But I bet I can manage."

This was something he never knew about her. He was learning a lot of things he didn't know about her, but he enjoyed the discovery. "Wow. Okay."

She lifted her chin. "So, it's a deal?"

How could he disappoint her? She looked way too excited, and her enthusiasm bandaged the anxiety in his chest. "Well, I don't want to scare away our guests."

She whacked his arm. "You might scare them away, but I don't plan to."

"Why am I just now finding this out?"

Her lips parted. Her fingers gave him a feather-soft brush along his jawline. "Because it's not something I ever wanted to do in front of a crowd." She waved her arm in the air. "I mean, I have at church and stuff, but I wasn't about to during our Christmas festivities."

He couldn't wait to experience this with her. His parents had played music together every year. Maybe this was a sign, and he and Remy would, too. "Okay, then. We'll do it. We'll make it our new tradition. Of course, that means you have to come back every year."

She smiled and settled her cheek on his chest.

He cringed. Come back next year? He never wanted her to leave. Why didn't he just admit it?

"Remy," he said, his voice cracking.

She lifted her face and glanced up at him, her eyes glowing and gleaming with warmth. His heart clumped to his feet.

Now was definitely the time to tell her, but anxiety twisted his stomach. He didn't know why. Everything about right now was perfect. And that's what scared him. If he confessed his feelings and read her wrong, she would run. It wouldn't be the first time. "What if I told you I never want you to leave?"

Her pupils dilated. A soft breathy sound escaped. Her gaze remained on his. "What if I told you I never want to leave?"

His heart hammered against his ribcage. They stopped dancing, but they didn't separate. He kept his palms stationed on her lower back. "I'd ask if you were sure. Or if the magic of Christmas makes you feel this way."

"I'd ask you the same."

He drew in a breath and held it. "I'd tell you I've never

felt this way about another person before. I'd tell you that I want to be more than friends and I'm willing to risk that friendship to tell you so. I'd also tell you that I never want someone like Carson to come into the picture and take you away from me."

"I'd tell you I don't need Christmas magic to see the truth of how happy I've been here. I'd tell you that Carson made me realize how much I didn't want to be with him or have that life. I'd tell you I want to share this with you and I love what we've done. And I'd tell you that I'm in love with you."

His breath stalled. He bumped his forehead to hers and stationed it there as if she was the only thing keeping him upright.

"You love me?" His voice squeaked, filled with shock and surprise and hope and anticipation.

She laughed, a giggly, shaky titter that landed straight in his gut. "I'd also tell you that you're supposed to say I love you, too."

"Oh, Remy. I love you, too. So much more than you could ever know." Then he kissed her, with no intention of letting her go anytime soon.

CHAPTER 18

Remy melted under his kiss. It was as if the whole world was falling into place.

They went inside for dinner and ate by candlelight.

They didn't make plans and they didn't speak of marriage, but Remy told him how she'd already decided she would quit her job.

"It's time for me to do what makes me happy," she told him.

She didn't want the night to end, but tomorrow would be a busy day, and they both needed their rest. Santa would visit on the night before Christmas Eve. Remy was glad he'd kept that tradition, although he wouldn't keep the one of him dressing up. His mom and dad had played Mr. and Mrs. Claus, but Seth preferred to be in the midst of things.

Seth drove her home in the Jeep. Stars burst and twinkled around them like firecrackers celebrating the wonder of winter love.

They parked, and Seth came around to help Remy down from the Jeep.

She smoothed her gloved hand over his beanie. "Such a gentleman."

He cupped her face. "I'm doing everything I can to be a gentleman tonight, but it's hard with you so near."

They kissed again. His fiery tongue burned away the cold from her skin.

Neither pulled away first, it just happened with the wondrous synchronicity of love. They gazed into each other's eyes under the dark moonlight.

"You know my family is going to say I told you so."

Seth's eyes glittered. "Yeah. Landon already tried to lecture me on how I should tell you my feelings."

Her skin tingled. "What? He knew?"

"He guessed. He thought he knew. Well, I guess he did know since he guessed right." Seth chuckled and tugged on her hand. "Come on, I'll walk you to the door."

"You'll come in and say hello, right?"

Their footsteps rasped under the snow. She stopped. He glanced at her, his brows arching. "What's wrong?"

"Let's tell them on Christmas Day. That I'm staying. That we're a couple."

His nose scrunched. "You wanna keep this a secret a while longer?" He pulled her into his arms and kissed her. "I'm okay with that."

Jingling bells approached, along with her family's raucous laughter in the carriage ride. Seth dropped her hand. He assisted Addie from the carriage and she threw her body into his arms.

"That was awesome, Seth!"

He returned her hug. "Great. Glad you enjoyed yourself."

Remy's heart was full.

Everyone took their turns saying thank you, and Landon ushered them to the door. "Let's go inside where it's warm.

They all followed him in and shed their coats and gloves.

Remy stood back and observed her family's boisterous chatter and actions, the way Tessa grabbed mugs from the kitchen, Addie twirled around the living room, and the men spoke with Seth about their insights on tonight's ride. Melissa and Ethan stood beside them, showing off pictures on her phone.

Euphoria filled Remy. Her gut pinched, nostalgia taking over for a moment, but she swallowed. Their parents would be so happy for them right now.

Tessa asked Seth if he wanted tea, but he held up his hands in a no. "I'm good. I need to get back home soon."

Addie tugged on his shirt, eyes wide but tired. "I thought we were going to Snowman Alley and show off our masterpiece?"

"It's late," Jason stooped to pick up Grayson, who had been leaning against him about to fall asleep. "We'll go tomorrow."

Addie's lip trembled. "But—"

"But Santa comes tomorrow," Seth interjected. "So it'll be fun to see him and then visit Snowman Alley, don't you think?"

Addie rubbed her eyes and nodded.

"I'm taking Grayson to bed." Jason said goodnight to everyone. Grayson's head lolled on his shoulder, eyes fluttering as if trying to stay awake. "Why don't you come on, too, Addie? It's bedtime."

Addie stuck out her lip in a pout and crossed her arms. "But I'm not ready for bed."

Jason curled his fingers at her. "We've got a long day tomorrow."

"Come on, Addie," Tessa said.

Jason stood in the door and stopped Tessa with a whisper. "I'll handle it. You stay up and visit with your sister. I'll be fine." He put up a hand and waved. "'Night everyone."

A chorus of *goodnights* followed, and Jason disappeared with his kids.

"I'll see you guys tomorrow." Seth made his way to the door.

Another chorus of *goodnights*.

Remy followed him to the door and kissed his cheek, keeping everything chaste for her watchful family, then shut and locked the door before a wave of cold air blew in.

"I think it's time for these kids to get to bed." Landon thumped his chest, then kissed his wife.

"Me, too," Ethan said. "Goodnight."

"The girls and I are having a cup of tea before bed." Melissa filled a pan with water and put it on the stove.

Once the men were gone and the tea was brewed, the three women sat on the couch, talking, giggling, and watching the lights on the tree.

"I'm glad we decided on blinking colored lights this year," Remy said. She loved the white lights, but many of the trees had them and she preferred lots of color and lots of blinking.

"The kids wouldn't have it any other way," Tessa said.

"I love the color," Melissa said.

Remy held up her mug and the three girls tapped them softly together. "Cheers to that."

"So, tell us about Seth," Tessa said.

Remy had expected this. She tucked her feet under her and dunked her tea bag. "Oh, is that why we're all curled up on the couch together? To gossip about me and Seth?"

"Of course!" Melissa said. "We want details."

Giggling, Remy rolled her eyes and settled the back of her head on the couch cushion, then upright. She and Seth had agreed to tell her family on Christmas Day, and she wasn't intentionally lying to her sister. She just wanted to keep this secret a little while longer. "I'm not sure there's much to tell."

Tessa nudged her shoulder. "Oh, come on, sis. There's plenty to tell."

"Well, we talked. A lot." Heat flushed through her body, heating her face.

"You're blushing," Tessa teased.

"Stop it. It's just hot under this blanket with you two on either side of me."

"Oh, come on," Tessa said. "The poor man is in love with you. Anyone can see that."

"And you're in love with him," Melissa asserted.

"We talked about our feelings, sure. But I don't know what's going to happen."

"What do you want to happen?" her sister asked.

Shrugging, she sipped her tea, then shifted her body to settle deeper into the couch. "I plan to quit my job and move here."

The women screeched, but Remy shushed them. "Let's keep this between us, shall we? We haven't made real plans yet. It's all just been in the moment. After the holidays, maybe we'll have more time and we both agreed we aren't ready to announce it, but we planned to tell everyone on Christmas Day."

Melissa shifted closer to her. "Oh, darling. You already have announced it. You just don't know it. By your actions and the chemistry between you both. Everyone sees it. Now you just have to make it official."

Seth loved playing Santa, but the night before Christmas Eve, when the jolly man visited the resort, he denied his father's tradition of dressing up. Instead, he preferred to have someone else do it so he could visit the crowd and share their joy. MacGregor volunteered, because he loved the role almost as much as Seth's father had.

Remy's niece and nephews were thrilled. Addie clutched Remy's hand and hustled the crowd forward, and Grayson burrowed into his mother's legs until she finally picked him up. Undoubtedly braver and more curious in his mother's arms, his eyes grew wide in wonder as they drew nearer.

"Ho, ho, ho," Santa said, waving to everyone. Children sat on his lap and whispered their wishes into his ears. Families gathered together to have their photos taken with him as Mrs. Claus, MacGregor's wife, stood by with a camera.

His chest tightened. He loved his family of employees and was grateful they had decided to join him and help with Christmas, even after his almost-betrayal.

Seth was thrilled when Remy's family invited him to dinner.

Addie could barely contain her excitement until after dinner, when they would meet with Santa and then head to snowman alley to reveal the snowman she and Remy had built yesterday.

"Let's take a picture with Santa," Addie said when their turn came.

"You've already seen Santa once this year," Tessa drawled.

"Yeah, but not with the entire family. Come on. You too, Seth."

Addie dropped Remy's hand and raced forward, toward where Santa held out his hands. She crawled onto his lap.

The family bunched together, but Seth lagged behind, close enough to hear the conversation.

"Merry Christmas, my child," Santa said.

"Merry Christmas, Santa. Can we take a picture with you?"

"Of course. Do you want to tell me what you want for Christmas first?"

Addie chewed her lip, worry lining her brow. "Well, I already told you everything, but now I've decided there's something else I really, really want. But I'm afraid it's too late."

Santa's belly shook with his *ho ho ho*. "And what's that?"

Addie's eyes flashed. "A camera!"

"A camera?"

Addie bobbed her head, and an idea immediately formed in Seth's mind. Seth's enjoyment of playing Santa was when he could exceed his guests' expectations on Christmas Day.

Addie fidgeted. "Like, a digital camera. Like my Aunt Remy has."

"Oh, okay. That's a gift for a good girl. Have you been a good girl?"

"Yes, sir." Addie glanced around, as if seeking her mom's endorsement.

Tessa sat down her son and cast a worry-glance to her husband. Her face was tight, lined in dissatisfaction of discovering her child wanted a gift she wouldn't have time to find.

Seth wouldn't tell them his plan, even if it would put them at ease. His surprise was for everyone.

Santa smoothed his hand over Addie's hair. "Well, I'll have to check with the elves. Like you said, it's very last minute."

Addie hugged Santa's neck and jumped down. "Grayson, do you have anything you want to say to Santa?"

Grayson pattered forward and touched Santa's leg as if he wanted to be noticed but was too afraid to be as bold as his sister.

Santa opened his arms.

Grayson pointed. "Take picture with Santa?"

"Yes, absolutely," Tessa said. "Come on. Let's get this picture so the other children will have time with Santa."

The family assembled behind Santa, and Seth stood back. Addie glanced around, frowning and then, pinpointing Seth, she waved him over. "Come on, Seth. You should be in this, too."

He glanced at Remy, his nerves tingling.

She waved, then called, "Come on."

His gut dipped. He was in love with Remy, but loved her family like his own and was proud they had asked him to join them.

Remy wrapped her arm around his waist.

He couldn't contain the grin spreading across his face. His pulse drummed out a racing rhythm of elation and gratitude. Tonight, on this special night before Christmas Eve, he wanted nothing more than to be surrounded by family and friends. This was what he lived for. This was the reason he had kept this resort open even at the worst of his times, and this was the reason he would never shut down again.

Once the photo was done, Seth shook Santa's hand, nodded at Mrs. Claus, and followed Remy's family toward Snowman Alley. Seth trailed behind, beside Remy.

A fence bordered the area and shimmered with lights. Short, decorative poles placed strategically amongst the decorations gleamed. Snowman Alley was almost full now, and most of the snowmen had remained intact, thanks to the suitable weather. They traversed the path of snowmen until Addie stopped and pointed.

"There it is, look, look! That's the snowman Remy and I built."

Jason bent on one knee and grabbed his daughter around the waist. "It's adorable."

Addie beamed. "Thank you."

Remy dropped his hand and kneeled on the ground with Addie, using her phone to take pictures of the two of them being funny in the snow.

Grayson kicked at the snow, his lip hanging out in a pout.

Ethan grabbed his hand before he knocked over any of the snowmen.

"I wannna make a snowman," Grayson said, his chubby cheeks a shiny red.

"We can, but it's a little cold tonight, don't you think?" Tessa asked.

He stomped his foot. "I wanna make a snowman now."

Jason stood. "Grayson James. You'll not be doing anything if you continue you throw a fit. Are we clear?"

Grayson lowered his eyes and nodded, his lips softening.

"Okay," Jason said. "We can build a quick snowman. It'll be fun. But only if you don't throw any more fits, okay?"

Seth's heart hitched as he watched the interaction between father and son. He appreciated the way Jason handled Grayson with love and discipline.

He wanted children to leave this place to one day, as his parents had done for him. Fear soured his stomach, but he slowly breathed in and out. His breath wisped in the cold, and he imagined the particles were the ghosts of his fear. Releasing and letting go.

He couldn't be afraid to dream.

His parents had built this place. Their dreams had come true, but they had died way too soon. Until now, he hadn't allowed himself to hope for anything. He had gone through the cycles of his days as if on a treadmill. Attempting to move forward but going nowhere, hoping for nothing while he tried to keep traditions alive and keep the resort active.

This family had slowly etched away his loneliness, and he was finally free to dream again. To imagine his own house-hold, Remy by his side with buckets of children. Or at least two or three.

He was an only child, but he wanted a large family. He wondered how Remy felt about that.

He continued to watch Grayson, his tongue poking out as

he clumped snow into a ball. Ethan sat beside him, working on his own mound. Landon and Melissa took turns throwing snowballs at each other, and Jason and Tessa built their own snowman together.

He caught Remy's gaze, his pulse jerking.

He cleared his throat, needing a moment alone before his emotions got the best of him. "How about I go get us some hot chocolate?" he offered.

Jason looked up. "That'd be great. Thank you."

"Everyone want one?"

"Yes, please," a chorus of voices said.

Remy jumped up and brushed snow from her legs. "I'll go with you."

"I wanna go," Addie said.

Landon winked at Seth. "Uncle Landon needs your help, Addie."

Addie put a hand on her hip. "With what?"

Landon threw a snowball toward her, and it fell at her feet. "Missy is beating me in this snowball fight."

Shrieking, Addie bunched snow in her hands and threw it toward Landon. "And I'll help her beat you!"

Seth chuckled before clasping Remy's hand and walking away. "I love your family," he said.

"They're okay," she teased.

He stopped and turned to face her. She eyed him, a questioning frown forming in between her brows.

He clasped her hands and pulled them to his chest, his cheeks puffing. So many emotions he was sick of bottling. Might as well bring it all out into the open. "I don't regret my memories with my parents and being an only child, but I love your big family."

Her lopsided grin gave away her confusion. Her head tilted, and she licked her lips. "I do too. Although they can be a pain sometimes."

He wasn't ready to ask her to marry him, only because he had a special moment planned in his head. And her next answer wouldn't make or break how he felt, but they needed to get everything they wanted in life out in the open.

"Do you want kids?"

Her face softened. She tweaked his nose. "Lots."

He posted his forehead on hers and blinked away the burn in his eyes, the heat radiating into his chest.

"You're a good man, Seth. A thoughtful man."

He withdrew, masking his feelings of dread and expecting the worst. Had she changed her mind? "Uh, thanks. Do I sense a but?"

She smoothed her hand over his arm and angled her head. "No, not at all." Her lips pursed. "I just wanted you to know. And you'll make a fabulous father one day."

He leaned into her. "You'll make an even better mother. I love you," he said before his mouth swooped down on hers.

His life had been pretty darn good. His parents' deaths had scarred him, but finding love with Remy stripped away the heartbreak.

CHAPTER 19

C hristmas Eve was another reason to celebrate, and everyone had their own way to rejoice. Some people went outside to ice skate, some gathered around the tree or moseyed through the Christmas village or the lighted path of trees Seth had finally revealed to everyone. Others preferred to stay indoors, out of the cold.

Seth had dinner with Remy and her family and afterward, he fulfilled his promise by playing his guitar in the bar. Remy sat at the piano, her presence filling him with joy. People gathered to sing along with them while they played Christmas carols. Remy's beautiful voice plucked his heart, and her fingers danced across the piano keys. He had no idea she was this talented.

They played a few songs together, then escaped outside with her family to the observatory. Three telescopes were lined up for guests to enjoy any time of day or night, but right now they had the place to themselves. The sky was crystal clear tonight and offered an unhindered view.

"Any sign of Santa?" Seth asked Ethan, who studied the sky.

"No, but this is awesome, man. Awesome."

"I think I see Santa." Addie pointed up. "He's moving pretty fast, though. Hard to keep up."

"Yes, it's definitely hard to keep up," Seth said.

"Wanna see." Grayson bounced up and down.

"Come on, Gray." Addie stepped away and helped her brother look through the lens.

"Yah, yah, Santa," Grayson said.

Seth wrapped his arms around Remy. She leaned her head on his shoulder, and together they observed the children.

Ethan was energized by the telescope. He wasn't hogging it, but he didn't want to leave. He showed his parents different stars and mentioned moon phases as if he knew what he was talking about.

"This night is perfect," Remy said.

"And your voice is perfect," Seth countered. He'd wanted to get her alone all night to praise her and her singing, but he also enjoyed his time with her family.

She crinkled her nose up at him and squinted. "Not at all. But I'm not afraid of perfect anymore."

He knew exactly what she meant and felt the same. He refused to let fear rob him of enjoying the moment. The way her hair wisped out of her cap and brushed across his cheek. The way her niece and nephew took turns peering through the telescope and babbling about the stars. The way Tessa and Jason carried on like children as they shared the other telescope with each other, exchanging kisses each time they switched. And Landon and Melissa going back and forth between the kids, then they stepped away and let Ethan continue his observations.

Melissa's voice carried to Seth. "I didn't realize he was this interested in astronomy. I guess we should have gotten him a telescope."

"Next year, for sure," Landon said.

Addie and Grayson moved away from the telescope, their shoulders slumping. Grayson blinked and rubbed his eyes, then leaned against his mom's legs, head lolling on her thigh. Addie covered her mouth, stifling a yawn.

Tessa picked up Grayson. "Since Santa is so close, we better get to bed, don't you think?"

Addie wrapped her hands over her stomach and bobbed her head. "I'm cold and tired."

Landon planted his hand on Ethan's shoulder.

Ethan didn't budge. "I'm not ready to go yet."

"I'll stay a bit longer with him," Seth offered. "If that's okay."

Ethan whirled around to face his parents. "Yeah, Dad. Please?"

Remy stepped away from Seth and toward Ethan. "I'll stay, too. I'm not quite ready, myself."

"Thirty more minutes, tops," Landon said. "Everyone is tired and we're going inside."

"I'll set my phone timer for twenty, and we'll head that direction then," Remy said.

Once everyone had gone, Remy, Seth, and Ethan had the observatory all to themselves, so each of them peered through their own telescope. Ethan oohed and ahhed over everything.

"You can see the town lights from here," he commented.

"Yes, you can," Seth agreed. "It's beautiful."

All too soon, Remy's phone pealed.

"Oh man," Ethan groaned, turning away from his telescope with shoulders slumped. "Guess it's time for bed so Santa can come," he murmured.

"We can come out again before you have to go home," Seth said.

"Yeah, that'd be cool." His footsteps drug as he walked

between Remy and Seth. "But I don't think Santa will be coming here tonight."

Remy's brow arched. "Why do you say that?"

"I don't think I believe in Santa anymore. I mean, I want to, but I'm too old for such nonsense."

"Now, Ethan, Santa isn't nonsense." Remy rested her hand on his back. "He represents the magic of Christmas. You can't ever let the magic of Christmas die, no matter what you believe."

"Well, I don't plan to tell Addie or Grayson, but kids at school talk. One day, when they get older, they'll hear that chatter, too, but I don't plan on being the one to say anything."

Seth listened to the conversation but didn't want to interrupt nephew and aunt. He laid his hand on the boy's shoulder as they continued to walk side by side.

Ethan's revelation saddened him. He loved everything about Christmas, and he knew exactly how to restore Ethan's joy.

He walked home with them, his heart stuttering at the sight of the house, the outside lights twinkling. The memory of his parents was always strong.

Remy invited him inside. He hated for the night to end. One day, he hoped it wouldn't have to. They would share a home, a life. But for now, Seth had to decline.

He had too much to do to get ready for a perfect Christmas morning. He loved surprising his guests, and his mind was running rampant on everything still to do. He imagined spending the night with Remy by his side next year.

He brushed his nose to hers for a split second, then backed away and waved. "Would love to, but I've got to get ready for Santa myself."

He returned to the resort, and he and his staff placed presents under the tree. Many of his guests brought a gift for their children to find in the morning, and Seth generally had something to put out for everyone, as well. He carried out the gifts for Ethan, Addie, and Grayson, his skin tingling in anticipation.

Then he hiked the path toward his home and smiled up at the night sky.

~

Christmas morning was nothing short of miraculous. Remy woke before everyone else and grabbed a cup of coffee, then returned to her room. She shifted the curtains aside, the snow floating in light and airy flakes. She sent a quick *Merry Christmas* text to Seth.

Her stomach fluttered when the phone buzzed. Like a child on Christmas morning eager to open presents, she couldn't wait to see him.

But he had guests to tend to, and she and her family already had plans for opening gifts before heading to the resort.

Will you let your family know Santa left some gifts under the lobby tree with their names on them?

Her palms were sweaty as she typed her response. *Of course, I will. See you later. XOXO.*

She wanted to say more, so much more than the *XOXO,* but that was better left for when she saw him in person. Anticipation kept her heartbeat—and her breath—choppy. She couldn't wait to see him.

She and her family would be gathering near the tree soon. She took a quick shower and put on her Christmas PJs. She and her sisters cooked breakfast while the kids shuffled through packages under the tree.

Tessa, standing at the stove, flipped a pancake and tossed a look behind her. "We're eating breakfast first."

Addie frowned. "We know. We're just looking."

Remy cracked eggs into a bowl. "Come on, Mom. Don't you remember those days? The smell of excitement? The rosy flush of anticipation?"

Tessa chuckled and slid a pancake onto a plate. "What are you now, a poet?"

Remy beamed and whisked the eggs.

"What exactly does excitement smell like anyway?" her sister asked.

"Peppermint and cocoa."

Tessa's brows arched. "Really?"

Remy shrugged. It was the first thought that came into her mind. She cocked her head toward the tree. "Even the men are under the tree like kids themselves."

Maybe next year there would be a third man—her man— but then again she and Seth would have to tend to the resort's festivities. She couldn't wait to make new traditions.

When breakfast was ready, they all gathered near the tree and ate.

"This is the only time Mom allows us to eat on the floor." Addie giggled, then stretched out her feet and wiggled her toes, which were covered in fuzzy Christmas socks.

Some traditions remained the same, such as everyone wearing pajamas while opening gifts. The kids all wore different ones, but each couple matched. Remy's was bright red and covered in white stockings. Tessa and Landon's were a mix of colors covered in reindeer, and Jason and Melissa were green covered in elves.

"I love the PJs," Remy told Addie, who wore polka-dots and candy canes.

"Mom lets us open one gift on Christmas Eve, and it's always Christmas PJs. Aren't these adorable?"

"They are."

Ethan grunted, but thrust his chest out in pride. His

looked tougher, a deep blue background covered in skiing snowmen, the masks they wore almost like they were in combat.

"Yours are cool, too," Remy said. "And Grayson. I love yours." Dark pants covered with the Grinch and a lighter top with the character and a Santa hat.

Grayson pointed at her. "Yours. Dorable."

She couldn't stop thinking about Seth, and next year. Them wearing matching PJs. Her heart skipped a beat.

After breakfast, Remy helped Tessa clean up the kitchen, and soon they were opening their gifts.

Remy held her breath as Addie opened the music box. Was it her place to tell her Seth had made it? She didn't want to do so until she talked to him about it. After all, she'd found it in the store, and the only reason she knew was because the store owner had told her.

Maybe he wanted to keep his talents anonymous. A shame.

Addie gasped at the gift and threw her hands around Remy's neck. "Thank you, thank you, thank you."

Tears burned her eyes, but she blinked them back. Her chest expanded. *Happy, happy.*

Ethan was pleased with his new baseball gifts and Grayson huddled in the corner to play with his trucks.

Remy clapped her hands together once before waving them in the air. "Was that an awesome Christmas, or what?"

Grayson threw up his hands in celebration. "Yay!"

As much as she loved this time with her family, she was eager to see Seth. "Seth texted to tell me Santa left some packages for us under the lobby tree."

Addie's eyes widened, chin trembling. "Can we go look?"

Tessa stood and clapped her hands once, reminding Remy of a drill sergeant. "We still have to get our teeth brushed and get dressed."

"Well, let's hurry up about it," Remy said. She couldn't contain her grin or hide her excitement.

And she didn't want to.

She sent a message to Seth to let him know they would be heading to the resort in about fifteen minutes or so.

Lovely, he said. *I'm down here with the crowd, but everyone is clearing out. See you soon.*

~

Seth loved watching his guests enjoy their time with family and friends. Most of his regulars always put something for him under the tree. Maybe a homemade afghan or gift basket of treats. He enjoyed each and every one and, with the help of his staff, he always had something under the tree for them, too. Usually a gift basket full of jerky, cheese and crackers, and wine along with something personal if he knew the guests well enough.

Remy stepped into the room, and Seth's breath stalled in his chest.

Addie squealed and rushed into his arms. Grayson followed, and Ethan—acting more grown up—strolled forward and shook his hand.

"Merry Christmas!" Seth said. "Guess what? Santa left more presents for you guys under the tree."

Beaming, Addie ducked her head and cupped her hands over her face, then she squealed and whirled around to her mother. "Can we open them now, Mom? Please?"

"Wait for everyone to get settled, then we can." Tessa glanced at Seth and mouthed *you shouldn't have.*

He only grinned, that grin spreading into all his limbs. She should have expected it, since he'd done it every year and his parents had before they died, but every year was always the same *you shouldn't have.* He giggled to himself, then clasped

Remy around the waist and murmured in her ear, "There's something for you under that tree, too."

She cocked her chin. "There's something for you, too. Several things, actually, in that package Tessa is carrying. I'm pretty sure the whole family bought you something individually."

Seth broke away from her. "We better get started. I think Addie is about to crawl out of her skin." He wanted to keep Remy in his arms, but he couldn't wait to see her open her gift.

Addie foraged under the tree and removed all the gifts with their names.

"Addie, settle down," her mom said.

"Can I hand everyone's out?" she asked. "Pretty please?"

Tessa glanced at Seth.

"I think that's a great idea." Seth settled on the couch next to Remy.

"Here's one for you, Aunt Remy," she said, handing her a silvery package with a huge matching bow on top. "And a couple for Seth from my parents and from Uncle Landon and Aunt Melissa. Here's one for everyone." She handed them all out and kept hers aside, then clapped her hands and settled on the floor next to her package.

"Shall we take turns or open them all at once?" Tessa asked.

"I say let's just open them," Seth said.

Everyone chorused an agreement.

Seth slowly opened his package, preferring to keep his focus on everyone else while they opened theirs. At Addie's ear-piercing squeal, he flinched.

She held up her gift. "Santa got me the camera I wanted!"

"Cool," Ethan said. "I got a telescope." His eyes widened, a smile broadening his face while he studied his gift.

"What did you get, Grayson?" Addie asked.

"Train!" Grayson yelled, happily tearing open his train set.

"What about you, Remy?" Addie asked.

Seth's palms grew sweaty, his pulse bouncing in his ears. If he could slow this moment down, take a small leap into the future to see her reaction and prepare himself, he'd do that in a heartbeat.

"Oh, I've been so busy watching you guys, I don't know."

"Wait," Addie said. "Let me get this camera together so I can take pictures of the rest of you."

"Do you need some help?" Remy asked.

"Sure. Thank you."

Remy got up from her perch on the couch and kneeled next to Addie. He chuckled. "You sure you can handle that?"

She shot him a cute scowl and scrunched her nose. "We can handle it."

Tessa scooted forward. "Seth, this was too much."

He cocked his head and grinned. "What do you mean?"

She nodded at the tree and at her children enjoying their gifts.

"Santa did all this," Seth said.

Tessa blinked at him and smiled, then tugged on his elbow and wrapped her arms around his neck for a side hug. "You're a wonderful man, Seth. And always part of this family. I hope you know that."

His belly flipped. "Thanks. I love you guys."

"And we love you, too." She nodded toward her sister. "There's one particular person I think loves you a bit differently."

He opened his mouth to speak, but couldn't get any words out.

"And I think you feel the same way."

"Well..." His throat clenched. Had Remy told her yet?

"Okay, I'm ready for pictures, guys," Addie announced.

He blew out a breath. Winked at Tessa. She shoulder-bumped him and went back to her seat. Remy bounced back beside him.

She tore into the package, which tore into his nerves. The feeling he'd had so long ago, when he thought she'd so easily discarded his friendship and affection, came back for a second. He breathed out his fears.

"Oh, Seth," she whispered, glancing at him as the camera flash blasted. Wrapped in tissue, in perfect working order, was the music box he had given her so long ago.

Time stood still as Seth fought the urge to kiss her. Not in this room full of her family. He tilted his head. "Is that what the package says? I thought Santa brought that."

She planted her forehead on his. "This time, I know it's from you."

Remy pulled it from the box, her skin glowing, the smile on her face one of pure pleasure.

Addie moved closer and pointed. "Hey. I got a music box for Christmas, too. But from Aunt Remy, not Santa."

He tugged on his ear and cocked his head. "You what?" he asked, thinking he must have misunderstood.

Remy nodded his direction, but spoke to Addie. "Yeah. Did you know that Seth creates these boxes?" Then she turned to him and crinkled her nose. "Yeah. I found it at a gift shop in town. And the clerk there told me you created these and sold them. Another talent of yours I didn't know about."

His eyes widened then he averted his gaze. So now she knew, but his nerves didn't go away. Everything he created was like sharing a piece of his soul, and sharing a piece of his vulnerabilities. For a moment, he felt like that young, insecure child who was just learning his way through the world.

He wanted to kiss her. They weren't the only two in the room, although right now, it sure felt like they were. Tessa sidetracked Addie by having her take pictures of Grayson and Ethan, likely to give Seth and Remy time for themselves.

She nudged his shoulder. "Why didn't you tell me?"

Her pursed his lips. "Tell you what?"

"That the music box was from you so very long ago?"

Why hadn't he told her? Why had he waited, using this moment, this gift to tell her all the things he should have told her years ago? If only he had an answer, but his only answer was one of fear. "I thought you had abandoned it. I thought you didn't want it."

She placed her hand on his cheek, their gazes locked. "Didn't your parents tell you we called looking for it?" Her voice cracked, and he wished he could remove the tears pooling in her eyes.

He shook his head, his throat burning. "No." He took the box and turned it over, showing her his engraved name. *Love, Seth.*

"Oh, Seth," she whispered, the warmth of his breath stroking his cheek. She touched the engraving. Her eyes pooled with moisture.

He put his forehead on hers and traced his fingers with hers, the depth of his name on the wood like a permanent mark of his love.

The click of Addie's camera whirred, flash going off, and they broke apart. They smiled and waved at the camera as Addie continued to click.

"Hey, there's some gifts for Seth here," Ethan scuttled forward and handed Seth several packages.

"Wow. Thanks, guys." His breath was choppy, spinning, spinning, spinning in his chest. He'd never know why his parents hadn't mentioned it, but he had been pretty good about keeping his feelings to himself as well.

No more secrets. He would tell Remy everyday how he felt about her.

He ripped open his packages, leaving Remy's for last. His heart halted, then rang in his ears.

Remy had unearthed old pictures and created a collage in a bronzed frame. The two photos of her he'd taken so long ago—one of her at the creek and one where she trailed behind her family—he'd snapped her side profile in both pictures, her hair billowing in the breeze. Then one of his family and hers together.

His chin dropped, eyes blinking as he studied the creation and bit back tears. "It's gorgeous," he said. "Thank you."

Addie sat beside them and looked at the photos. She tapped the glass. "Hey, that's a picture of Aunt Remy when she was younger."

"Sure is," Seth said.

"Did you take those photos?" she asked.

He nodded. "I did. When I was a bit older than you."

"Awesome!"

"Snow!" Grayson waddled to the window.

Seth was grateful for the distraction. As much as he enjoyed the moment, he didn't want to burst into tears.

"Okay, guys." Tessa clapped her hands. "Let's get our coats and gloves on and go play in it."

"Wait." Melissa stood. "I have one more gift to give everyone." She ambled toward the tree and grabbed Landon's hand then faced everyone, rubbing her stomach.

All the adults gasped.

"This time next year, we're going to have another bundle of joy. Landon and I are pregnant!"

The whole family rushed forward to offer their congratulations.

Seth stood back, watching the crowd as his heart burst open in joy.

CHAPTER 20

Everyone bundled up for the cold and darted outside to play before Christmas lunch. Remy strolled hand in hand with Seth through the crowd, greeting those she had already met and meeting those she hadn't.

"I have something else to give you," he told her.

They stopped in the back part of the resort where the trees bunched together and opened into a path. The sun was high in the sky, so the lights weren't twinkling, but gold twined the trees.

"Oh, Seth. That music box..." She lowered her gaze and placed her hand under her breastbone. "When I found the one at the shop in town and the cashier told me you made them, I wondered..."

He planted his fingers under her chin and lifted her gaze to meet his. "I'm sorry you lost it," he said. "I'm sorry you were looking for it. And I'm sorry I abandoned our friendship so many years ago."

"Is that why?"

"Partially. But it's also because I was so attracted to you. I wanted more than friendship. And I want more than friendship now."

Her breath hitched, her pulse blooming in her core and broadcasting to her limbs.

When she didn't reply, he said, "If you don't..."

She nodded and put her arms around his neck. "I do, Seth. Haven't you already figured that out?"

He shuffled backward and took her hand. "Then come on. I have something else to show you."

Thrilled at what else he would have to show her, she walked with him toward his house. She couldn't imagine what else could possibly make this Christmas better.

Her throat burned with unshed tears. What might have happened if she had known Seth had given her that box so long ago? They wouldn't have been ready for each other. Not back then. They were both too young and had a lot of growing up to do.

She had a lot of growing up to do. But her life dreams were clear to her now.

Their footsteps planted in the freshly fallen snow as if establishing them as a fixture. And she hoped to be a fixture here.

Inside, his house was hot. She shrugged off her coat and gloves and hung them beside his on the rack near the door.

"Now I understand how gratified my parents must have felt running this resort." Seth grabbed a stocking hanging from the mantel.

"You've done an amazing job." She meant to say more, to gush over everything she admired about him, but he turned and handed her a stocking. "What's this?"

"Well, you have to look inside to find out, silly."

She buried her hands in the stocking and pulled out a small jewelry gift box. She gasped, then almost choked on a deep breath. It was just a small box. It could be anything, but her mind churned with the possibilities.

She blinked rapidly and tried not to hyperventilate.

He took over, opening the lid to display a ring.

Her throat swelled. She gulped down a breath, then stuttered. "It's...b...beautiful," she said, sniffling through her tears.

"It was my mother's. I have my father's. They wrote it in their will, too. Of course, if you prefer your own, I totally understand. And I know they would. She always said I could make a necklace out of it when they died, but I hadn't had time to find an engagement ring and didn't want to wait. I thought it would be nice for us to go and choose one together. I mean, if you agree."

"No." She fingered the ring.

"No?" His voice dropped, body hunching.

She giggled, then snorted, the raspy sound of her tears chortling through her voice. "No, I mean, this is way too beautiful to refuse. I wouldn't want anything else."

He grabbed her around the waist and tugged her forward. "You are way too beautiful to refuse," he said. "I love you. I always have. And I'll love you for the rest of my life."

She nodded, breathless. She wanted to say the words but sensed he wasn't finished, so she waited, mesmerized.

He bent down on one knee. "Will you marry me?"

She swayed. "Yes. Yes, of course."

He slipped the engagement ring over her finger, then stood and kissed her.

"I think I've always loved you, too. That's why I've had such a hard time dealing with things. I never thought I'd see you again. I want to spend the rest of my life with you, right here, helping you run this resort every single day of our lives together."

He nodded at the door. "Then come on. I think we have another gift to give your family."

"Our family." She cupped his face and planted kisses along his cheeks. "But we can tell them later."

Remy sat outside with her family later that evening. The horizon sparkled in radiant colors of purple and gold as the sun descended, creating a soft glow around the earth that mirrored Remy's contentment. A crackling fire kept them warm, and everything was quiet enough to hear kids hollering and playing in the resort's park behind them.

Seth was beside her on the bench, he and Landon planning their next fly-fishing tournament.

Her gaze wandered to the brush of snow along Seth's beanie, a flock of birds singing together in the glistening trees, and her sister's smile as she talked to her husband.

She let out a satisfied sigh.

Addie approached, startling her. She jumped and turned, then tweaked her nose. "Hey sweetie."

Addie handed her a gift bag.

"What is this?"

Addie bounced up and down, eyes gleaming. "You gotta open it to find out."

Chuckling, Remy opened the bag and pulled out a framed photo. One of the first Addie had taken with her new camera. Remy had just opened the music box, and Addie had captured the look of love as she gazed at Seth. "Oh, sweetheart, you did a fabulous job." She nudged Seth with her elbow and showed it to him. "Look at this."

He studied it, blinking, then ran his fingers across the glass. He glanced at Addie. "It's amazing."

Addie beamed and tottered from side to side.

"We've got an announcement to make to the family," Seth told her. "Do you want to get their attention?"

Her eyes widened, and she nodded then started climbing to stand on the bench.

Seth took her arm and helped. "Careful, it's slippery up here." He continued to hold onto her so she didn't fall.

Remy's pulse raced. Good thing she was sitting. Her body was weak. Not because she was nervous about telling her family about her and Seth. Most of them already knew anyway. A swarm of butterflies expanded in her chest.

Addie clapped her hands. "Mom, Dad, Uncle Landon, Aunt Melissa. Shush a minute, please. We've got one more nenouncement to make." She pointed at Remy, then Seth helped her off the bench. She sat beside her mom, folding her hands in her lap in rapt attention.

Remy grinned at Addie's mispronunciation and grasped Seth's hand in her right, then held up her left. "Seth and I are engaged. I'll be staying here, helping him with the resort."

"Took you long enough," Tessa called as everyone cheered.

"Let's keep it a secret a bit longer," Seth said. "I plan on telling my staff tomorrow."

They rushed forward to give hugs, nearly barreling them both over with their enthusiasm.

Remy laughed as flakes of snow fell around them, an applause from the sky.

They gathered near the tree and sang carols with the rest of the guests.

Remy moved into Seth's arms and placed her cheek on his shoulder. They danced together as everyone sang.

"I love you," he said into her ear.

She lifted her chin and gazed into his eyes. "I love you, too."

They sang together, their voices carrying the night. With her head planted firmly on Seth's chest, the thrum of his voice buzzed into her. She was exactly where she was supposed to be. Forever.

She surrendered to complete joy. The song lifted into the wind, spiraling to the clouds, and flakes of snow drifted down. The spirit of Christmas still lingered, would always linger, at this resort. The presence of hope and memories. She pictured their parents, hovering above and granting their blessing with each kiss of snow.

THE END

ABOUT ANGELA

Angela Smith is a Texas native who, years ago, was dubbed most likely to write a novel during her senior year in high school. She always had her nose stuck in a book, even hiding them behind her textbooks during school study time. Her dream began at a young age when her sister started reciting 'Brer Rabbit' after their mom read it to them so often. She told her mom she'd write a story one day and never gave up on that dream even though her mom was never able to see it come to fruition. By day, she works as a certified paralegal and office manager at her local District Attorney's office and spends her free time with her husband, their pets, and their many hobbies. Although life in general keeps her very busy, her passion for writing and getting the stories out of her head tends to make her restless if she isn't following what some people call her destiny.

Find out more at www.loveisamystery.com, www.facebook.com/authorangelasmith, or www.twitter.com/angelaswriter.

OTHER BOOKS BY ANGELA

Burn on the Western Slope

Fatal Snag

Final Mend

One Last Hold

One Wrong Move

Solace

Liberation

Dark Ride

Dark Justice